GRIM

Satan's Fury MC- Little Rock

L. WILDER

GRIM

Satan's Fury MC- Little Rock

L. Wilder- 2024

Without limiting the rights under copyright reserved above, no part of this publication or any part of this series may be reproduced without the prior written permission of both the copyright owner and the above publisher of this book.

This book is a work of fiction. Some of the places named in the book are actual places found in Arkansas. The names, characters, brands, and incidents are either the product of the author's imagination or are used fictitiously.

The author acknowledges the trademarked status and owners of various products and locations referenced in this work of fiction, which have been used without permission. The publication or use of these trademarks is not authorized, associated with, or sponsored by the trademark owners.

This e-book is licensed for your personal enjoyment only. This e-book may not be re-sold or given away to other people. *All Rights Reserved.*

Book Cover Details:

Model: Dean Stannard

Cover Design: Mayhem Cover Creations

Editor: Marie Peyton

Proofer- Rose Holub

Personal Assistant: Natalie Weston

Catch up with the entire Satan's Fury MC Series today!

All books are FREE with Kindle Unlimited!

Summer Storm (Satan's Fury MC Novella)

Maverick (Satan's Fury MC #1)

Stitch (Satan's Fury MC #2)

Cotton (Satan's Fury MC #3)

Clutch (Satan's Fury MC #4)

Smokey (Satan's Fury MC #5)

Big (Satan's Fury #6)

Two Bit (Satan's Fury #7)

Diesel (Satan's Fury #8)

Falling for the President's Daughter (Satan's Fury #9)

Q (Satan's Fury #10)

Blaze (Satan's Fury MC- Memphis Book 1)

Shadow (Satan's Fury MC- Memphis Book 2)

Riggs (Satan's Fury MC- Memphis Book 3)

Murphy (Satan's Fury MC- Memphis Book 4)

Gunner (Satan's Fury MC- Memphis Book 5)

Gus (Satan's Fury MC- Memphis Book 6)

Rider (Satan's Fury MC- Memphis Book 7)

Prospect (Satan's Fury MC- Memphis Book 8)

T-Bone (Satan's Fury MC-Memphis Book 9)

Q (Satan's Fury MC- SG)

Bones (Satan's Fury MC- SG)

Wrath (Satan's Fury MC- SG)

Savage (Satan's Fury MC- SG)

Rooster (Satan's Fury MC- SG)

Day Three (What Bad Boys Do Book 1)

Damaged Goods- (The Redemption Series Book 1- Nitro)

Max's Redemption (The Redemption Series Book 2- Max)

Inferno (Devil Chasers #1)

Smolder (Devil Chaser #2)

Ignite (Devil Chasers #3)

Consumed (Devil Chasers #4)

Combust (Devil Chasers #5)

The Long Road Home (Devil Chasers #6)

Naughty or Nice (Mistletoe, Montana Collaboration)

My Temptation (The Happy Endings Collection #1)

Bring the Heat (The Happy Endings Collection #2)

His Promise (The Happy Endings Collection #3)

Ties That Bind (Ruthless Sinners #1)

Holding On (Ruthless Sinners #2)

Secrets We Keep (Ruthless Sinners #3)

Widow's Undoing (Ruthless Sinners #4)

Claiming Menace (Ruthless Sinners #5)

Tempting Country (Ruthless Sinners #6)

Jagger's Choice (Ruthless Sinners #7)

Viper's Demands (Ruthless Sinners #8)

Lynch's Rule (Ruthless Sinners #9)

The Butcher (Ruthless Sinners #10)

❦ Created with Vellum

Character List:

Preacher- President
    Sons- Beckett and Memphis

Creed- Vice President
    Seven- Sergeant of Arms
    Grim- Enforcer
    Ghost- Brother
    Memphis- Brother
    Rusty- Brother
    Goose- Brother
    Gash- Brother
    Duggar- Prospect
    Jonesy- Prospect
    Skid- Prospect
    Smitty- Prospect

Prologue

"Funny thing about the carotid." I pressed the sharp end of my blade against his throat. "Once it's severed, it only takes a couple of minutes for you to bleed out."

"WAIT! STOP!" he pleaded. "Just tell me what you want."

"I want to know who came up with the idea."

"What are you talking about, man?"

"Amy." It had been months, but the simple sound of her name still made my blood boil. Amy was Beckett's girl, and she was caught off guard when Deshawn and his buddies barged into her home. She was just letting her damn dog out and had no clue that these men were about to do what they did. "You know, the girl you and your buddies raped and murdered."

"I don't know what you're talking about."

"You know damn well what I'm talking about, you piece of shit."

Getting Deshawn alone hadn't been easy. Seemed like he was always with his crew or at work or at some corner dealing with a couple of his boys. But I'd watched and waited, waited and watched, and tonight, luck was on my side. I spotted him making a deal in an alley right outside of his apartment. Once it was done and the coast was clear, I didn't hesitate. I grabbed him up and slammed him into the back of the building, dazing him right before beating the hell out of him.

He was a tall, lanky dude, so it didn't take much to rough him up. Hell, I didn't even break a sweat, and he was bruised and bloody, pleading for me to stop. I needed him alive, so I stopped and pinned him against the building. I could feel his pulse quicken beneath my fingertips when I growled, "Lying is only gonna make it worse, kid."

"I was just going along... I didn't know."

"That didn't stop you from fucking her, now did it?"

"It wasn't like that."

"Oh? What was it like then?"

"They were watching me." His breaths came in shallow gasps as the cold steel of the knife dug into his skin, reminding him of the imminent danger he was in. "I had to."

"You didn't have to do shit. You chose to rape and kill that girl, and now, you're gonna pay for that shit."

I sliced his throat ever-so-slightly, but it was enough to send him into a panic. "It was Ruben! It was his idea."

"Keep talking."

His eyes darted frantically, searching for a way out, but there was none to be found. "Ruben had a thing for her, but she blew him off. He's the one. It was him! All him!"

"What about Jimmy and Clayborn?"

"They came along for the ride. T-Ride and Macon, too."

"Good boy."

I took hold of his shirt and gave him a hard shove towards the back parking lot. "Whoa. Where we going?"

"Gonna take us a little ride."

"But where? Why?" I unlocked the back of the SUV and opened the back hatch, revealing a layer of thick plastic sheeting and the ominous large pine crate resting on top. "Ah, shit. What the fuck is that?"

"That's for you." I gripped the edges of the crate before giving Deshawn a hard shove. "Get inside."

"Please, man. Don't do this."

His words were a desperate plea for mercy, but I had no mercy to give. I put the barrel of my Glock against his temple and demanded, "Get inside."

A sense of foreboding hung heavy in the air as Deshawn did as I ordered and crawled up into the back of my SUV. As he got into the crate, I warned, "You can scream and knock around all you want, but it's not going to do you any good. No one's coming for you, and your screaming is just gonna piss me the fuck off. So, do us both a favor and keep your trap shut."

"Please, man. Don't do..."

Before he could say anything more, I closed the top of the crate and secured the latch, making certain that there was no way he was getting out. Minutes later, I was on my way to Washington. This wasn't the way I usually did business, but I was a firm believer in things coming full circle.

It just so happened that this particular situation needed a little nudge.

Beckett deserved that. Amy, too.

I just had no way of knowing that *coming full circle* would bring an end I never saw coming.

Grim

38 HOURS LATER....

❦

"Take off your clothes."

She was scared. I could see it in her eyes. I couldn't exactly blame her. I was twice her age, big and muscular with scars and tattoos that would intimidate the fiercest of men. But she was used to that. She'd been a Fury hang-around for a while, but she didn't know anything about me—just that I was an enforcer from another chapter.

Seeing that she needed a little encouragement, I gave her a little smile and pushed, "Come on, darlin'. You don't have to be scared of me. I'm gonna make us both feel real good. You'll see."

She nodded, then dropped her hands to the hem of her fitted sweater and eased it over her head. Seconds later, her skirt was gone, and she was standing in front of me bare and waiting.

She was too young, too skinny, too submissive for

my liking, but Washington was a hell of a drive from Little Rock, and I was in dire need of a cold beer, a good lay, and a soft bed. I'd already had my beer, and that bed was calling my name.

"That's a good girl." I started unbuckling my jeans as I commanded, "Now, come here."

As she approached, I gave her a half-smile and said, "Let's see what you got."

Her eyes locked on mine as she lowered herself to her knees, and a hiss slipped across my teeth when she took me in her hand. Her fingers barely wrapping my girth as she began teasing me with soft, easy strokes. My cock grew harder with every flick of her wrist, and while it felt alright, I needed something more.

I was about to tell her to get to it when I felt the tip of her tongue rake against me. I reached down, taking her hair in my hands, guiding her as she finally took me in her mouth. Her mouth was soft, warm and wet, and I won't deny that it felt pretty damn good. Unable to fight the urge, I pulled back on her hair and forced her to take me deeper.

She struggled for a moment but quickly recovered and carried on. "That's it. *Take all of it.*"

Her strokes became firmer and quicker with a slight twist of her wrist, and she sucked harder as she took me deeper. She was getting into it, really into it, and fuck. The girl had a mouth on her, and it damn near had me going over the edge.

I took a step back and pulled myself free from her

grasp, and she looked at me with surprise as I reached down and picked her up. "Enough of that."

I carried her over to the desk and settled between her legs. I grabbed a condom from my wallet and then ditched my jeans. I wasn't sure if she was ready for me. I didn't really care. I gathered some spit on the tip of my fingers and raked them across her center.

Her breath caught when I drove deep inside her with one hard thrust. She wasn't new to this. She'd had her fair share, but she still felt pretty fucking good as I worked myself in deeper. Relishing the sensation, I let out a low growl as I slowly withdrew.

A slight hiss slipped through her teeth as I drove into her again and again—each time a bit faster and more unforgiving. Her heels dug into my back, and she gasped, "Oh, my God, you feel so good!"

Still buried deep inside her, I slipped my hands under her ass and lifted her from the desk. I carried her over to the bed and dropped her onto the mattress as I commanded, "On your knees."

She quickly complied, and as soon as she was on all fours, she glanced over her shoulder and eagerly watched as I stepped behind her. I reached over and fisted her hair in my hand, giving it a hard tug, and she cried out when I plunged inside her once again. Unable to control myself, I drew back and plowed into her again and again, giving her everything I had.

"Fuckkk!" I shouted out as my throbbing cock demanded its release too fucking soon. I continued to drive into her in a demanding rhythm until, at last, she twisted the sheets with her hands and let out another tortured groan. Her body clamped down around me like a vice as my hips collided with hers, and I was done.

I drove into her once more, then finally came deep inside of her. I took a moment to collect myself, then withdrew and told her, "You can go now."

"But wait... Are you gonna be around later?"

And there it is. She wanted more. Unfortunately, I didn't have the time nor desire to give it to her. "Heading out first thing tomorrow. Maybe next time."

Without saying anything more, I turned and went to take a shower. By the time I got out, she was gone, and I was pleased to see that there was no trace of her left in the room. The girl knew her place. I liked that.

I laid down on the bed, and it wasn't long before my mind drifted to Beckett. He was the reason why I'd traveled thirty-some-odd hours from Little Rock to Washington. He was Preacher's kid. He was only nineteen and the youngest of three. That came with its advantages, especially when your father is the president of the MC. He got anything he wanted, and when he got into trouble, we were there to bail him out.

Over the years, he grew to feel entitled.

He thought he had a say in what we did or didn't do, but he couldn't have been more wrong. He learned just how wrong a few months ago when his girl was killed by a local gang.

They hadn't just killed her.

They'd done a real number on her, and that was putting it mildly. Beckett was all fucked up about it. He was angry and hungry for revenge, and he expected Preacher to feel the same. He wanted the gang taken care of—even if it meant declaring war.

Preacher refused.

Not because he was cold-hearted.

He knew it was a horrible thing that they did to Amy, but at the end of the day, they'd only been dating for a couple of months. She wasn't an ol' lady, and the club had no real ties to her. Preacher tried explaining that to his distraught son, but the kid's emotions had gotten the best of him, and he couldn't see the forest for the trees.

Fearing he might do something he'd regret, Preacher sent him to hang with the Washington chapter for a couple of months. Maverick and the boys took him under their wing, and every time we checked in with them, they seemed to think Beckett was doing better. Preacher wanted him home for the holidays, so I agreed to go get him.

When I arrived, it was late, and Beckett had already crashed for the night.

I had a little fun with the cute hang around and crashed as well.

I woke up the following day much later than I had planned.

The long drive and my night with the pretty young lady had taken their toll, and I slept until almost noon. I got up, took a quick shower, and as soon as I was dressed, I went to track Beckett down. I'd barely started down the hall when I spotted Stitch.

He'd been the chapter's enforcer for as long as I'd known him, and while he had a hell of a replacement, it was strange to find that he had stepped down and was now just another brother. He was about to step out the back door, so I called out, "Yo, Stitch. You seen Beckett?"

"The boys aren't working today, so they partied a bit last night. If I had to guess, I'd say he's probably still in his room." He motioned his head down the hall. "Third door on your right."

"Appreciate it."

He nodded, then continued out the door. Once he was gone, I made my way down to Beckett's room and knocked on the door. Seconds later, I heard, "I'll be out in a minute."

I wasn't in the mood to be kept waiting, so I opened the door and stepped inside. The room was a fucking mess. There were bags at the door, empty bottles strewn around the room, and dirty towels tossed in the corner. I glanced over to the bed and immediately spotted Beckett's hair peeking out from the tangled mess of blankets. I tossed them back as I yelled, "Rise and shine, sleeping beauty."

"Hmmm," he groaned with a slight stretch.

"Beck!" My tone was gruff and carried a hint of

impatience as I pushed, "Get your ass up! It's fucking noon."

"Grim?" He cracked one eye open. "I thought you were coming tomorrow."

"I made it hear early. Now, get up."

His voice was laced with irritation as Beckett whined, "Ah, man... What's the fucking rush?"

"I've got something you're gonna wanna see." I crossed my arms and leaned against the doorframe as I watched him start to stir. I liked Beckett. He could be a lot at times, but he was a good kid. I was looking forward to showing him what I'd brought, so I pushed, "Now, stop fucking around and get up!"

With a sigh, Beckett finally swung his legs over the edge of the bed, facing me with a scowl. "Okay, what is it?"

"You'll see."

Without any further argument, he got up and put on his clothes. Once he was ready, I led him out of his room and down the hall. When we started outside, he asked, "Where the hell are we going?"

I didn't answer. I just kept moving forward, and he followed. It wasn't long before we'd made our way out to Wrath's workroom. Beckett followed me over to the two-way glass, and his eyes grew wide when he spotted the man in the center of the room. His hands were bound above his head, and it was difficult to see his face. Confused, Beckett asked, "Who the hell is that?"

"Deshawn Michaels." Before he could ask, I explained, "He's one of 'em."

"Seriously?" His eyes grew wide. "He's one of the guys who raped and killed Amy?"

"I wish I could've brought them all, but he'll have to do."

"What are we supposed to do with him?"

"That's up to you." I motioned my head to the door. "He's all yours."

"Seriously?"

"I'll be back in a couple of hours." I gave him a pat on the shoulder, then said, "Go get the closure you need and let's put this shit behind us once and for all."

He still looked bewildered when I turned and started back down the hall. I was beginning to think he was going to pass on my offering when I heard the door open. I glanced over my shoulder and relief washed over me as I watched Beckett disappear inside the room. I left him to it and went to the kitchen for some coffee.

Maverick and his boys were off doing their thing, so I did my best to just stay out of the way. I went out to my truck and cleaned it out. I tossed the crate and plastic into their burn pile, then tossed in a match. Once it was lit and the flames were rolling, I headed into the bar.

I grabbed a beer from the cooler and kicked back at one of the corner tables. I pulled out my phone and saw that I had a message from Tyrone. He was one of our distributors, and while he'd always come through for us, there always seemed to be some kind of drama that came with the take.

Apparently, this time was no different, and he'd sent me a cryptic message about a possible delay. We didn't do delays, so I gave him a call. As soon as Tyrone answered, I snapped, "Are we gonna have a problem?"

"No, man. I got it all under control," he assured me. "It's all here and ready for you and your boys to come pick up."

"And what about your message last night?"

"It was nothing. I got it handled."

"You sure about that?"

"Yeah, man. It's all good."

There was something about his tone that didn't sit right with me. Something was up, and that pissed me the hell off. "You're telling me the goods are there and are up to par, and if that's the case, we'll take our fucking money and go. But if it turns out you're lying and we got some shit like we did last time, then I'll take every fucking dime of that take, and I'll use it to fuck you up. I'll go after your crew, one by one, and I will mess them up in ways you can't begin to imagine."

"It's all good, man. You'll see."

"You better fucking hope so."

I ended the call and grabbed my beer, kicking it back for a long drink. Once I'd finished It off, I stood and tossed the empty bottle in the trash. Rooster and Savage were still at the bar, so I walked over and asked, "How you guys making it today?"

"Can't complain. What about you?"

"I'll be better when I can get back home and wrangle in a couple of assholes, but I can't do that until I sort out this shit with Beckett."

"Maybe this thing today will help out in that department."

"I don't know, Savage. I've got a feeling he's not gonna let it go, but maybe working this guy over will do him some good."

"How long has he been back there with him?"

"An hour." I glanced over at the clock. "Maybe two."

"Might be time to go check on him and see how things are going?"

I nodded, then followed them both back out to Wrath's workroom. When we arrived, the place was completely cleared out. All that was left was Michael's body hanging from the rafters, and I had to give it to Beckett. He'd done good. He'd given the guy exactly what he deserved.

Savage and I remained at the window while Rooster went in to see about Beck. He was sitting on a stool in the corner, smoking a cigarette, and he didn't seem to notice Rooster had walked in. He called out to him, but Beckett didn't respond. So, he walked over to him and placed his hand on his shoulder, trying once again to pull him from his thoughts.

He didn't speak.

He simply nodded and kept staring at what was left of Deshawn.

His wrists were bound in chains, and he was hanging from a rafter in the ceiling. He still had on his shirt, but his pants were down around his ankles. There were multiple lacerations all over his body, and blood was dripping down from beneath the hem of his shirt.

Both of his shoulders were dislocated, and his head hung low with his chin resting on his chest. He didn't look like he was still conscious or even breathing, but even if he was, I wouldn't be able to tell. Both of his eyes were completely swollen shut, and his face was covered in blood and bruises.

Rooster said something else to him, and eventually, Beckett muttered a response. They spoke for a moment longer, then Beckett got up, and his eyes never left the ground as he walked out of the room. He walked past me and Savage and muttered, "Gonna take a shower."

"Take your time."

Once he was gone, I nodded to the window and said to Savage, "We're gonna need to take care of him."

"We'll handle it."

"Good deal. I appreciate you boys taking care of Beckett these past few months. We're always available if you need us to return the favor."

"I'll be sure to let Prez know."

Savage and Wrath gave me a hand loading Beckett's things, and after giving him some time to say his goodbyes, we were on the road home. We'd gotten a later start than I'd hoped, but there was little I could do about it. Things had to be done.

We shared a little small talk along the way, but it was short-lived. Beckett grew quiet and remained that way all the way to South Dakota. We stopped for the night, ate and filled up, and then, we were back at it.

After a few hours, the silence was getting to me, so I asked him, "How's it going over there, kid?"

"It's going."

I glanced down, and I couldn't help but notice the cuts and bruises on his knuckles. As the club's enforcer, I'd had my own fair share of wrecked knuckles and knew they hurt like a bitch. "You good?"

"Yeah." Beckett kept his focus on the view out the side window. "Just ready to get home."

I glanced down at the GPS as I told him, "I hate to break it to you, but we're still about eight hours out."

"Figured as much."

"We'll stop in an hour or so to fill up and grab a bite to eat."

He didn't respond.

I didn't expect him to. The kid was a million miles away. I didn't want to push. He'd been through a lot over the past few months, and it had been a hell of a ride.

I'd already tried asking him how things had gone in Washington, but he wasn't exactly forthcoming. He mentioned working at the construction site and hanging out with Rooster and Torch. His spirits seemed to lighten at the mention of their names, but only momentarily. In a blink, his somber mood returned, and he was back to staring out the window.

And he'd been like that for hours.

I'd tried to be patient and all that bullshit, but the silence was too much for me. When I couldn't stand it a moment longer, I gave him a nudge and said, "Any plans for when we get back?"

"Probably sleep for about three days."

"I know your dad and the rest of the brothers are looking forward to having your back."

"Hm-hmm."

And with that, my patience broke. "What the hell was that?"

"Nothing. I'm good."

"The hell you say," I argued. "You've hardly said two words since you got in the fucking truck."

"Yeah, I know. I got a lot on my mind." I thought that was all he was going to say until he glanced over at me and continued, "I'm not sure I'm ready for this."

"Ready for what?"

"All the Christmas bullshit." His eyes drifted to his lap as he confessed, "Not sure I can do the whole holiday thing without Amy."

"You won't have to handle that alone."

"You say that, but I've been handling it alone for months."

"I'm here."

"Yeah, I appreciate it more than you know." He

inhaled a deep breath, then added, "You didn't have to bring him to me, but it meant a lot to me that you did."

"Wish I could've done more..."

"I know. I get it." He gave me a half-hearted shrug. "They'll get theirs in the end. Assholes like that always do."

"Yeah, they definitely do." I finally had him talking and didn't want him to stop, so I said, "I bet you're ready to get home and sleep in your own bed."

He grimaced as he answered, "About that... I'm gonna be staying over at Amy's place."

"No. That's not gonna happen."

"I've put a lot of thought into it... It's sittin' empty and most of my shit's still there. Just makes sense to hang there until things settle down."

"It's almost Christmas. You gotta know that being there is gonna fuck with your head."

"Maybe it will. Maybe it won't."

"And what about Prez?"

"What about him?"

"He wants you home with him for the holiday."

"And I will be. I just won't be right up under his fucking nose." Beckett shook his head and sighed. "I know he won't like it, but he should be happy that I agreed to come back at all. Things were good in Washington. Those guys treated me like I actually mattered."

"Don't even start with that shit. You know damn well that you matter here," I snapped. "Hell, everyone bends over backward for you."

"Yeah, right." His brows furrowed. "I'm nothing there. Just the Prez's kid, spoiled and entitled, and that's all I'll ever be."

"That attitude isn't gonna do you any favors."

"*It is what it is*." He shrugged with a scoff. "But it's all good. I'm over all the bullshit."

"You sure about that?"

"Might as well be. It's not like me bellyaching is gonna change anything."

"No, it won't."

"See?" I felt a sense of relief when he said, "I'm just ready to put all this shit behind me."

"Not sure how staying at Amy's place is gonna help you do that."

"I've just gotta figure some things out."

"Like what?"

"If I wanna keep my ties to the club or if I wanna do something else. I can't do that living under Dad's shadow."

"You're seriously thinking about walking away from the club?"

"Yeah, I am. I've been thinking about it a lot."

"Well, I'll be damned." I couldn't believe my ears. Beckett had been a fixture in our clubhouse since the day he was born. We'd all just assumed that he would follow in his father and brother's footsteps and patch in. "What would you do?"

"I don't know." He shrugged. "I'll figure something out."

"You better be ready cause Prez is gonna lose his shit. Memphis, too."

"This isn't about them. It's about me," he argued. "It's time for me to stand on my own."

"You can do that and be a brother, too."

"Not as long as Dad's the president." Regret marked his face as he grumbled, "I'll always be a kid to him and nothing more, and I can't live like that. I gotta prove to him that I can take care of things on my own."

"I get it. I just don't want you to make a decision you will regret."

"What's life without regret?" Beckett scoffed.

"Beck."

"I get it. I really do." He leaned his head back and closed his eyes as he muttered, "But I need to do this. I've gotta prove that I can handle things on my own."

With that, he let out a breath and settled back in his seat, signaling that he was done with our conversation. I left him alone and turned my focus back to the road ahead. I figured he could use the sleep, so I didn't bother waking him when I stopped for gas. I grabbed a quick bite and just kept trucking.

By the time we made it back to Little Rock, I was wiped. Even though I knew Prez was gonna give me hell about it, I did as he'd asked and dropped Beckett off at Amy's place. It was the first of many mistakes I would make over the next few days—mistakes that would cost us dearly.

Jenna

"Jones just puked in the hallway. Go clean it up."
"Take this here."
"Go there."
"Clean up this shithole."
"Go out there and show Benny a good time."

I'D HEARD IT ALL BEFORE. DONE IT ALL BEFORE. SO, I wasn't surprised when Steven appeared in my doorway and demanded, "Take this over to Jimmy's first thing in the morning."

He tossed a large duffle bag onto the bedroom floor. I didn't have to ask. I knew what was inside, and I also knew I didn't want to deliver it—not to Jimmy or anyone else. "What? I have to work. You know that."

"So? Do it on your way."

"What about Luna?"

Steven was two years younger than me, and there was a time when we were thick as thieves. There wasn't anything my brother wouldn't do for me and I for him, but everything changed when he joined the Assassins, a vicious gang who wreaked havoc on the city. Now, he was covered in tattoos, and all muscled up like he was on steroids, and the only thing he cared about was himself and them. He certainly didn't care about me or his niece, so I wasn't surprised when he spat, "What about her?"

"You know I have to take her to daycare?"

"So?" Aggravation marked his face as he sassed, "Drop it off on your way."

"I'm not taking that in the car with Luna."

"You like having a roof over your head?"

It was a common threat. He used it anytime he wanted me to do something for him. I wanted no part of it. I was a mother, and I was doing everything I could to raise my daughter right. I hoped that I could worm my way out of it, so I started, "You know I do, but..."

"I don't wanna hear your bullshit, Jenna." He turned and stormed out of the room as he shouted, "Either take the fucking bag or get the fuck out."

I wanted to tell him to go to hell, but I didn't have that luxury. I was basically homeless and was at the mercy of my brother's hospitality. Unfortunately, that mercy came at a cost. I had to do things for his stupid gang, or he'd put me and Luna out on the street.

I hated it.

I knew what he was doing was illegal, and I wanted nothing to do with it.

But I had no choice. We needed a place to live. It was either here or on the streets, and I couldn't do that to Luna.

It wouldn't have been so bad if the house wasn't such a dump. The paint was peeling, revealing the weathered, crumpling wood beneath. The front porch was falling apart and creaked with every step. Several windows were broken and boarded up like the house was already condemned, and the worn-out sofas and mismatched chairs looked like he'd picked them up off the street.

And our little room wasn't much better. It accommodated a twin bed and a rickety wooden dresser. The wallpaper was dull and peeling at the edges, and it was a far cry from the pretty pink bedroom she'd once had.

I'd done what I could to arrange our few possessions in a way that made the small room feel like home, but it did little to help. Thankfully, Luna was only three and wasn't old enough to realize that we were in such a bad spot. I glanced over at Luna lying next to me, and she was sleeping soundly, all sweet dreams and innocence.

Just looking at her made my heart smile.

That little girl meant everything to me. I don't know what I would've done without her. Every little smile, every giggle, every hug gave me the strength to keep going. She was the reason I did the things I did, and I would keep doing them if it meant keeping her safe.

I ran the tips of my fingers through her curly hair, brushing it away from her sweet, angelic face, and guilt washed over me when her big brown eyes flickered open. In barely a whisper, she muttered, "Momma?"

"It's okay, sweetie." I leaned down and kissed her cheek. "Go back to sleep."

She didn't need much encouragement. She was exhausted and fell right back to sleep. I reached over and turned out the light, then curled up next to her. I wanted to put the day behind me and drift off myself, but the second I closed my eyes, I saw his face—Officer Simon Reynolds.

He was the man who showed up at my doorstep one early morning and delivered the news that would change my life forever. It wasn't a good memory. It was the opposite. It was one of the worst days of my life, and I still hadn't recovered. I just wanted to sleep, so I inched closer to Luna and listened to the soothing sounds of her breathing. It wasn't long before my exhaustion took over, and I drifted off.

The next morning, I woke to my alarm going off and Luna nudging my arm, "Momma... Momma."

"Okay, okay." I reached over and turned off my alarm. "I'm up."

I tossed the covers back and rubbed the sleep from my eyes. After a quick stretch, I stepped over to Luna's plastic tote full of clothes and asked, "Overalls or..."

"Overalls," she answered, cutting me off.

"You got it."

I pulled them out of the bin and grabbed her favorite white top, then tossed them onto the bed. Once I'd gotten her dressed, I braided her hair and put on her shoes. "Okay, sweetie. You're all set. Now, it's Momma's turn."

I was just working as a cashier at a small drugstore, so thankfully, there was no need to get dressed up. All I had to do was throw on some jeans and a sweater, brush my hair, and dab on a little makeup. As soon as I was done, I gathered our coats and bags, then quietly slipped out of the room and headed to the kitchen.

Luna would get breakfast at daycare, so I grabbed myself a granola bar and we were on our way. I took her out to my car and put her into her car seat. As always, Luna was accommodating and helped me buckle her in. Minutes later, we were on the road and headed to her small daycare center.

I was living paycheck to paycheck, so I couldn't afford some of the nicer centers in town. After a great deal of searching, I finally came across *Little Feet*—a family-owned daycare with less than twenty kids. It was far from perfect, but the people there were wonderful and took amazing care of Luna.

When we arrived, I parked and helped Luna out of her seat. Her tiny fingers gripped my hand as I led her up to the daycare's front door. Before going inside, I crouched down in front of her and adjusted the straps of her little overalls as I said, "I'm sorry, sweetie. I've gotta get to work. I want you to be a good girl today, okay?"

Luna nodded, her two little, braided pigtails bouncing as she replied, "Okay, Momma."

I led her through the front door, then bent down and gave her a tight hug. "I'll be back as soon as I can."

"Okay, Momma!"

Luna smiled as she took her teacher's hand and walked over to join the others. I watched her for a moment, then headed back out to my car. I needed to be at work within the hour and still had to drop off the duffle bag at Jimmy's, so I wasted no time getting back to my car.

I'd only been to Jimmy's place a couple of times, but I knew exactly where it was. It was on my way to work, and the old green siding stuck out like a sore thumb. My entire body tensed when his house came into view.

I disliked all of Steven's friends. They were ruthless criminals who had no regard for anyone but themselves, and Jimmy was the worst of them all. He was tall and lanky with long, greasy hair, and he was cranked out on meth or coke, and that made him handsy. He was always touching me and making lude comments, and I feared one day he would take things too far.

And now, I had to go into the creep's house and take him a bag full of God knows what, and I couldn't have dreaded it more. I hesitated at his doorstep, glancing nervously over my shoulder to make sure no one was coming up behind me. Thankfully, no one was in sight.

I knocked, but no one answered.

I knocked again, harder this time, but again, no sign of Jimmy.

I had to get to work, so I checked the door, and it was unlocked. After taking a deep breath, I pushed the creaking door open, revealing a dimly lit and cluttered living room. I stepped over a stack of old pizza boxes and discarded chip bags as I called out, "Jimmy?"

I continued forward but stopped when a tall, slender man with dark clothing stepped out of the shadows. "Who the fuck are you?"

"I'm ah... I'm Steven's sister," I answer nervously. "He told me to bring this bag over to Jimmy."

"Hmm." He gave me the once over, then motioned his head towards the doorway. "He's down the hall."

His voice was deep and menacing, which only amplified the anxiety that had been building inside of me. I moved further into the house and the distant sounds of a television and the occasional creak of the floorboards had my stomach in knots. And with each step, that knot grew tighter.

When I finally made it to his room, I knocked softly on the door. Seconds later, the door opened, and Jimmy appeared with disheveled hair and sleepy eyes. Knowing I'd just woken him, I tried to play nice and smiled as I whispered, "Hey, Jimmy."

"It's seven in the morning."

"Yeah, I know." I held up the duffle bag as I told him, "Steven told me to bring this by."

"Fuck." His gaze shifted from me to the bag as he grumbled, "You were supposed to bring it last night."

"I'm sorry." I shrugged. "I was just doing what he told me."

"It's cool." He took the bag and tossed it on the table, then turned his attention back to me. His eyes skirted over me as he said, "It's pretty cold out there. Come in and warm up for a minute."

"Thanks, but no thanks."

"I wasn't asking." He reached out and grabbed my arm, jerking me towards him. "You don't have to make this hard, babe. I know you're into me."

"I think you need to ease up on the drugs, Jimmy."

"You uptight little bitch." The fury in his eyes sent a shiver down my spine. "You wanna think you're better than me, but you're not. And one day, I'm gonna fuck some sense into you."

"Go to hell."

I yanked my arm free and charged for the door. I didn't get far before I heard him coming after me. I picked up the pace, but I wasn't fast enough. I'd just rounded the corner when he grabbed hold of my hair and gave it a hard jerk, forcing me to fall back on my ass. "You best watch your fucking mouth."

"Screw you, Jimmy."

"You live with an Assassin. That makes you Assassin property. We're gonna fuck you good and hard, each and every one of us, and when we're done, you'll be all used up." He reached down and grabbed hold of my throat, squeezing it tightly as he forced me to my feet. "Then, we'll go for your little girl. Won't no one want either one of you when we're done."

"I'll die before I let that happen."

"The clock's tickin'."

Horrified, I stormed out of his house and raced outside. I jumped into my car, and tears streamed down my face as I started the engine and sped towards the drug store. That was it. The time had come.

I had to get away from Steven, Jimmy, and the rest of those asshole Assassins before they made good on Jimmy's threats.

I just had no idea where I was going to go.

And to make matters worse, Christmas was right around the corner, and we were going to be on the streets.

Damn.

I couldn't catch a break.

Grim

Relief washed over me when I spotted the familiar lookout tower in the distance. The clubhouse was just around the bend, which meant after two and a half days of driving, I was finally home.

The building used to be an old, abandoned textile mill. It was right on the river and a prime spot for coming in and out of the city—which is why we'd bought it and converted it into our clubhouse. Eager to get inside, I pulled through the gate and parked. I'd just gotten out of the truck when I noticed Prez walking towards me.

Surprise marked his face as he asked, "Where's Beck?"

"Took him over to Amy's place."

"Why the fuck would you do that?"

The vein in Prez's neck pulsed with anger, and that wasn't something I wanted to see, especially when that anger was directed at me. While I was more than capable of holding my own, Prez was not a man I'd want to throw hands with—not that it would ever come to that. I respected him too much for that. Doing my best to de-escalate things, I told him, "It was what he wanted. I know it's fucked and I tried to talk him out of it, but..."

"Goddamn it," Prez grumbled under his breath. "I thought we were past all this bullshit."

"So did I but seems he still needs some time to himself."

"At his dead girl's house?" he snapped. "At Christmas? That's just asking for trouble."

"I thought the same thing, but he said he needed the time." I could tell by his expression that he didn't like my answer, so I added, "After everything, it didn't feel right not to give him that."

"Yeah, I get it." He ran his hand over his goatee. "Guess that means he's still pissed at me."

"I don't know if I'd say that, but he's still going through something."

"Isn't he always?"

"Yeah, but this seems different. He's trying to come into his own or something. Hell, maybe he's finally growing up."

"Wouldn't that be something?" Prez shook his head and smiled. "Love the kid, but damn. He can be a real thorn in my side."

"Bet you could say that about all of us at times."

"No doubt." He chuckled, but his laughter quickly faded into concern. "You really think he's doing okay?"

"Hard to tell, Prez. In some ways, he seemed to be holding his on, but in others, he seemed a bit off. Either way, he was a hell of a lot better than he was a few months ago."

"Well, there's that."

"If you want, I can go back over there tonight and see how he's making it."

"No, I'll go. It's time he and I hashed this thing out once and for all." He placed his hand on my shoulder. "Appreciate you going to get him. Now, go take a load off, and I'll get with you in the morning."

"Sounds good." Prez turned, and as he started towards his truck, I told him, "Later, Prez."

"Later."

Once he was gone, I made my way inside the clubhouse. I let out a deep breath as I stepped through the front door. It felt good to be back. It was my second home, and at times, it felt like more than that. I'd been here since we first started working on the place.

We'd spent months tearing down walls and completely overhauling the inside. We'd done what we could to hold onto the building's historic elements and kept exposed brick walls and industrial accents. There were twenty or more small bedrooms, a full kitchen with all the works, a hangout room with sofas and TVs, and a large bar.

The heart of the clubhouse was undoubtedly the

bar. It was where all the brothers gathered, especially when we needed to let off some steam, and I was in dire need of doing exactly that.

As soon as I walked inside, I was hit with the familiar scent of cigarette smoke and whiskey. It was late, so I wasn't surprised to find that Goose, Rusty, and a couple of prospects were the only ones there. I was okay with that. Rusty and Goose were always a good time.

Rusty was a bit of a wise ass. He was tall and built like a fucking refrigerator, and he was as stubborn as the day was long. You never knew what was going to come out of his mouth.

Goose was a bit more even-tempered. He always played it cool, and he had the looks to match. He had one of those kid faces that made him look ten years younger than he really was, and he would've looked even younger if it wasn't for all the fucking muscles and tattoos.

Neither of them had an ol' lady, so there was no urgency for either of them to get home. And from the looks of their heavy eyelids and sagging shoulders, they should've gone home hours ago.

As soon as Rusty spotted me, he flashed a smile. "Hey, brother. When did you roll in?"

"Just got here." I grabbed a bottle of Wild Turkey from the shelf as I told him, "And if anyone's asking, I'm not going anywhere any time soon."

"Can't blame you there."

The low hum of country tunes played from the jukebox in the corner, barely covering the thud of my boots as I walked across the room and sat down next to my brothers. I'd just started to pour myself a drink when Goose looked towards the doorway and asked, "Beck not with ya?"

"Afraid not." I topped off the glass, then took a long drink. "He decided to hang out at Amy's place for a bit."

"No shit?"

"No shit." I took another sip, then said, "You know how Beck is when he gets something in his head."

"Yeah, he can really dig in the heels." Rusty's brows furrowed as he said, "Surprised Prez was okay with him staying over there."

"He wasn't."

"So, what's he gonna do about it?"

"He's on his way over there now." I shrugged. "Maybe he can talk some sense into him. If not, I'll go back in the morning and try again."

"I can try, too," Goose offered. "If you think it'll do any good."

"Might take you up on that."

He reached for my bottle of Wild Turkey and poured it into his glass. "So, how were our boys in Washington doing?"

"They seemed to be making it alright." I chuckled as I said, "A lot's changed, and they seem to be adjusting to it all, but I don't think I'll ever be able to see Cotton as anything but the president. Same goes for Stitch. He was one hell of an enforcer, and it's hard to think of him as anything else."

"Yeah, we've all heard the stories about Stitch, and the crazy shit he's done." Rusty's eyes skirted over to me. "But then again, I'm sure they've heard the same shit about you."

"I doubt that."

"Seriously? Remember what you did to those Benton brothers?" Rusty cleared his throat. "I never knew acid could do that. Fucked me up for months. Just like hearing about Stitch and the blowtorch. Fuck. That shit was all kinds of fucked up. I don't know how you two do the things you do."

"Be interestin' to see you two working together."

Goose smirked as he said, "It'd be even more interestin' to see you two go against each other."

"That'd never happen."

"Yeah, but it would definitely be a fight worth watchin'." Rusty gave me a smirk. "I know he's a legend and all, but I think you could take him."

"I appreciate the vote of confidence."

Rusty and Goose continued with the pestering as we poured another drink and then another. It seemed like I'd barely sat down when an hour had passed, and the booze had caught up with me. I decided to call it a night, and the boys followed after. Since I'd been drinking, I skipped driving home and stayed in my room at the clubhouse.

It wasn't much, just a bed, dresser, and TV, but it

came in clutch on nights like these. I got undressed and crawled into bed, and I was out the second my head hit the pillow. I was sleeping like a baby when there was a pounding on my door. Without waiting for me to answer, Seven opened my door and charged into my room. "Grim! Gonna need you to get up."

"Yeah." The look on his face was enough to have me jump out of bed and start getting dressed. "What the hell is going on?"

"It's Beck."

"What about him?"

His voice trembled with urgency. "Ah, shit, brother. He fucked up. *He fucked up bad.*"

"What the hell are you talking about?"

"Gash got a call from one of his buddies, and he told him that he'd heard some rumor that Beck had gone over to Ruben's place late last night."

Ruben was an Assassin and not just any Assassin.

He was one of their main guys, and he wouldn't think twice about going to throws with anyone who tried any shit with him or his boys. Everyone knew that, including Beckett. My throat tightened. I already knew the answer before I asked, "Why the fuck would he go there?"

"He'd gotten into another round with Prez and took off. Guess he decided to go over there and confront the guys who killed Amy. They weren't expecting him, so he was able to barge right in and start shooting. Managed to take out a couple of them, but that's as far as he got."

Again, I already knew the answer when I asked, "What are you saying?"

He didn't respond.

He didn't have to. I could tell by his expression that Beckett was gone, and that revelation hit me like a ton of fucking bricks. I felt an overwhelming sense of regret, guilt, and grief. It was hard enough to lose someone close, but it was even harder to lose someone knowing that I'd had a part to play in it.

I started replaying different scenarios in my head, trying to figure out where I might've been able to intervene or offer some kind of help, but I just found one dead end after the other. I took a step back and shook my head. "No, that can't be right. He was fine. He was..."

"Gash didn't believe it either. He went looking for Beck early this morning. Found his car a few blocks away from Ruben's. They'd shoved him inside and tried to torch it, but the flames didn't take. Sloppy bastards."

"Goddamn it!" I turned and slammed my fist into the wall, busting through the drywall. I'd fucked up, and it weighed on me in ways I'd never be able to explain. Understanding my anguish, Seven remained silent and gave me time to process. "I need to see him!"

"I don't think..."

"I wanna fucking see him!"

Without arguing any further, I charged past him and out of the room. I saw nothing but red as I made my way down the hall and into the infirmary. When I stormed in, Beckett was lying lifeless on a gurney. His eyes were closed, and at first glance, he looked to be sleeping. But then, I saw that his clothes had been cut from his body, and he was covered in blood. Blade was standing over him, cleaning him little by little.

I walked over, and bile rose to my throat when I saw the bullet wounds in his chest and head. Fuck. He was just a kid. He had his whole fucking life ahead of him, and he was lying on that gurney because I wasn't there to stop him from going into that house. "This shit should've never happened. It's on me. I should've done more to make sure..."

"Nah, brother. Don't do that to yourself. This shit isn't on you." Blade sounded sincere as he said, "Beck was always a live wire. You never knew what the hell he was gonna do."

"No, it was my job to protect him, and I failed."

"Prez and Memphis both said the same thing." Blade placed his hand on my shoulder as he tried to reassure me, "This whole thing is fucked up. You don't need to make it worse by putting blame where it doesn't belong."

"This couldn't get any worse."

"You best go and check in with the others." He glanced down at Beck, then said, "They're trying to figure out what the hell we're gonna do about all this."

I nodded, then made my way out of the room and down the hall to the conference room. I could feel the tension crackling around the room as I walked over to my place at the table. I looked around at my brothers, and like me, they seemed to be just as stunned and enraged by the news of what had happened to Beck.

I was hoping to have a moment with Prez, so I could give him my condolences and assure him that we would avenge his son's death. But he wasn't there. Creed, our VP, stood in his place. His expression was stoic as he called us to order.

"I know you're all eager to speak with Prez and give him your regards, but it's best to give him some space. He needs it and deserves it, and I expect you all to respect that."

"Understood."

"I know they aren't all involved in this, but Ruben is one of their leaders. If we go after him, we gotta go after them all."

"Agreed."

"Shep has already started working on finding us all the names and addresses of every known Assassin in town, and he'll track their phones to find their current locations."

Shepard was the club's hacker. He used his computer as a way of looking out for us in a way that no one else could, and he did it well. From tracking folks down to breaking into the FBI's database, there wasn't anything he couldn't do on that computer, and that included finding anyone associated with the Assassins.

"We'll use what he finds to decide how we want to move forward." Anguish marked our VP's face as he confessed, "You should all know upfront that this whole thing is a goddamn clusterfuck. These guys are spread out all over town, so when we hit, we gotta hit hard and fast. Their hangout. Their homes. Their fucking cars. We've gotta be everywhere at once, or they're gonna get the best of us."

"Not gonna happen." I showed no emotion as I told them, "We're gonna get these motherfuckers. One by one. And everyone around will be better off when we do."

"You're right about that." Creed turned his attention to me as he asked, "How are you wanting this thing to go?"

"We hit the bar first, see who we can take out there. Then, we split up, go to the addresses Shep finds for us, and hunt down whoever's left."

"Fuck yeah. Let's do it."

And with that, Creed stood, and we all followed him out to the artillery room. It was hidden beneath the garage, and it contained everything we could possibly need for battle—from guns and knives to bulletproof vests. We'd gathered what we needed, then headed out to the parking lot.

We were loading everything into the back of the SUVs when Shep came running up behind us. The big brute looked relieved as he rushed over and handed me a folder. "We got 'em."

"All of them?"

"Every last one."

"Good work, brother." I motioned my head toward the SUV as I asked, "You coming with?"

"Absolutely."

Without hesitation, he whipped around to the side of the truck and got in. He'd just closed the door when Prez and Memphis, Beckett's brother, stepped out of the clubhouse and started walking towards us. As expected, they both looked visibly shaken, but more than that, they looked enraged in a way I'd never seen before.

Prez didn't say a word as he got in the front seat of my SUV and closed the door. When Memphis started over to Duggar's truck, I called out to him, "Memphis?"

"Yeah."

"You sure this is a good idea?"

"We're going, Grim."

His determined tone made it clear that he couldn't be dissuaded from coming along to seek revenge for his brother's death, so I gave him a nod and finished loading the last of our gear. Once I was done, I closed the back hatch and got inside with Prez and Shep. I started the engine, and as soon as I started through the gate, Creed followed behind with Ghost, Gash, and Memphis. Duggar was the last to roll out with Smitty and several prospects.

We hadn't gotten far when I felt compelled to turn to Prez and say, "I'm sorry, Prez. I should've..."

"Don't," Prez ordered, cutting me off.

The truck fell silent, and the already tense moment

became excruciating. I should've listened to Creed and kept my fucking mouth shut. We all rode in silence for several long minutes, and I thought we would remain that way until Prez finally said, "What happened to Beckett isn't on you."

"But it is." My shoulders tensed. "I spent the last two days with him. I should've known."

"I'm his father, and I didn't know." Prez shook his head, his eyes reflecting the pain we both felt. "None of us could've seen it coming. Beckett knew what he was doing. He knew what would happen if he went in there, and he went anyway. That's on him. Blaming yourself won't bring him back."

I felt my chest tighten as I said, "I let you down."

"No, I let myself down." Prez let out a breath. "I'm his father. I shouldn't have pushed so damn hard, but I did and here we are. I just need us to get through this thing without losing anyone else. Can we do that?"

"We'll do the best we can," Shep answered from the back.

"That's all I ask."

With that, the conversation ended, and I took the moment to mentally prepare for what lay ahead. It was going to be a hell of a fight, but then again, it always was. I didn't mind it. I liked the rush that came with the hunt, but I didn't like having my brothers in the line of fire.

Unfortunately, this wasn't a fight I could do without them. We weren't just seeking revenge on the Assassins.

We were setting an example for anyone else who might consider going up against Fury, and we had to do it in a way that would leave an impression.

It was still daylight when we pulled into the gravel-strewn parking lot. It was a risk to go in without the cover of night, but it was the best way for us to maintain the element of surprise. We pulled around back and parked, and even though I'd never been inside, I could tell the place was a dump.

Some of the bricks on the exterior were busted or cracked, the roof needed replacing ten years ago, and there was trash and weeds scattered all over the lot. A dozen or so cars were parked out front, and several were sporting the Assassins' black and red colors on their rearview mirrors. I hoped that was a good sign as I parked and started to get out of the truck.

As soon as everyone had gathered around, I started with the rundown. "Seven and I will be the first ones going in. We'll need Duggar and Ghost to cover us until we're inside, and once we get into position, all bets are off. I'm gonna shoot who I can, and I'm gonna need you boys to do the same."

"You two aren't going in there without me," Memphis interjected. "Beck was my brother, and..."

"That's not going to happen," Prez interrupted. "I've already lost one son today. I'm not taking a chance on losing another."

"You can't keep me from going in there..."

"I can, and I am. You're not going, and I don't wanna hear another fucking word about it."

"Fuck."

Memphis slammed his fist into the side of Creed's SUV, denting the hell out of it before walking away from the group. I gave Prez a minute to collect himself, then asked, "We good?"

"We're good."

I gave him a nod, then looked back at my brothers and was pleased to see that they were locked and loaded. Like me, their thirst for revenge had them eager to get inside. With them following closely behind, I made my way up to the door.

I stopped and looked in the window, and just as I expected, there were two guys stationed at each entrance, making it impossible for us to get inside unnoticed. I wasn't about to let that stop me, especially when I spotted Ruben at one of the back tables. He was laughing and drinking a beer, and just the sight of him had my blood boiling.

I took another quick scan of the bar, then turned back to Seven as I announced, "Change of plan."

"What do you need me to do?"

"Nothing." I reached into my back pocket and grabbed a second clip. "Just hold tight until I give you the signal."

He nodded, and he and the others watched as I slammed the butt of my gun against the window. As soon as the glass shattered, I started shooting, killing the two guards at the front, then moved to the two in the back. I was still shooting when I heard Seven shout, "Damn, brother. Didn't know you were gonna play it like that."

"You gonna help me out or what?"

"Waiting on you to give me the signal."

"I just gave it."

"We got you, brother."

I was still firing off at the window when Seven and the others positioned themselves at the door. I gave him a nod and covered them as they made their way inside. I quickly followed, and it was instant mayhem.

Bullets whipped through the room—some came a little too close, but I was too cranked up on adrenaline to care. Like a man possessed, I continued to charge further into the room, firing off round after round as I took out anyone who was still breathing.

With each body that dropped dead to the ground, I gained a sense of satisfaction, and that satisfaction grew even stronger when I spotted Ruben on the floor. He was face down and dragging himself across the floor. I was considering how I was going to get to him when silence fell over the room. The shooting had stopped just as quickly as it had started.

I glanced around the room, and we were the only ones standing. It was done. I was in the clear, so I stormed over to Ruben and planted my feet in his path. Panic marked his face as he looked up at me and pleaded, "Come on, man. Just finish me off."

"And what would be the fun in that?"

I could've pulled the trigger and ended it right there, but when I thought about what he and his boys had done to Amy, and then to Beckett, I just couldn't do it. He deserved to hurt the way he'd made Beckett hurt for all those months, and I was going to make sure that he did.

I knelt down as I snarled, "You and I are going to spend some quality time together. But don't worry. I'm gonna get you patched up first." I gave him a wink. "Wouldn't want you to go and die on me before we get the party started."

"It ain't gotta be like that."

"Oh, but it does. You killed one of ours, and now, you're gonna pay for that shit." I turned to Gash and Jonesy, one of our prospects, and ordered, "Take him to the clubhouse and secure him in one of my rooms. Have Doc check him out and tell him I want him alive when I get back."

"You got it."

Even though we were in a rough side of town where the cops don't always come running, I wasn't going to take any chances. I turned to Seven and announced, "We need to get the hell out of here."

He nodded, and then we both quickly gathered the rest of the prospects and a couple brothers and ordered them to torch the place. Even the slightest bit of evidence could be detrimental, so I wasn't surprised when Prez stopped Duggar and ordered him to stick around and keep an eye on things.

The rest of us headed outside, where we met up with Shep. He was on his laptop, shaking his head as he went through the list of names he'd generated. We needed to know who was left and where to find them, and I hoped he had it all figured out until I heard him say, "I can't be sure. Even with all their tattoos, it was too hard to identify some of them."

"Do the best you can."

He nodded and scanned his screen once more, then said, "Looks like we've got four left with two, maybe three, places to hit."

"Just tell me where we're going."

"Billy Mathos and Gael Santos are over on Remington Cove, and Jimmy and Clayborn are over on Glenn."

Jimmy and Clayborn were names I'd heard before. Deshawn told me all about them when I'd caught him in that alley. They'd started this whole mess with Ruben, and I was ready to end it.

"I've got Jimmy and Clayborn, and I'll take Ghost and Gash with me." I looked over to Seven as I said, "You take Smitty and Creed over to the cove."

"You got it."

"And what about the rest of us?" Prez asked, sounding pissed.

"We need you to go to the clubhouse and hold tight." I understood that Beck was his son and he felt the need to be in the thick of things, but he'd already put himself in enough danger. "If one of these guys isn't where Shep thinks they are, then we'll need you to go take care of them."

"You got it."

I gave him a quick nod, and we all dispersed.

As I got back in the truck, I had an uneasy feeling that we were about to encounter something unexpected—something that could change everything. That feeling should've had me turning that truck around.

It didn't.

Nothing was going to stop me from finishing off the Assassins, once and for all.

Jenna

I'd had a bad feeling all day.

It wasn't the first time.

I'd felt it countless times since moving in with my brother. He'd put me through the ringer with all his craziness, so it made sense that I was always on edge.

But today was different.

All the bells and whistles were going off in my head, and I knew I had to get Luna and I out of there before something terrible happened. As soon as I got off work, I rushed to the daycare and picked up Luna, then drove straight home. I rushed to our room and quickly started gathering everything we owned into a black garbage bag.

Luna sat huddled in a corner, clutching a stuffed animal as she watched me pack our belongings. Her eyes were wide and full of fear as she muttered, "What's wrong, Momma?"

"We've gotta find somewhere else to live, sweetie." I was terrified that Steven or Jimmy would show up and cause trouble, so I kept glancing over my shoulder every few seconds, making sure we were still alone. "I've got to get us somewhere safe."

"Why?"

"It's complicated, sweetie." I continued shoving our things into the bag as I told her, "But don't you worry. Momma is going to take care of it."

"Can I take Boo?"

Boo was her favorite stuffed animal and most prized possession, so I told her, "Of course you can. You can take anything you want."

I opened another garbage bag and quickly filled it with Christmas presents I'd bought for Luna. It wasn't much, just a doll she'd been begging for and a small kitchen playset. I'd used the last of my savings to buy it, but I had no choice. I had to get her something for Christmas.

I was just about to pack the last of my clothes when the front door burst open. Panic washed over me when I heard Jimmy and Steven's voices, followed by footsteps coming down the hall.

I darted over to Luna and pulled her off the bed. "I need you to hide under the bed. Just for a few minutes, and I need you to be really quiet. I mean it. Not a word. Do you understand?"

With brows furrowed, she nodded and did as I asked. Once she was safely hidden, I dropped the comforter over the foot of the bed, concealing her even more. I continued closing the bag, praying that they would leave us alone, but when I saw my doorknob turn, I knew that wasn't the case.

The door slowly creaked open, and Steven scowled as he stepped into the now barren room. "What the hell is all this?"

"We're leaving," I answered.

"Leaving?" he scoffed. "Where the fuck you think you're gonna go?"

"That's not any of your business."

"You can come stay with me," Jimmy snickered. "I'll take real good care of you and your little girl."

"I don't think so."

"See?" Jimmy nudged Steven. "The stuck-up bitch thinks she's too good for me."

"She's got no reason to think that shit," Steven snapped. "Bitch don't even got a place to live."

"Steven," I pleaded.

"You've always thought you were better," he snarled. "And for no reason. Hell, look at ya. You're nothing, and you'll always be nothing."

Jimmy took a step over to me and wrapped his grubby hands around my waist, pulling me against his chest. "I'm gonna fuck you so good."

"That's not happening." I jerked free from his grasp. "Not now. Not ever."

"It's time for you to have an attitude adjustment."

He raised his hand and smacked it across my face,

busting my lip. His face was flushed with anger, and even though I knew more was coming, I sassed, "That all you got?"

"You little bitch!"

This time, he reared his hand back into a fist and plowed it into my eye, sending my head flailing back. Steven took the moment of opportunity to punch me in the stomach. It wasn't the first time he'd put his hands on me. My dear brother was an asshole and could care less who he hurt—even his own flesh and blood.

I hunched over and wrapped my arms protectively across my chest, but it did little to help when he kneed me in the gut, taking my breath away. I was still trying to recover when Jimmy grabbed me and shoved me back, pinning me against the wall with his knife pressed against my throat. I could feel the blade cutting into my skin as his free hand dropped to my thigh.

"Not so tough after all." He started inching towards my crotch, groping me as he said, "I'm gonna fuck you long and hard."

"Fuck you, Jimmy."

When I tried to push him off me, he tightened his grip on my throat and called out to Steven, "Help me get her on the bed."

Steven stepped over and grabbed my hands, tugging me towards the bed. They'd just gotten me on my back when the front door flew open with a hard thud, like someone had just kicked it in. Jimmy shot up and looked over to Steven, "What the hell was that?"

"Fuck if I know."

They both started for the door, and as soon as they stepped out of the room, Jimmy shouted, "Woah, who the hell are you?"

"Jimmy?"

"Yeah. Who the fuck…"

Before he could finish his thought, gunfire exploded through the house. I heard Steven wail as the bullets rattled through his body, and he dropped to the ground. A small part of me felt a slight pull to rush out into the hall and check on him. But that feeling quickly faded into a cold, numb relief. The past couple of years with him had been rough, and over the past few weeks, I actually started to fear for my life and Luna's.

Tonight, he proved that feeling right.

All thoughts rushed from my mind the second I heard footsteps coming down the hall. Whoever had killed my brother and Jimmy was coming for me and my precious daughter, and there was nothing I could do about it. I was a sitting duck.

I considered darting under the bed with Luna, but it was too small. I would never fit, so I let my back slide down the wall. As soon as my rear hit the ground, I drew my knees up to my chest and wrapped my arms around my legs. I lowered my head and braced myself for what was to come.

Seconds later, I heard the men enter the room. One of them continued over to me, stopping just inches from my feet and nudged my calf with their boot. "Hey."

I lifted my head, and as I looked up, my eyes were met with the most fierce, terrifying, unbelievably gorgeous man I'd ever seen. He had dark hair and even darker eyes, and he was broad and muscular in a way that let you know he could handle whatever came his way. He'd just killed my brother, and I had every reason to believe that he would do the same to me and Luna just for having ties to him.

I wasn't sure how to answer, so I remained silent.

He studied the marks on my face for a moment, then asked, "They do that to you?"

I nodded. "You killed them."

"Yeah, well, we had our reasons." He glanced back at his two friends at the door, then turned his attention back to me. "You got a name?"

"Jenna."

"I don't know what you're doing here, Jenna, but..."

His words trailed off, and I had no idea why he'd stopped talking until I felt Luna's little hand on my thigh. She'd crawled up next to me without me even knowing it. "Oh, sweetie. You should've stayed under the bed."

"I was sck-ared, Mommy."

"I know. I am, too." I pulled Luna close as I looked up at the man and said, "This is my daughter, Luna. Just let us go, and you'll never see or hear from us again."

"Go, but just know, if you breathe a word of any of this..."

"I won't say anything. I swear it." I gave him a slight shrug. "Besides, it was only a matter of time before someone did it."

Worried he might change his mind, I quickly stood and picked up Luna. I settled her on my hip before grabbing the bags filled with our things and rushing for the door. I eased past the stranger's friends, and as soon as I stepped into the hall, I saw my brother's feet and stopped dead in my tracks.

I put my mouth to my daughter's ear and whispered, "Close your eyes, sweetheart. Close 'em tight."

I waited for her to close them, then said, "That's my good girl. Now, keep them closed until I tell you to open them. Okay, sweetie? Can you do that for Momma?"

"Um-hmm," she mumbled with a nod.

I quickly stepped over Steven's lifeless body and then Jimmy's. Once I was in the clear, I rushed down the hall and out the front door. I continued out to my car and put Luna in her car seat. I put our bags in the back seat next to her, then hurried over to the driver's side and got in.

I put the key in the ignition and turned it, expecting it to turn on, but got nothing more than a strange clicking noise. I turned it again, and relief washed over me when the engine roared to life. I quickly threw it into gear and started backing out of the driveaway. Unfortunately, I didn't get very far.

I thought we were in the clear until a loud, thunderous boom came from the front of my car, followed by a thick, billowing smoke. The car abruptly died, leaving an eerie silence in its wake. Even though I knew it was pointless, I turned the key again, praying it might get us a little further down the road, but no such luck.

It was only a matter of time before those men came outside, so I reached for my door handle and was about to pull it open when Steven's front door opened. The three men came filing out, and the last one tossed a lit match into the house. In a blink, the entire living room was engulfed in flames.

The three men started down the front steps, and it wasn't long before the man who'd freed me and Luna spotted us sitting in my car. He said something to his friends, then started over to us. When he reached my car, he motioned to my window, but that wasn't going to happen. My car was dead, so I eased the door open, and he immediately snapped, "Why the hell are you still here?"

"My car," I muttered nervously. "It's not starting."

He glared at me with annoyance, and I feared he'd kill us right then and there. Instead, he asked, "Where were you headed?"

"I don't know."

"Don't play games with me. I don't have the time nor the patience."

"I don't really have a place to go," I confessed. "I was going to try one of the shelters for a night or maybe sleep in my car, but now, my car isn't an option and where we were staying is now on fire and..."

"Yeah, yeah. I get it." He let out a frustrated breath, then turned to his two buddies and said, "Call Skid and have him meet us over at my place."

"We're taking them to your place?"

"I didn't stutter."

"You gotta be kiddin'." His friend gave me a once-over. "We don't know anything about this chick. Hell, she could be one of them for all we know."

"Yeah, she could." His eyes drifted to the backseat, and they locked on Luna's as he said, "But I'm not sending them to one of those shelters. Hell, you know how they are. No way in hell they'd survive the night."

"And why the hell does that matter?" the blond scoffed. "These two ain't nothin' to us."

"They're going to my place, and that's the end of it."

And just like that, all eyes were on me. There was clearly some unease between the men, and I didn't want to add to it. I just wanted this whole thing to be over, so I looked to the man in charge and said, "I appreciate the offer and all, but that's not necessary. We can..."

"It's not up for discussion." He opened the back door and grabbed our bags as he ordered, "Now get the kid and let's go."

I got out of the car and grabbed Luna from the backseat, then followed the men over to their SUV. I had every reason to be completely terrified, but I wasn't. These men seemed different than Steven and his friends. None of them would've given two shits about me and Luna going to a shelter. For that matter, they would've been happy to see us go—as long as I did a stupid drop along the way.

I had no idea who these men were or what they were about, but something in my gut told me I'd be better off with them than in some shelter. As soon as we were settled inside the SUV, Luna looked up at me with worry in her eyes and whispered, "I don't wanna go."

"It's okay." I reached over and placed my hand on hers, squeezing it gently. "Momma's here. I won't let anything happen."

I glanced over to the two men in the front seat and then to the man to my left, and while they all three looked intimidating as hell, I felt oddly safe with them. I prayed I wasn't wrong; otherwise, Luna and I could be worse off than we were before, and I didn't think that was possible.

Grim

"You know, we could just give her some cash and drop 'em off at a hotel somewhere."

"Yeah, we could, but we're not. At least, not yet."

"What about Prez?"

"What about him?"

"You gonna tell him about the girls or let it ride?"

I'd called Prez right before we torched Clayborn's place and told him that we'd gotten our two guys and were on our way back. I'd made no mention of Jenna or her daughter, and Ghost knew it. He also knew I didn't keep secrets, especially from Prez.

I glanced up at my review mirror, and my stomach did a nosedive when I found two sets of dark eyes staring right back at me. They were scared, and I couldn't really blame them. They had no idea who we were or where we were truly taking them.

I wanted to assure them both that they were safe,

but I doubted they would believe me. So, I turned my attention to Ghost as I told him, "I'll tell Prez everything as soon as we get them to the house."

"How long are you planning on keeping them there?"

"You'll know when I know. Now, how 'bout you get off my fucking back?"

"Sorry, brother. I was just..."

"I know what you were doing." He was just trying to look out for me, so I softened my tone as I said, "And I'm telling you it's not necessary."

I was eager to get these two dropped off, so I pressed my foot against the accelerator and sped over to my house. It wasn't long before my driveway came into view. My place wasn't fancy by any means. It was a brick ranch-style house with a wrap-around front porch. That was about all it had going for it.

There were four bedrooms, but I only used the master. It had a decent-sized living room with a sofa and a recliner, and there was a large flat screen hanging over the fireplace. The kitchen was alright. It needed some updating, but I was rarely there and hadn't taken the time to do anything with it.

The other rooms were basically empty—other than a bed and few random boxes of shit I never put away. Needless to say, I wasn't worried about anyone messing up the place, especially when it came to this chick and her kid. They both looked relatively harmless, and I had no intention of them staying more than a couple of days

—just long enough for me to figure out what to do with them.

When I pulled into the drive, Skid was already there and waiting on the front steps. I got out, grabbed the garbage bags full of Jenna's stuff, and carried them over to the porch. I could tell by Skid's expression that he was wondering why I'd called him there.

We had other prospects, but he was the only one I trusted to not only watch over Jenna and her daughter, but to be in my house. He knew my expectations and would abide by them better than any of the others. I handed him the key to the house as I told him, "Got a lady and her kid that's gonna be staying here for a couple of days, and I want you to watch over them while they're here."

"Okay. I can do to that."

"Her name's Jenna, and the kid's Luna. That's about all we know about them so keep a close eye on them. There's food in the fridge but get them more if they need it."

"You got it."

"If anything comes up—*and I mean anything*, call me."

I motioned my hand, signaling for them to get out. Seconds later, the door opened, and the beautiful brunette got out with her daughter. As soon as they started walking towards us, Skid gasped, "Holy shit. She's a fucking stunner."

He was right.

She was indeed stunning.

And she didn't even have to work at it.

She was just wearing jeans with a simple sweater, but she looked like she'd stepped out of one of those beauty magazines. Her hair was dirty blonde and curly in a sexy, windblown sort of way, and she barely had on any makeup.

She didn't need it.

She was a natural beauty—just the kind of girl Skid would be interested in, so I leaned in closer as I asked, "You gonna be able to handle this, or should I get someone else?"

"Yeah, I got it."

"I'm gonna hold you to that."

"Who worked her over?"

"The assholes she was staying with."

Before he had a chance to respond, they walked up. Jenna held her daughter close as she nervously looked around the house. Her eyes darted over to me when I said, "You two make yourself at home. I'll be back when I'm back."

"Wait. You're just going to leave us here?"

"Skid's gonna be here." I held her gaze for a moment, then added, "If you need something, let him know and he'll take care of it."

"But my car... I have work and..."

"It'll be taken care of."

"But why?" she pushed. "Why would you do that? Why would you help me? Do you want something from me? Are you going to do something to us?"

"I've been in a tight spot before." I looked over at the kid in her arms, remembering how scared I was when my mother and I had to live on the streets. It was rough, and there were times I didn't think we were going to make it. "Someone helped me and my mother out, and I'm just doing the same for you."

"But I can't pay you or anything like that."

Her vulnerable tone got to me in a way I didn't expect, and I had to collect myself before answering. I inhaled a deep breath, then said, "Didn't ask you to. Just go get settled, and let Skid know if you need anything."

Without saying anything more, I turned and walked back to the SUV. As soon as I was behind the wheel, I threw it into reverse and whipped out of the driveway. When we got back to the clubhouse, everyone was gathered in the conference room. Shep was on his laptop, searching for any news on the Assassins, while Prez and Memphis hovered over his shoulder.

There was no missing the concern in Prez's voice when he asked, "Are we good?"

"It's looking that way." Shep continued to type away at his keyboard. "I just want to check a few more things."

"Let me know if you find anything." Prez stood, and the second he spotted me and Ghost, he walked over and asked, "Are you just now gettin' back?"

"Yeah, we just rolled in." I could tell by his expression that he was going to ask what held us up, so I added, "We ran into a complication over at Clayborn's place."

"What kind of complication?"

"There was a woman and kid there."

"You get rid of them?"

"We took 'em over to my place."

I clenched my jaw, bracing myself for his response, and just as I expected, he was pissed. *"You did what?"*

"I had my reasons, Prez."

"So, you know this chick?"

"Never laid eyes on her."

His brows furrowed. "So, you know nothing about this girl."

"I know those guys had roughed her up and had her scared out of her fucking mind." I kept my tone steady and showed no emotion as I continued, "I know her car was a piece of shit and wouldn't start, and I know she had no place to go and was planning to take her kid to one of the shelters in town. She's got no money and nobody to turn to. A chick like her isn't gonna have the means to cause trouble."

"She's a woman," Prez scoffed. "She has plenty means."

"I can handle her."

"I certainly hope so. She's at your place now?"

"Yeah, Skid is with her. He'll watch over things until I can get back."

"You sure he can handle that?"

"He's come too far not to."

"I know this hasn't been easy on either of you. I know that firsthand, but it will be worth it in the end."

I was just about to respond when my burner started ringing. I quickly reached into my pocket, and when I glanced down at the screen, I was surprised to see that the number had a Washington area code. Curious, I looked up at Prez and said, "I need to take this."

"Go ahead. I'll catch up with you later."

I nodded, then stepped away and answered, "You got Grim."

"Hey, man. It's Rooster."

"Hey, brother."

His words were laced with apprehension as he asked, "I know you guys have a lot going on, but I was wondering if you'd seen or talked to Beckett today. I've been trying to call him but couldn't get him to answer."

"Yeah, well, there's been a bit of a situation, and it's left us all scrambling."

"What kind of situation?"

"Beckett went after the guys who hurt Amy."

"He did what?"

"Yeah, he just went barreling in there and got himself killed."

"Damn, brother. That's all kinds of fucked up. I knew he wanted his revenge, but I never dreamed he'd do something like that. You got any idea what Preacher's gonna do?"

"We're taking care of it."

"Just say the word, and we're there. We'll help get these guys..."

"I appreciate it, brother, but we got it covered."

Rooster was silent for a moment, then said, "I sure wish I'd gotten his message sooner."

"What message?"

"It was a text he left on my personal, but with everything we've had going on I didn't see it." Rooster sounded broken up as he explained, "Looks like he sent it the night you guys got back... Told me he was done walking, but I doubt that's gonna make much sense to you."

"No, afraid not."

"He was having a tough time, so I told him you gotta go through hell to get to the good stuff, and even though it's hard, you gotta keep walking. I'd reminded him of that the day he left, and I hoped he would. Guess he just didn't have it in him."

"He let his demons get the best of him and left us with a hell of a mess."

"I can imagine, and I hate that for you guys. Beckett was a good kid. I'm sure it's been rough."

"Yeah, it has been, especially for Preacher and Memphis."

"I sure hate that. Give Preacher our condolences, and remember, we're here if you need us."

"Thanks, Roost. I'll be sure to let Prez know you called."

After I hung up the phone, I made my way back

over to Prez and told him about Rooster calling. I told him about the message Beckett had sent and what Rooster had told him. I could tell from his expression that it meant a lot to him that Rooster had tried to get through to him.

But he didn't say anything.

He simply turned and walked out of the room.

I got it. He needed a minute. I needed one, too but I needed to check in with Shep first. I made my way over to him, and he was still hacking away at the laptop when I peered over his shoulder. "How's it looking?"

"It's all good. We did it." Shep glanced over his shoulder. "But I found something you might be interested in."

"Oh?"

"Yeah, it turns out that Clayborn had a sister." After pushing a few keys, Jenna's picture came up on his screen. She was younger and her hair was darker, but it was her. "And looks like she might've been staying at his place with her daughter."

"She was. We found her there."

"So, she's the one you took over to your place?"

"Yeah, that's her."

"You think we're gonna have a problem?"

"No way I can answer that." I sounded like a fucking asshole. I don't know what the hell I was thinking letting this chick and her kid into my home, but what was done was done. I didn't want to make matters worse, so I told him, "Find out everything you can on her and get it to me within the hour."

"You got it."

I gave him a pat on the shoulder, and as I started out of the room, I told him, "Appreciate it, brother."

I was still amped up and needing to wind down. I considered heading to the bar, but I knew there was only one thing that was going to knock off the edge. And that was paying Ruben a visit, so I made my way out back, where my interrogation rooms were located.

As I walked up to the first two-way mirrored glass, I caught a glimpse of myself, and it occurred to me that I'd never seen God. But right then, at that very moment, I saw the devil staring back at me.

I'd seen him every time I walked into that room, and today was no different.

I looked at him for a moment, then shook it off and continued inside. There, I found Ruben bound to a table with his arms pulled tightly over his head and his legs spread wide. He heard me coming towards him and tried to raise his head, but it was taped down to the table. I remained out of his view as I told him, "We meet again."

"If you know what's good for you, you'll let me go."

"Not gonna happen." I placed my hand on one of the bandages covering his bullet wounds and pressed down on it firmly, causing him to bellow out in agony. "Looks like doc's been in to see ya."

"Why the fuck you wanna patch me if you're just gonna end up killin' me?"

"Like I told you before. We're gonna spend some quality time together. I'm going to make you feel every ounce of pain you've inflicted on others. *Every. Fucking. Ounce.*"

"My boys will come for me, and when they do, you're as good as dead."

"No one's coming for you," I scoffed. "Your boys are dead. Every last one of them."

"You sick motherfucker."

"You're right. I am." I wanted him to get better. It was the only way he would live through the hell I had planned for him, but I couldn't stop myself from slamming my fist into one of his wounds. "By the time I'm done with you, you'll wish you'd never laid eyes on that girl. And you'll sure as hell wish you'd never killed our boy. You can count on that."

I knew I'd kill him if I stayed in that room, so I left things there and headed straight for the bar. My heart was still pounding with frustration as I made my way over to the counter and grabbed a beer. I wasn't surprised to find that the place was packed with brothers and hang arounds. We'd had an eventful day, and like me, they were looking to blow off some steam.

I'd just popped the cap and was about to take a drink when I spotted Memphis sitting alone at one of the tables in the back. Even from across the room, I could tell he was having a rough go of it, so I headed over to have a word with him. As soon as I approached, he glanced up and muttered, "Hey, brother. How's it going?"

"It's going." As I sat down, I motioned my hand toward his bottle of whiskey. "Skipping the beer straight to the rye?"

"Needed something a bit stronger."

"Having a hard time of it?"

"You could say that." He took a sip before adding, "This whole thing has turned me for a loop."

"It's gotten to all of us. I can only imagine how it's been with you."

He shook his head. "Beckett was a pain in the ass, but he was my brother, and I would've done just about anything for him. But that whole thing with Amy was a cluster. You know?"

"It definitely was."

"Looking back, I can't help but think we should've just gone on and dealt with the Assassins the second all that happened. Maybe then, Beck would still be here and..."

"What's done is done. We can't go back."

"Don't start with that bullshit! I know we can't go back!" he roared. "I know I can't change anything! I'm saying it should've never happened! None of it! He should still be here! And if we'd just done what we should've done, he would be! And I wouldn't be sitting here feeling like..."

He grabbed the bottle of whiskey and flung it at the

wall behind us, shattering it into a million pieces. He sat there for a moment, just staring at the mess he'd made, then stood with a stricken look on his face. "I'm sorry, brother. I just can't do this right now."

Without saying anything more, he turned and walked out the back door. Damn. I should've just left it alone. I took it as my sign to call it a night. I took my beer and finished it off before tossing it into the trash. As I started for the door, I gave Ghost and Gash a nod, letting them know I was leaving.

I went straight to my room, took a long hot shower, and when I got out, my worn-out mattress was calling my name. I slid under the cool sheets, and as I settled back on my pillow, I had high hopes for a good night's sleep. But as soon as I closed my eyes, my phone chimed with a message.

I quickly grabbed it, and my chest tightened when I saw that it was a message from Shep. He was sending me what he found on Jenna, and I wasn't sure I wanted to read it. She'd been lingering in the back of my mind since I'd left her at my place, and I had a feeling that what Shep sent was only going to make matters worse. Damn. It had been a long time since a woman had gotten under my skin the way she had, and I didn't like it—not one fucking bit.

Jenna

The details of that day had etched themselves into my memory—the way the sunlight filtered through the trees, the distant sounds of a lawnmower, the brim of his hat, the remorse in his eyes, and the somber voice cadence. They haunted me in my dreams, especially when I was going through a rough patch, so it was no surprise when I dreamed of those familiar words...

"Hello. Are you Ms. Jenna Clayborn?"

A navy officer stood on my doorstep in his freshly pressed uniform, and I could tell by his stoic expression that he was about to deliver some terrible news. I knew what was coming. He was going to tell me that Jeremy had been killed in the line of duty and had left me alone to give birth and raise our daughter.

It was news I didn't want to hear, and I had to fight the urge to close the door and force him to leave. I swallowed hard, then answered, "Yes, I'm Jenna. How can I help you?"

"I'm Officer Simon Reynolds. I'm here about Sergeant Jeremy Graves."

Everything around me stilled as he spoke. His words fell like lead, and my hopes and dreams disappeared in the silence that followed. My fingers trembled as I clutched the doorframe, bracing myself as my world crumbled beneath me.

I watched his mouth as he offered his condolences, but I hadn't heard a word he'd said. I was too lost in disbelief to respond. I was too busy trying to figure out what I was going to do.

I loved Jeremy.

We'd met in high school and became best friends.

I was going to marry him.

We were going to have a family together.

Neither of us had great lives. His father was an abusive asshole who ran off his mother. My folks were both drug addicts who barely survived the day, much less took care of me and Steven. Jeremy joined the military as our ticket out. He had it in his head that we wouldn't have to stay in the projects with the gangs and constant killings and that we'd have a chance at a real future together. Even though I wasn't happy about him enlisting, I went along with it. I thought I'd just have to bide my time until he came home.

Only that day never came, and it never would.

Losing him changed everything.

I was twenty-one, pregnant, and completely alone. I was also broke and unable to pay rent with what I made working at the laundry mat. I got a second job and tried to manage my finances the best I could, and I was doing okay. But when Luna came along, everything changed.

When I didn't show up for work, I lost my second job.

And even though I was able to take Luna with me to the laundry mat, I couldn't make enough money to cover all my bills. Once I got behind, it started to snowball, and I lost my apartment. Even though I knew it wasn't a good idea, I moved in with my parents, but the nightmare continued. I tried to make the best of it, but I couldn't raise an infant in such a volatile environment.

That's when I turned to my brother.

I spent two horrific years with him, and now, I was sleeping in a stranger's bed and praying I wouldn't wake up to find myself in another bad spot. I knew nothing about the men who'd brought me here, but I'd been around long enough to know that you don't trust anyone—especially men who kill other men.

When I woke up the next morning, I was relieved to find that the house was quiet, and Luna was still sleeping soundly next to me. Being careful not to wake her, I eased out of bed and put on some fresh clothes. I was in dire need of coffee, so I eased the bedroom door open and whispered, "Hello?"

When I didn't get an answer, I stepped out and tiptoed into the kitchen.

I called out again, and still no answer.

I saw no sign of Skid or anyone else. I also saw no coffee. It didn't feel right to go through some stranger's cabinets, but I was desperate. I walked over and started opening cabinets, and to my surprise, most of them were empty. He just had a few glasses, plates, and a few pots and pans. I continued with my search until the back door swung open, and Skid stepped inside.

He smiled and held up a cup holder full of various coffees as he proudly announced, "I got coffee."

"I see that."

"I wasn't sure if you liked that girly shit or not, so I got a little of everything."

"That was very sweet of you."

Even though he'd been nothing but nice, I was still a little apprehensive as I walked over and took one of the cups of coffee. He placed the remaining cups on the counter and asked, "Did you sleep alright?"

"Yeah, I guess." I didn't get it. He and his friends were rough, tough, murdering biker guys, but he was so friendly. And with his blond, wavy hair and boyish charm, he was kind of cute. I liked that he was being nice and didn't want him to stop, so I played along. "How about you?"

"Not too bad." He motioned his head over to the living room. "The sofa's a little short for my long legs, but I managed."

"You could've slept in one of the guest rooms."

"Yeah, but that would've made it harder to keep an eye on things."

"So, what exactly are we doing here?"

"I was going to ask you the same thing."

"I have no idea."

Skid grabbed one of the coffees and leaned against the counter. "I guess we're just supposed to hang out here and wait for Grim to come back."

"But what about my car?" I argued. "And my job?"

"Grim said he'd take care of it."

"Yeah, and?"

"If Grim says he'll take care of something, he'll take care of it."

"And what if I don't want him to take care of it?"

"I guess you're outta luck on that one," he scoffed. "Besides, you need your car. Might as well let him do what he's gonna do."

"This whole thing is crazy. The man doesn't even know me, and he's brought me to his house and is fixing my car."

"That's Grim."

"Any idea when he'll be coming back?"

"A couple of days? Maybe more."

"So, what am I supposed to do until then?"

"That, I don't know."

"Well, I can't just sit around here all day."

He gave me a goofy shrug, then said, "You could take a nap? Or watch TV?"

"I'm not a nap kind of person." I thought for a moment, then asked, "I could make breakfast?"

"I'd be good with that."

"I'll have to see what's in the cabinets first."

"Go for it."

I gave him a nod, then walked over and started opening cabinets again. After a bit of hunting, I was able to find some flour, sugar, and a mixing bowl. I grabbed a frying pan and then, I was ready to roll.

I grabbed some eggs from the refrigerator and started tossing ingredients into the bowl. I'd just started whipping the batter when a sleepy-eyed little girl stumbled into the kitchen. Luna rubbed the sleep from her eyes as she muttered, "Momma?"

"Good morning, sweetie." I lowered the whisk into the bowl, then went over and lifted her into my arms. "How's my sweet girl this morning? Did you sleep okay?"

"Um-hmm," she answered with a nod.

"Are you hungry?"

She nodded once again.

"Good, 'cause I'm making us some pancakes." I carried her over to the kitchen counter and sat her down on one of the stools next to Skid. She glanced over at him but then nervously turned her attention back to me. Knowing she needed a little reassurance, I smiled and told her, "Skid's going to eat with us. Is that okay?"

"Um-hmm."

"Good. How about some juice?"

"Um-hmm."

"You got it."

I made her a sippy cup of juice and placed it in front of her, then got back to work on our pancakes. Luna and Skid watched as I poured the batter onto the sizzling skillet. Once they were golden brown, I stacked them on a plate and started on the eggs. Minutes later, we were all sitting at the counter and quietly eating. I couldn't help but notice that Luna kept glancing over at Skid. Like me, she wasn't sure what to make of him.

He must've noticed that she was unsure of him because he gave her a warm smile and said, "You're a lucky girl. Your momma is a real good cook."

She didn't answer. She just sat there staring at him, so he kept at it.

"Your mom and I were talking about some things we could do today." Skid glanced over at me as he said, "I was thinking we could watch a movie or something. Do you have a favorite movie?"

"Can-to."

"Canto?" His brows furrowed. "I'm not sure I've heard of that one."

"It's *Encanto*," I interjected. "It's a Disney movie."

"Sounds good to me. We could watch after we eat."

Luna turned to me with a hopeful expression. "Can we, Momma?"

"Sure, we can do that, but you gotta finish your breakfast first."

That's all it took to get her to dive into her pancakes. As soon as we all finished eating, Skid helped me clean up the kitchen while Luna piddled with her sippy cup. She was still in her PJs, so I took her back to the room where we'd slept and got her dressed for the day. It didn't look like we were going anywhere, so I put on her play clothes and headed to the living room to find Skid.

When we walked in, he was flipping through the channels. "What was the name of the movie?"

"Encanto."

"That's right."

Skid searched for the movie while Luna and I got settled on the sofa. Luna was all smiles when she saw her favorite movie pop up on the screen. She settled back, and it wasn't long before both she and Skid were wrapped up in the show. I, on the other hand, was restless and couldn't get into the movie. I was usually working at this time and felt like I needed to be doing something.

I glanced around the room, and I couldn't help but notice that everything was covered in a thick layer of dust. Grim had a really nice place—much nicer than any place I'd ever stayed, but it needed some TLC. I had nothing better to do, so I turned to Skid and asked, "Any idea where he keeps the cleaning supplies?"

"If I had to guess, I'd say he didn't have any."

"Really?"

"Grim's not the cleaning type."

"I see. Well, that's too bad. I was going to try and tidy up a bit to thank him for letting us stay."

"Ah, man." He sighed. "Guess that means you want me to make a run, huh?"

"Would you mind?

"After the movie?" I gave him a pleading look, and he quickly recanted, "Okay, I'll go now."

Like a kid who'd just lost his lollipop, he got up with a pout and started towards the door. He was just about to walk out when I remembered that Christmas was just a day away, so I shouted, "Hey, Skid! Hold up."

"What's wrong?"

"Just give me a second." I rushed into the room where we'd slept and grabbed my wallet from one of the bags. I took what little cash I had and carried it to Skid. "Do you think you could grab a little Christmas tree and maybe some lights?"

"Yeah, I can do that." He glanced down at the small wad of cash I had in my hand and said, "Keep your money, doll. I'll get it."

"Are you sure?"

"Yeah, I'm sure."

"Thanks, Skid."

"No problem."

He walked out, and I was pleased to see that Luna didn't seem to mind his absence. I knew he wouldn't be gone long, so I used the opportunity to do a little snooping. I slipped down the hall and went into the master bedroom and found a nice-sized room with a king-sized bed and a nice dresser.

I stuck my head into the master bath, and it was equally as nice. It was also in great need of a good cleaning. I went and checked the other rooms, and like the one where Luna and I had slept, there was a bed, a few pieces of furniture, and an assortment of unopened boxes—all of which were dusty and had a weird smell.

I was going to have my work cut out for me, but it was something that would keep me busy until Grim came back. The thought made my chest tighten. At the moment, Luna and I were relatively safe. We were staying at a nice place in a nice neighborhood with no gunshots going off in the middle of the night, and Skid had been nothing but sweet to us both.

But that all could change at any moment. Grim could return and sell us both off to the highest bidder, kill us, or kick us out onto the streets. I hated being so vulnerable, but I had done it to myself. I should've gone on to college and tried to make something of myself instead of relying on Jeremy to fix everything. It was a mistake, and sadly, there was little I could do to fix it.

I had just made my way back into the living room to check on Luna when Skid came charging into the house with an arm full of cleaning supplies and a Christmas tree. He'd even bought lights and ornaments. "Wow! Did you buy out the store?"

"I came close." He walked over and dropped everything on the counter. "I figured I'd save myself a second trip."

"Smart idea."

Skid grabbed the tree and ornaments, "Hey, kiddo. Look what I got!"

"It's a tree!"

"That's right, and I'm gonna need you to help me

decorate it."

He placed it in the corner of the room, and Luna hopped off the sofa and rushed over to check out what he'd bought. She was practically beaming as she looked at all the shiny ornaments. With Luna's favorite movie playing in the background, they began putting the lights on the tree.

While Skid seemed like a good guy, I wasn't sure I could trust him alone with Luna, so I kept a side-eye on them as I started working on the kitchen. It was quite the undertaking. On the surface, everything looked pretty good. Things were put away and seemed tidy, but the second I started wiping down the counters and cabinets, I realized the place hadn't had a deep cleaning in months—*maybe never*.

It was going to take some time for me to get everything clean, but I was okay with that. I needed a distraction from the daunting feeling in the pit of my stomach, so I cleaned and cleaned some more. It was really starting to look good, especially with the little tree in the living room.

One day rolled into the next. We celebrated Christmas. Luna played with her gifts, and we watched movies. The down time was getting to me, so I asked Skid about all the boxes Grim had in the bedrooms. He assured me that it was okay to open them up and to put things where I thought they should go.

So, I did.

That was a mistake—a big, giant, terrible mistake.

Grim

It had been an absolute shit day.

We'd buried Beckett. It was brutal. I don't even know how we got through it, but we did. Afterwards, the entire chapter went on a run in his honor, and then the girls and ol' ladies made a big meal for the families. We spent the better part of the night celebrating his life.

At least, we tried to.

It was Christmas, and Prez buried a son and Memphis a brother. We all felt their pain—I felt theirs and my own. Beckett was a good kid with a lot of potential, and Prez had high hopes for him becoming a member of the club. That was all shot to shit when he decided to go over to Ruben's place, and I was still riddled with guilt because of the part I played in his death.

That guilt led me to drink too much, so I stayed

yet another night at the clubhouse. The following day, we had business to attend to, and by the time we were done, it was late. Once again, I decided to stay at the clubhouse. The next day, there was another reason and another. Before I knew it, I'd been there a week, and I'd only called to check in with Skid a handful of times.

I wasn't exactly worried. I knew he could handle things, but I'd put my problem off on him and it was time to rectify that. I needed to get Jenna's car to her, so I went to track down Ghost. The man was a brick house and was always eating, so I started in the kitchen. And just as I suspected, he was standing at the fridge, searching for something to eat.

"Need your help with something."

"Sure thing." With a chicken leg in hand, he turned to me and asked, "Whatcha need?"

"You to drive a car over to my place."

"Okay. Sounds easy enough."

He followed me out to the garage, and once I had the keys to Jenna's car, I tossed them over to him and said, "It's the blue Buick out back."

"Do what?" He leaned to the side for a better look. "Damn. Whose clunker is that?"

"It's not that bad. Just go easy on her and get her to my place in one piece."

"Yeah, whatever you say, Boss."

Begrudgingly, he did as I'd asked and followed me over to my place. Once I'd parked, I waited for Ghost to get out of Jenna's car, and then we both headed for the front door.

Something felt off as I opened the door and stepped inside the house.

There was an unfamiliar scent of lavender and bleach in the air, and as I looked around, I was surprised to find that everything seemed oddly clean. There was even a Christmas tree in the corner of the living room.

I'd lived in that house for almost five years, and I'd never seen it look like this and I'd certainly never had a fucking tree. And for reasons I couldn't explain, it infuriated me. "What the ever-loving hell?"

"Wow." Ghost's eyes were wide with surprise. "You finally fixed the place up."

"I didn't do shit." A low growl slipped through my lips when I spotted Jenna standing in the corner. Her hands nervously wrung the edge of her shirt as she listened to me say, "What is all this?"

"I just cleaned up a little."

"And who asked you to do that?"

"No one. I was just trying to..."

"I let you into my house, kept you and your daughter off the streets, and this is what you do?" I advanced towards her, my footsteps echoing off the polished floors. "You just take over and rifle through my shit like you own the damn place?"

"No! It wasn't like that." Jenna's eyes widened, her body instinctively retreating as she stammered, "I'm sorry. I didn't realize that..."

"Woah! Hold on, now!" Skid shouted as he came rushing into the room. "This isn't on her. I told her she could do it."

"And why the fuck would you do that?"

"I thought it was time."

"You know how I felt about this shit!" I glanced around the room once more and spotted pictures, books, and sit-arounds that I'd kept packed away in boxes—which only intensified my anger. I hadn't emptied those boxes for a reason.

I didn't want those memories haunting me every damn day.

And now, they were all out and in my face. And to make matters worse, she'd seen everything. Touched everything, and the sense of violation enraged me. *"Goddamn it!"*

I glanced over at Jenna, and shame washed over me when I saw that she was cowered in the corner like a kicked puppy. Her daughter was next to her, and the sight of them both standing there looking utterly terrified knocked the wind right out of me. Fuck. What the hell was wrong with me? They hadn't meant any harm. If anything, they were trying to do a good thing, and I'd been an asshole for making her feel bad about it.

Jenna looked like she was on the brink of tears, but then, she did something that surprised me. Her back straightened, and her eyes narrowed as she took a step forward. "You know what? Screw you! I busted my ass to clean this place up, and instead of thanking me, you come in here and try to make me feel like shit about it?"

"It's my house."

"Yeah, and it had a year's worth of dust on everything in here." She threw her hands up in the air. "Now it's gone!"

I didn't respond.

I simply stood there glaring at her beautiful face.

"You're welcome!" She rolled her eyes as she grabbed her daughter's hand and charged out of the room. "Gah. What an asshole."

"I like her," Ghost announced with a chuckle. "The girl's got grit."

"You can go now."

"You sure about that?" he snickered. "She's a bit feisty. You might need some help handling her."

"Go." I looked over at Skid as I said, "You, too."

"Look, I should've never told her that she could go through your shit." I could hear the remorse in his voice as he told me, "Don't hold it against her. It's totally on me."

"Um-hmm."

"So, on a scale from one to ten, how bad of a fuck up this?"

"That depends." I cocked my brow. "You gonna get the hell out of here, or are you going to keep standing there pestering me?"

He started out the door as he mumbled, "I'm going. I'm going."

"Appreciate you watching over things while I was gone."

"No problem."

He and Ghost loaded up into his pickup, and then they were gone, leaving me alone to deal with my house guests. I was still at the door, staring at Jenna's beat-up car parked in the driveway, when I heard footsteps behind me. I turned and found Jenna and Luna standing there with their garbage bags full of belongings, and neither of them seemed all that pleased to find that I was in their way.

"What's this?"

"We're leaving," Jenna answered.

"I see that." I tried not to sound like a dick as I asked, "Where you gonna go?"

"I don't know. We'll figure something out. Maybe try a shelter like we were going to do before, maybe just sleep in the car for tonight."

"No."

"What do you mean, no?"

"It's not safe."

"Seriously? Like it's safe here?" Before I had a chance to answer, she laid into me, "Two seconds ago, you were flying off the handle."

"Yeah, I was," I started. "This is just a lot and..."

Her voice trembled as she added, "We should go."

"No."

I knew her history. I'd read all about it in the file Shep had sent. She'd had a hard time of it, and just about the time it looked like she might've caught a break, things would fall apart. She grew up with two drug addicts for parents. They were in and out of jail. Met a guy and got away for a little while, even got pregnant, but ended up back at her folks' place when he was killed. They were nothing but fuckups, so she tried her brother, and that didn't play out well for her, either.

The last thing she needed was me making matters worse by doing something we'd both regret, so I told her, "I've got the room. Use it."

She didn't respond.

She just stood there staring at me as she weighed her options.

Knowing she needed a little push, I added, "Just until you find a better option... Hell, I'll even ask around and see if I can find a place for ya, but for Christ's sake, don't go piling up in your car or shacking up in some shelter. The kid deserves better than that."

A look of humiliation washed over Jenna's beautiful face, making me feel like a dick for pushing so hard. The poor girl looked like she wanted to crawl under a rock when she glanced down at her daughter and muttered, "Okay, I ah... I appreciate you letting us stay here. I know it's a lot. I'll do my best to stay out of your way."

Before I could try and fix things, Jenna turned and led her daughter back to their room. She closed the door, and I was once again left feeling like I'd shit on the parade. I was frustrated and annoyed, and I really needed a minute to just shut out everything. I walked over and grabbed a beer from the fridge, then headed into the living room.

I got in my recliner, kicked back, turned on the TV, and was immediately hit with the blaring soundtrack of some kid's movie. I quickly turned it down and changed it to the news. I settled back, and it wasn't long before the monotone sound of the newscaster's voice and the low hum of the ceiling fan had me dozing off. I was enjoying a momentary siesta when I felt an uneasy sense that someone was watching me.

I inhaled a deep breath, then eased one eye open and found a little figure standing next to me. Luna's big brown eyes were wide and filled with innocence, and even though it was dark in the room, I could see that she was sporting a pout. I had to give it to her. The kid was cute.

"Hey, kid." My voice was low and thick with sleep as I stretched and asked, "You need something?"

Her bottom lip trembled slightly as she shrugged.

"Well, you either do or you don't. Which is it?"

"I'm hungry."

"Hungry?" My initial grogginess started to dissipate when I looked around the room and found no sign of her mother. "Where's your momma?"

"She's sleeping."

"Ooo-kay." I sat up in the recliner with a huff. "Well, if you're hungry, what do you want?"

Luna shrugged, her pout deepening. "I don't know."

"You aren't making this easy, kid."

No response.

Damn.

I stood with a groan, then told her, "Okay, how 'bout we go see what we can find."

I started for the kitchen, and she trailed behind like a shadow. I walked over and opened the pantry door, and I was disappointed to find a sparse collection of canned goods and a few boxes of cereal. Luna peered inside, and her brows furrowed as she surveyed what was inside. I scratched my chin as I told her, "Damn. Looks like I need to make a trip to the grocery."

My chest tightened when Luna's face fell, and she let out a small sigh.

"Hey, now. No more of that poutin' stuff. I'm not gonna let you go hungry." I opened the fridge, and like the cabinets, there wasn't much there. I was hoping I could come up with something to put together, but no such luck. I looked back over at Luna as she was standing there with a hopeful look in her eyes.

I didn't want to let her down, so I asked, "How 'bout pizza?"

"Cheese pizza?"

"Whatever you want, kid."

"Can we get cheese sticks, too?"

"Sure thing." I had to give it to her. She was a cute kid. She had these big brown eyes with freckles dappled across the bridge of her nose, and she had this lopsided grin that got you right in the gut. I grabbed my phone from my back pocket. "I'll get some for your mom and me, too."

As I dialed the number for the local pizzeria, I looked over to Luna and couldn't help but smile when I saw the excitement in her eyes. She was a cute kid, and I hated that she and her mother were going through such a tough time. There were things I could do to help them—things like letting Jenna and her stay at the clubhouse and become hang arounds, but I had a feeling Jenna wouldn't be up for that.

I wasn't so sure I was up for it myself.

I felt an unexpected need to protect them both, and the idea of all the brothers having access to Jenna didn't sit well with me. It didn't sit well with me at all. I shook the thought from my head and placed our order. When I was done, I hung up the phone and turned my attention back to Luna. "Alright, kid. Your pizza is on its way."

"Okay."

She didn't move.

She just stood there looking up at me.

I had no clue what to do with her, so I asked, "Now what?"

"I could draw you a picture."

"Yeah, you could." I glanced around the room as I told her, "But you're gonna need some paper and crayons and shit."

"Shit is a bad word."

"Yeah, it is, and I say it a lot."

"You shouldn't say bad words."

"Yeah, well, I do, and I doubt that's gonna change any time soon." I could tell by her expression that she wasn't pleased with my answer, so I added, "How 'bout we pretend bad words aren't so bad—just while you and your mom are staying here with me."

She gave me a nod and watched as I searched through my desk for some paper and a pen. Once I had a couple of things, I carried them into the living room and laid them on the coffee table. "There you go."

And just like that, she knelt down and got to work on her picture. There was something about having her there doodling on that notepad that was strangely comforting. I sat back down on my recliner and started flipping through the channels, searching for something kid appropriate that wouldn't make my fucking skin crawl.

It wasn't easy.

Seemed like everything on had some kind of shooting or cussing, and I'd already exposed her to enough of that. When I found an old sitcom, I dropped the remote on the table and kicked back. I'd just relaxed when I felt the energy in the room take a dramatic shift. I didn't even have to look to know that Jenna was standing in the doorway, and just like that, my peaceful moment had come and gone.

Jenna

I rolled over from my nap and panicked when I discovered that Luna was no longer lying next to me. I sprang from the bed and frantically went to look for her. When I opened the bedroom door, I could hear the TV playing, so I quietly crept down the hall and headed to the living room. My breath caught when I walked in and found Grim lying back in his recliner and Luna sitting cross-legged coloring at his feet.

I didn't know what to make of it.

They both looked perfectly content like they'd done this kind of thing a hundred times before, and the sight stilled my heart as I stood there watching them. Luna's small fingers moved with purpose as she doodled on her notepad. Her little brows were furrowed, and her head was slightly tilted, showing just how engrossed she was in her artwork.

She didn't even know I was standing there.

I wasn't sure that Grim knew it either.

His broad frame was sprawled back in his recliner with his feet perched high. He was watching an old TV series, and even though he didn't seem to be paying her any mind, I wasn't sure how he felt about Luna sitting in the room alone with him, especially after our earlier exchange.

The last thing I wanted to do was disturb him further, especially when he was trying to relax. I was trying to figure out how to get her when he mumbled, "She's fine."

"She can draw in the bedroom."

"Or she could stay where she's at." He turned his head slightly, and a cold chill ran down my spine when his dark eyes met mine. "No reason to move her. She's good."

"Okay. As long as she isn't bothering you."

"No bother." He turned his focus back to the TV, and I'd thought that was going to be that until he announced, "Pretty low on groceries, so I ordered pizza."

"Oh, yeah. Skid had a list and was going to grab some stuff this afternoon but didn't get the chance."

"Where's the list?"

"I'm pretty sure it's still on the fridge."

"I'll take care of it."

"I can do it," I volunteered. "It's the least I can do after all you've done."

"Hmmm."

An awkward silence fell over us, and I wasn't sure what to do or say. The last thing I wanted to do was set him off again, but there were things that needed to be said. I swallowed hard, then forced myself to say, "I didn't get a chance to mention it earlier, but thanks for fixing my car. I don't know what I would've..."

"It was nothing. Don't sweat it." He turned his head slightly—just enough to get a good look at me, then said, "You know, you could sit."

"I don't want to bother you."

"Sit, Jenna."

I nodded, then skirted past him and made my way over to Luna. I ran my hand over the top of her head as I whispered, "I thought I told you to stay in the room with me."

"I not sleepy anymore."

"But you didn't tell me..." She was too focused on her drawing to pay me any mind, so I decided to just let it go. "Whatcha drawing?"

"A kitty-cat for Mr. Grim."

"Oh, that's sweet." I glanced over at Grim. "I'm sure he will love it."

I gave her a quick kiss on the forehead, then continued over to the sofa and sat down. I got the feeling he wasn't in the mood to talk, but I felt compelled to say, "I want you to know that I really appreciate you doing this... I appreciate all of it. Letting us stay here. The car. Everything. And I'm so sorry about earlier with the cleaning. I should've never overstepped..."

"Don't," he interrupted. "It's done. No sense going on and on about it."

"Well, if I could change it, I would. I just want you to know that."

"Understood." He turned his attention back to the TV as he asked, "How much longer before she's in school?"

"It won't be long. She's almost four, so I plan to enroll her in pre-K this fall."

"Hmmm. Thought she was older."

"I've heard that a lot. I think it's because she talks so well and is so polite."

"You teach her that?"

"I'd like to take the credit, but I'm not so sure." I shrugged. "I think it comes kind of naturally or something."

"That kind of thing doesn't just come naturally. It's all you, and you should be proud of that." He looked over at Luna as he stated, "You should be proud of her."

"Oh, I'm over-the-moon proud of her. She's the only thing I've done right in this world."

"I highly doubt that."

"It's true." I ran my hand through my hair, brushing it from my face. "Otherwise, I wouldn't be sitting here right now."

"But you are sitting here. Things might not be going

your way, but you're alive and well, and your daughter is, too. You're doing alright."

"I have no job. No money. And..."

"But you're trying. There are plenty of folks who would've given up a long time ago, so give yourself credit where credit is due."

"I guess." I got the feeling that there was something he wasn't saying, but Grim didn't seem like the kind of man who could be easily persuaded, especially when it came to talking about things he didn't want to talk about. I wasn't sure if he would tell me, but I felt inclined to say, "You mentioned that there was a time when someone had helped you and your mother out."

"Yeah?"

"Was she trying like I'm trying?"

"She was." His expression softened. "Like you, she wanted to give her kid a good life, but it seemed like there was always something standing in her way—until she met Gus."

"Gus?"

"He's the president of Satan's Fury in Memphis. He crossed paths with my mother at a diner that they ran. He gave her a job and place to stay until she got on her feet."

"Sounds like a good guy."

"He is." His lips curled into a slight smile as he said, "He made a real impression on me back then. So much so, I decided to join the MC."

"Wow, that's some story."

"Yeah, and one day, Luna will have a story like mine."

"I hope that's true."

"It will be. Just wait and see."

We went back to watching TV, and I'd all but forgotten that he'd ordered pizza until I heard a knock at the door. Grim stood and twisted his back, cracking his spine as he announced, "That must be the pizza."

I figured he might need some help with the boxes, so I followed him into the kitchen and waited as he opened the door. The delivery guy stepped in, balancing two large pizza boxes precariously in one hand while clutching a receipt in the other. "That'll be thirty-seven fifty."

Grim took the boxes and placed them on the center of the table, then grabbed some money from his wallet and offered it to the delivery guy. "That should cover it."

"Thanks, man." The kid took the wad of cash and shoved it in his back pocket. "You folks have a good one!"

"You, too."

I watched with curiosity as Grim opened the pizza box, revealing a steaming hot pizza topped with various meats and cheeses, and the sight had my mouth watering. Noting my expression, Grim smiled and asked, "Looks good, huh?"

When I nodded, he chuckled.

The man actually chuckled.

I couldn't get over it. If I didn't know better, I'd say

an entirely different man had come into the room, and this man was smiling as he placed a slice on a plate. *Smiling!* I almost felt like I had whiplash when he offered the plate to me and said, "It's the best in town."

"*Okay.*" I glanced down at the plate, and my stomach started growling in anticipation. I took a quick bite, and I couldn't help but let out a contented sigh as the flavors exploded on my tongue. "Oh, wow. You were right. This is really good."

"Told ya."

He chuckled again, and the deep rumble sent shivers down my spine.

Yep.

Definitely a case of whiplash.

I made a plate for Luna before calling out, "Hey, sweet pea! Your cheese sticks are here."

"Yay!" Seconds later, Luna came racing around the corner and made a beeline for Grim. "I want all of 'dem."

I offered her the plate full of cheese sticks and pizza, and Grim watched with a slight smirk as she crawled up into her chair. After grabbing a couple of drinks, I sat down next to Luna and started eating. Grim followed suit, and it wasn't long before we were all reaching for seconds. "This is really good, Grim. Thanks for ordering it for us."

"You're more than welcome."

"Thank you," Luna mumbled with a mouthful of food. "It's weally good."

"I'm glad you like it."

He gave her a quick wink and went back to eating. We were all enjoying the delicious meal when suddenly Grim looked over to me and asked the question I'd been asking myself for days. "So, what's your plan?"

"Pfft. Isn't that the question of the hour?"

"Well, I figured you'd been thinking about it. Just wondered if you'd come up with anything."

"Not really. I lost my job at the drugstore because without my car I haven't been able to make it in to work, so I've been going through the want ads. I've found a couple of possibilities, but the pay isn't all that great."

"I might be able to help you out with something." He took a sip of his beer before asking, "How are you at bartending?"

"No idea. I've never done it."

"They make good money."

"I've heard." I motioned my head over at Luna. "But with Luna and all, I haven't really had a chance to try it."

"Hmmm."

"Why? Do you have a place in mind?"

"Yeah, I might know a place. It's small, but the folks there are good people and I'd bet they'd be willing to work with you."

"That sounds great, but I don't know anything about bartending."

"You can grab a beer from a fridge, can't ya?"

"Well, yeah."

"Then, you know enough."

"I don't know about that."

"I'd teach you what you need to know."

"Seriously?" I couldn't believe my ears. He'd already done so much, and now he was offering to do even more. "You really would do that?"

"It wouldn't take long to teach ya the basics."

"Okay. That would be great."

We both continued eating, and it wasn't long before we were all stuffed. I helped Grim clean up the mess, and then we all made our way back into the living room. We watched a little TV, and when it started getting late, I went over to Luna and said, "It's time to get ready for bed."

"But I'm not..."

"It's time for bed," I interrupted. "We have a busy day ahead, and you need a good night's sleep."

Her bottom lip perched into a pout, but she didn't argue. She simply got up and made her way into the bedroom. As I followed her out, I turned to Grim and asked, "Are you still up for some lessons later?"

"Sure thing. I'll check my liquor cabinet and see what I have on hand."

"Great. I'll be back in a bit."

I gave Luna a quick bath and put her in her pajamas, then put her into bed.

It was funny. I'd been staying at Grim's house for over a week, and from the start, I'd felt oddly safe. I'd thought it was because Skid was there watching over us, but as I sat there across from Grim, I realized it wasn't him at all.

It was Grim.

All Grim.

He was this big, bad, tough biker, and while he clearly handled his own, there was an unexpected warmth and kindness in his eyes, especially when he looked at Luna. I was almost jealous that he didn't look at me the same way.

Luna was still a little wound up, so I laid down with her and pulled her close. "Did you have a good night?"

"Um-hmm." She looked up at me and smiled. "Grim has good pizza."

"Yes, he does." I toyed with her hair as I said, "I've really made a mess of things, and I'm really sorry. I'm going to work really hard to get us back on track, and when I do, we'll get us a cute place that's all ours. You'll have your own room and your own things, and we can have pizza any time we want."

"Can we have a kitty-cat?"

"Yes, we can have a cat and whatever else you want." I leaned down and kissed her on the forehead. "I love you so very much, and I'm going to do everything I can to give you the life you deserve. It's going to take me some time, so I need you to be patient. I also need you to be sweet and respectful while we are here. Grim has been really nice to let us stay here, and I don't want him to..."

I stopped talking when I looked down and found that Luna had drifted off to sleep. My heart swelled at the precious sight. I couldn't imagine loving anyone more than I loved her. She was my everything, and I had every intention of making good on my promises—no matter what the cost.

Grim

❧

I'd spent years living in this house alone.

I liked it.

I didn't have to worry about pleasing anybody but myself, and that's the way I'd planned on keeping it. But there I sat, listening to Jenna and Luna talking in the guest room. Their voices filled the empty places in the house, giving me a sense of comfort I didn't expect. Having them there made my house feel like a home—a feeling it'd been missing since the day I'd moved in.

I closed my eyes and reveled in the strangeness of it all, and when their voices grew quiet, I knew it wouldn't be long before Jenna would return. She would be expecting her lesson, so I got up and made my way into the kitchen. I'd just started pulling the liquor bottles from the cabinet when Jenna walked in, and the sight of her nearly took my breath away.

She'd changed into a pair of shorts and a long-sleeved t-shirt, and her hair was pulled up into a messy bun, revealing her warm smile. In another time or place, I would've tried to work the old magic and make a move. But I was no good for a girl like her. So, I'd do what I'd promised. I'd help her get on her feet, and then, I'd cut her loose.

As she approached, she motioned her head towards the bottles of liquor and said, "Wow. You have quite the setup."

"Can't practice without the goods."

"This is true." Her smile widened. "So, where do we start?"

"With the basics." I reached for a bottle of vodka. "For starters, you gotta know the good stuff from the cheap stuff, and you gotta know the right time to use them." I took a moment to name off some of the more expensive brands and then listed some of the cheaper ones. "Just because It's expensive doesn't mean it's always better. Lots of times, it's just the opposite."

"How am I supposed to know the difference?"

"After a few drinks, you'll figure it out." I poured a shot of vodka into a shaker, followed by a splash of soda water. I did my best to move at a slow, steady pace so she'd be able to follow without much confusion. "When you mix a drink, you don't want to overdo it with the pour. Needs to be an exact shot. You want to taste the alcohol, but you don't want it to overpower the drink."

"Okay. Makes sense."

Jenna watched closely as I shook the shaker then

strained the mixture into a glass filled with ice. I slid the glass over to her as I announced, "This is my take on a vodka soda."

"Okay." She picked it up and took a sip. "Vodka has never been one of my favorites, but this is actually pretty good."

"Thought you might like it." I reached for a bottle of whiskey as I told her, "Time to try something a little harder."

She nodded, then watched as I started pouring a shot into a glass and added a splash of sweet vermouth with a few dashes of bitters. I stirred the ingredients gently, then strained the mixture into a glass over a large ice cube. "The key to this one is patience. You want to take your time and let the flavors meld together."

I garnished the drink with a twist of orange peel before sliding it over to her. She picked it up, and after a cautious sip, she gave me a sexy smile and teased, "Hmmm. Not bad for an old man drink."

"Old man?" I scoffed.

"Am I wrong?" Her eyes skirted over me as she leaned against the counter and asked, "How old are you?"

"If you can't tell, I won't share either."

"Okay, fine. Let's just say it's a guy drink."

"That it is." I picked up the bottle of gin as I told her, "Let's try something a little more girlie."

I was about to start mixing a new concoction when

I noticed Jenna's smile had faded. "Can I ask you something?"

"You can ask. Won't promise that I'll answer."

"Why did you kill them? Jimmy and ... Steven?"

I wasn't exactly surprised that she'd asked about her brother. I knew she had to wonder what had gone on with us, but I wasn't in a position to answer her. She must've noticed my resistance and added, "I know he and those guys he ran with did bad things. I know they were running drugs and hurting people, and I know they must've done something terrible to you and your friends. I was just wondering what that was."

"How do you know what they were doing?"

"Because they made me do some of the runs." She grimaced as she admitted, "I didn't want to do it. I knew there was a chance I could get caught or killed, but I had no choice. I was at my brother's mercy."

"I get it."

"So, what was it? What did they do to you?"

"It's club business, Jenna. And I don't discuss club business."

"Yeah, Skid said you'd say that."

"You talked to him about it?"

"I tried, but he said the same thing you did."

"Because it's true."

"But it's not just club business. It's my business, too. I was there," she pushed. "I saw it. I know what happened. I'm just asking why it happened."

I was torn. I'd always been a firm believer that you

don't discuss club business outside of the club, but she was right. She was there. She'd seen everything, and it was her brother. She knew the kind of crap he was into, so I ignored my better judgment and told her, "Your brother and his friend raped and killed a girl. My president's son went after them for what they'd done, and they killed him, too."

"Oh, Grim. I'm so sorry." Her voice trembled. "I had no idea."

"You've got nothing to be sorry about." Anguish marked her face as she listened to me say, "You didn't kill him."

"I don't know what to say."

"He was a good kid. He didn't deserve that shit."

"I'm so sorry."

My throat tightened. "It was my fault. I let it happen."

"You let what happen?"

"I... It doesn't matter."

I picked up the drink from the counter and tilted it back, drinking what was left in the glass. As I put the glass down, I glanced over at Jenna and found her staring back at me. She studied me for a moment, then said, "I don't know if this will mean as much to you as it did me, but my grandmother used to say that death can't take everything from us. It can't take our memories, and if you had good memories about them, there's a pretty good chance that they had good ones about you, too."

"Your grandmother sounds like a smart lady."

"She was. I miss her." Her tone turned somber as she added, "She was the only person who really seemed to love me without wanting something in return."

"Mind if I ask you something?"

"Sure."

"What's going on with Luna's dad? Why isn't he helping you two?"

Even though I already knew the answer, I wanted to see if there was more to the story. I didn't want to admit it, but I was curious to see if she was still in love with the guy. "He would if he could, but he died a few months before she was born."

"I hate to hear that."

"The whole thing was crazy. He joined the military because he thought it would help us get out of the city, but it ended up costing him everything. We weren't married, so I couldn't get any of his benefits."

"What about Luna?"

"There was no way to prove that she was his, and I didn't have the money or the know-how to contest their ruling."

"Damn. That's rough."

"Yeah, well, it was a long time ago." Her dark eyes met mine, and a warmth settled over me as she said, "And while we aren't any better off, we're still here and trying."

"That's right. You are." This girl was something. Without even trying, she'd gotten under my skin, and that was something I didn't need. Not now. Not when everything had gone to shit. I needed to put some distance between us, so I glanced up at the clock and said, "It's late. We should call it a night."

"Oh, okay."

"We'll pick up from here later."

Disappointment marked her face as she muttered, "That would be good. Thanks."

"You still good with going to the grocery?"

"Of course."

"Good deal." I started putting the liquor bottles back in the cabinet as I told her, "I'll leave you some cash on the counter."

"You won't be here?"

"Afraid not... I've gotta get to the clubhouse first thing, and I'm not sure when I'll be back."

"Oh."

"I'll leave you a key so you can come and go and all that."

"That would be great. Thanks." She lingered for a moment, then turned and started out of the room. "I guess I'll see you when I see you."

"You, too."

I finished putting the bottles away and then headed to my room. After a long, hot shower, I put on a clean pair of boxers and collapsed on the bed. It had been a long day, but as soon as I closed my eyes, my mind drifted to Jenna. There was so much about her that intrigued me.

Her laughter echoed in my ears, her smile was etched in my mind's eye, and the warmth of her eyes still lingered on my skin. There was no doubt about it. She was getting to me. I couldn't seem to help myself. She'd been through so much, but she hadn't let it destroy her. She'd kept fighting.

A man like me had no business giving her a second thought, so I forced myself to shake her from my mind. It wasn't easy. Hell, I tossed and turned until my sheets tangled around my legs, but thankfully, my exhaustion eventually kicked in and I was able to finally sleep.

The next morning, I got up early and threw on my clothes. On the way out, I left Jenna the key to the house, some cash, and a note with my number on it, letting her know to call if she needed anything. I grabbed a juice from the fridge and was on my way.

Once outside, I walked over to my bike and swung my leg over my Harley. We were still in the thick of winter, but one of the many advantages of living in the south was our mild weather. There were only a few weeks out of the year that were either too cold or too hot for riding, and even then, there are those who tough it out.

On that cold morning, I couldn't imagine getting into a cage, so I turned the key and let the engine roared to life. Its rumble echoed through the quiet streets of my neighborhood, but I wasn't all that worried about the noise. I'd been living there long enough for my neighbors to know it was me backing out of the drive.

The cool morning air bit my skin as I started towards the clubhouse, but I liked it. It helped wake me up and get the blood pumping. By the time the clubhouse came into view, I was feeling ready to face the day. The feeling quickly faded when I pulled through the gate, and Creed and several of the brothers were talking in the parking lot.

It was early—way too early for Ghost and Skid to be there unless something was wrong. I quickly parked and killed the engine. There was a notable tension in the air as I dismounted my bike and made my way over to the group. The conversation halted as they turned to acknowledge my arrival. "Hey, what the hell is going on?"

Silence lingered for a moment before Ghost stepped forward and announced, "Memphis is in the ER."

"What?" My pulse quickened. "Why am I just hearing about this?"

"We just found out ourselves." Ghost hesitated, exchanging a glance with Creed before answering, "Apparently, he's been there for a couple of hours."

"For what?"

"He's pretty sure he broke his hand."

"Quit giving me bits and pieces. I wanna know what the fuck happened."

"He and Goose went out last night to blow off some steam, and apparently, he ran into a couple of the Brass

Kings. One of them got to mouthing, not sure who, but one thing led to another, and they got into a brawl.

"Damn." I looked around, searching the lot for Preacher's bike, but saw no sign of it. "Does Preacher know?"

"Yeah, he left a few minutes ago to go see about him."

"Fuck. This is the last thing he needs right now."

"There's more."

"Of course there is," I grumbled with a shake of my head. "Spill it."

"There are whispers of a retaliation from the Kings."

"A retaliation for what?"

"From the sounds of it, Memphis did a real number on one of their guys—broke his nose and collar bone and couple of ribs which ended up puncturing his lung. Dude is barely hanging on, and they're pissed."

Memphis had barely spoken two words since his brother's death. The guilt that festered in the pit of my stomach churned at the thought. I knew it had fucked him up. Hell, it fucked us all up, but Memphis was a ticking time bomb, waiting for a chance to blow. That chance came last night, and he took it.

Concern marked Ghost's face as he explained, "We don't know when or what they got planned, but they're coming."

"Let 'em," I growled. "It'll be the biggest mistake they've ever made."

Even as I said the words, I couldn't shake the feeling

that there was more to this than any of us knew, and if we weren't careful, it could become a real problem. It was my job to make sure that didn't happen, and that was exactly what I was going to do.

Hell, after the week I'd had, I was looking forward to it.

Jenna

"Can we get some animal crackers?"

"Yeah, I think we can manage that."

I knelt in front of Luna, and her little eyes were still heavy with sleep as I slipped on her shoes. Once they were tied, I reached up and fastened the buttons of her pink cardigan. Luna yawned as she twisted and stretched, letting out a little groan. She was doing her best to wake up as she asked, "And some ice cream, too?"

"I don't know. Maybe. We'll have to see if there's enough money for that." I pulled her hair up in a ponytail, and after a quick adjustment to her pink bow, I took a step back to make sure she was ready for our day out. "You're looking pretty good, squirt."

"You look pretty, too, Momma."

"Well, thank you."

I turned and gave myself a quick check in the mirror

and was disappointed to find that my sweet daughter was sadly mistaken. My hair was a frizzy mess, and my clothes were too big and hanging off me. My black eye was fading, but I still had massive dark circles under my eyes that made me look sickly. I grabbed my concealer and dabbed a little on the darkest spots, then blended it in, hoping it might help.

No such luck.

"Ready to go, sweet pea?" Luna nodded eagerly, her eyes sparkling with anticipation. "Okay. Let me grab the list and my keys, and we will be on our way."

Luna followed me into the kitchen and over to the counter where Grim had left the list and the money. I picked it up and gasped when I saw that he'd left us over four hundred dollars for groceries. I couldn't believe it. I couldn't ever remember spending this kind of money on groceries. It seemed crazy to me. "Holy moly."

"What, Momma?"

"Oh, nothing. I just... I think we can get that ice cream after all."

"Yay!"

I took the key he'd left and shoved it into my purse with the list and the cash. After making sure I had everything we needed, I took Luna's hand and led her out to the car. Once I had her buckled in, I got in the driver's seat and started the engine. It kicked on and purred in a way it never had before, and that never would've happened without Grim.

That thought led me to think about the night before.

He was so calm and patient with my lesson, which was unexpected for a man like him. I'd thought he would just barrel through without stopping to explain, but he took his time and was patient with me.

And when he smiled at me, my knees all but buckled right there on the spot. I had no idea what had come over me. Grim was a stranger—a killer and God knows what else, but he was also incredibly handsome. And the fact that he was being so nice and taking such good care of us only added to his draw.

It had been a long time since I'd encountered someone like him—if ever. He was the kind of man who could do a real number on my heart, so I would have to work hard not to let myself get carried away.

I put Luna in the front of the cart, and her tiny hands gripped the handlebar as I made my way down the first aisle. Luna's eyes were wide as she gazed around at all the various foods. We walked down aisle after aisle, gathering everything that was on the grocery list, and it didn't take long for us to fill the cart.

We were almost done when Luna sat up straight and pointed at the freezer section. "Ice cream."

"Yes, honey. I know."

I opened the door, and Luna's eyes sparkled with joy as she watched me grab a container of chocolate ice cream and drop it in the cart. I double-checked the list before making my way to the checkout. The cashier started scanning our items, and my throat tightened as I watched the total go up with every swipe.

"That'll be one-eighty-ninety-two, please."

"One what?"

"Eighty and ninety-two cents."

"Okay." With my heart pounding, I handed her the two crisp one hundred-dollar bills and waited for her to give me the change and the receipt. Once she'd placed them in my hand, I smiled and said, "Thank you."

She didn't respond. She was already busy scanning the next round of groceries. Luna seemed tickled as we made our way back out to my car. She watched with an excited gleam in her eyes as I put everything into the trunk. I was putting the last bag in when Luna gasped, "That's a lot, Momma."

"Yes, it is. We will have to thank Grim when he gets home."

She nodded with a smile, and all the way home, she chatted about the treats we'd bought, only they weren't really treats—just some fruits and crackers that I couldn't typically afford. I tried not to let it bother me, but it did. I wanted to be able to get those things for her all the time, and I hoped that one day I could.

Once we were back at Grim's, I unpacked the groceries while Luna played in the living room. I wiped down the counters and placed the receipts and Grim's change on the counter. I'd just started towards the living room when I heard the rumble of a motorcycle.

Thinking it was Grim, I stopped and waited for him

to come to the door. I saw a figure come into view, and disappointment washed over me when I realized it was Skid and not Grim. He eased open the door, and a smile crossed his face when he spotted me. "Hey there. How's it going?"

"Hey. It's going okay. Um, Grim's not here."

"Yeah, I know. He's ah... he's taking care of something."

"Oh, I hope everything's okay."

"It will be. So, how have you two been doing?"

"Okay. And you?"

"Can't complain. I was just out and about and thought I'd come by and check on my girls."

There was something about the way he said 'my girls' that didn't sit well with me, and I wasn't sure why. Skid was a nice guy—handsome, too, especially with his shaggy brown hair and smoldering, dark eyes. But that was about as far it went. Even so, I liked him and was glad he'd stopped by. "It's been quiet around here. We just got back from the grocery, and..."

"Oh, man. I was going to do that for you, but..."

"No, it's fine," I interrupted. "I was glad to get out for a bit."

"So, the car is working good?"

"Yes. It's great. I don't think it's ever run as good as it does now."

"Good, good. I'm glad to hear that." He leaned back against the kitchen counter. "So, how'd it go last night?"

"Okay. Better than I expected."

"So, he cooled off?"

"Eventually, but it took him a minute. Regardless, I still feel bad about it all. I shouldn't have gone through his stuff like that. I don't know what I was thinking."

"That was on me," he argued. "I'm the one who told you that it was alright to do it. The heat should've been on me. *Not you.*"

"Well, it's all a wash now. Grim seems to have let it go, but I've learned my lesson. I won't be meddling with things that aren't mine anymore."

Skid glanced around the house and smiled when he spotted one of the pictures on the wall. "He left it all up."

"Yeah, but he hasn't really had time to put it away. I was thinking I might just put it all back and be done with the whole thing."

"Do whatever, but I think it adds a little charm to the place."

"I do, too, but it doesn't really matter what I think. It's not my house." I shrugged. "But I get to stay here for a bit, and I'm very grateful for that. Actually, I'm grateful for a lot. Grim has been so sweet, and..."

"Woah. Wait a minute... *Did you just say sweet?*" Skid scoffed. "Are we talking about the same guy here 'cause there is nothing sweet about the Grim I know. I mean, don't get me wrong. He has his moments, but all and all, he's one I'd never wanna go up against."

"I feel you there." I walked over and opened the

fridge. "Can I get you a drink or something? We've got coke and juice. There's beer, too."

"A coke will be fine." I grabbed us both a can and offered him one. "Thanks... So, where's Luna bug?"

"She's in the living room watching TV."

"Mind if I go say hello?"

"Of course."

He gave me a nod, then made his way into the living room. Luna was sitting cross-legged in front of the TV, and she was so enthralled in her show that she didn't notice Skid when he sat down on the floor next to her. He gave her a little nudge as he said, "Hey, kiddo. How's it shakin'?"

Luna glanced up briefly, her face lighting up at the sight of Skid. "Hi, Skid!"

"Hey." He gave her a warm smile as he asked, "Whatcha watching?"

"Frozen."

"Again." Skid chuckled, his eyes skirting over to the television screen for a moment, then returned to Luna. "Haven't you watched that about twenty times?"

Luna nodded, and her attention went right back to the television. Skid watched her for a moment, and it wasn't long before he was drawn into the show's whimsical storyline. Luna giggled at a silly part, and Skid couldn't help but laugh right along with her.

He sat with her for several minutes, then nudged her with his elbow. "I gotta get going, kid. You be good to your momma."

"Okay." He got up, and as soon as he started out of the room, Luna called out, "Bye, Skid."

"Bye, kid." Skid was sporting a wholesome smile as he made his way back over to me. "You gotta a good kid in there."

"Yeah, she is pretty great."

His eyes skirted over me flirtatiously as he added, "Her momma is pretty great, too."

"Oh, thanks, Skid." I didn't want to give him the wrong idea, so I skimmed right over the compliment and asked, "So, where you headed off to?"

"Gotta make a run downtown to pick something up for one of the brothers."

"They keep you busy, don't they?"

"Yeah, but that's just part of it." He shrugged. "Hopefully, it won't be long before I get my patch, and I'll be done with the bullshit. Until then, I've gotta keep bustin' it, which is why I've gotta get to gettin'."

Before I realized what he was doing, Skid leaned in and gave me a quick kiss on the cheek. It was a sweet gesture, but there was meaning behind it. I knew that. He knew that. But he just played it off with a wink and made his way for the door. "I'll see you girls later."

And that was it.

He was gone, and I was almost relieved.

I couldn't help but wonder why I wasn't drawn to him like I was Grim. I knew the answer. I was drawn to the darkness in Grim. I had a similar darkness inside of me, and somewhere deep inside, there was a piece of me that wondered if we could help each other find the light.

It was a silly thought.

I knew that, too, but I had it just the same.

It was that feeling that later led me into the kitchen. I was going to cook Grim a home-cooked meal. I figured it was the least I could do since he was the one who'd paid for all the groceries. I grabbed the pork chops from the fridge and set to work, and it wasn't long before Luna came in to give me a hand.

We made fried pork chops, little green peas, and Luna's favorite mashed potatoes. We set the table and put dinner on the warm stove, thinking Grim would arrive at any moment. But he didn't.

We waited until after seven, and there was still no sign of him.

Luna was hungry, so we made our plates and ate. After she was done, I gave Luna a bath and carried her to bed. With a heavy sigh, I tucked her into bed and kissed her softly on the forehead. "Goodnight, punkin."

"Night, Momma."

I turned out the light and returned to the kitchen. I cleared away the remnants of our dinner and wiped down the counters. I wasn't quite ready for bed, so I went into the living room and watched TV. One hour rolled into the next, and still no sign of Grim. It was clear he wasn't coming home, so I turned off the TV, locked the doors, and headed into the bedroom.

I crawled into bed next to Luna and quickly nestled

in the covers. The bed was super comfortable, and with the sound of Luna's rhythmic breathing, it didn't take long for me to become drowsy. I was just starting to feel that tingle of approaching sleep when I heard a loud thud at the front door.

My eyes snapped open, and my heart pounded against my chest as I tried to listen for another thud. I didn't hear anything more, but I still felt the urge to go check it out. I glanced down at Luna, and she was still sleeping peacefully, so I was careful not to wake her as I eased out of bed.

The floorboards creaked beneath my feet as I tiptoed down the hallway. I looked around but didn't see anything in the living room or kitchen. I walked over and looked out the window, and yet again, I saw nothing. I thought my mind was playing tricks on me until I glanced down and saw a pair of boots on the bottom steps.

I leaned in for a better look and gasped when I found Grim leaning back against the door with a bottle of liquor in his hand. I eased the door open as I whispered, "Grim? Are you okay?"

He looked up at me with red eyes and grumbled something under his breath. I opened the door further and stepped outside. Grim's words were slightly slurred as he said, "Awe, hell, I'm sorry. I... I didn't mean to wake ya."

"It's okay. I wasn't asleep."

The scent of alcohol hung heavy in the air. It was on

his breath, on his clothes, and he was struggling to keep his head up. The sight of him tugged at my heart. I wanted to help him but wasn't sure how. He tilted his head back and muttered, "I stopped by the bar."

"I see that." I noticed some blood on his shirt and more on his knuckles, so I inched a little closer as I asked, "Are you okay?"

"Yeah." Grim let out a bitter laugh. "I'm peachy keen."

"Please tell me you didn't drive here."

"Prospect."

"Well, at least there's that." My heart ached at the sight of him in such a state, and I just wanted to get him inside and into bed. I reached out my hand as I said, "Come on. Let's get you inside."

"Naa-aah, I'm gooood right here."

"I'm not leaving you out here alone," I argued. "Now, come on, and let me help you inside."

Grim hesitated for a moment but eventually took my hand.

I helped him to his feet, and then together, we made our way back into the house. I closed and locked the door before leading him into the living room. Once we got over to the sofa, he plopped down and grumbled, "You shouldn't be so nice to me... I don't deserve it."

"You deserve it just as much as anyone else would."

"You're wrong." His voice was heavy with emotion as he grumbled. "I have blood on my hands."

I had a feeling he wasn't talking about the literal

blood on his hands. It was something else altogether. Maybe it was the guy who Steven and his buddies murdered or someone from his past. I hoped he would give me a little more, but all I got was some incoherent muttering. Grim laid back on the pillow and closed his eyes with a sigh. "You should stay away from me. Far, far away."

"I'm good where I am, thank you." I knelt and placed my hand on his, slightly squeezing it as I told him, "Now, settle back and sleep it off."

I started to stand but stopped when I heard him mutter, "Why do you have to be so good? So, so good."

"No, you've got it wrong. I'm not good. I'm nothing. I'm just..."

"No, baby," he interrupted in barely a whisper, with his breath growing heavier by the second. "You're everything, and don't ever let anyone make you think different."

And with that, his hand dropped to his side, and he passed out cold.

It tugged at my heart to see him look so sweet and vulnerable. It felt wrong to see him at such a moment of weakness, so I covered him with a blanket and headed back to my room. I crawled into bed, and I couldn't stop myself from wondering what he'd meant when he said he had blood on his hands.

He could've been talking about anyone, and that was somewhat unsettling. Don't get me wrong. I had no misconception about Grim and what he was about. I knew he was a killer. His brothers were, too. I saw that the day they killed my brother, but I couldn't shake the feeling that his murder was just skimming the surface of the things he'd done.

It was a feeling that hung with me as I drifted off to sleep, and it was still hanging with me the next morning when I got up. Luna was playing quietly with her toys, so I used the opportunity to go check in on Grim. I expected him to still be passed out on the sofa, but when I walked into the living room, there was no sign of him. I checked the kitchen, and he wasn't there either. I was beginning to think he'd left until I saw that his bedroom door was closed.

He was still there, so I tried to be as quiet as possible as I made my way over to the counter and started making a pot of coffee. I made Luna some breakfast, and she and I spent the next couple of hours trying our best not to wake Grim. It wasn't easy. It seemed like every noise echoed through the entire house.

Thankfully, he eventually got up and came into the kitchen. He was dressed and no longer reeked of alcohol. I was glad to see that the extra sleep had done him well. "Good morning."

"More like good afternoon."

"Yeah, I guess you're right about that." His brows furrowed as he motioned his head to the end of the counter. "What's that?"

"It's your change from the grocery and the receipt."

"I didn't ask for the change."

"I know, but it's yours and..."

"You're the one who went to the store," he argued.

"And?"

"The change is your compensation."

"There's over a hundred dollars there."

"And it's yours."

"You can't be serious."

"Take the damn money, Jenna."

"Okay, fine, but..."

Before I could finish my thought, he announced, "We're going over to Rosie's today."

"Rosie's?"

"The bar I told you about."

"What about Luna?"

"Skid is on his way over. He can keep an eye on her until we get back."

While I liked Skid, I barely knew him, and I wasn't sure how I felt about him watching Luna. "I don't know."

"It'll be fine. Skid's a good guy. Besides, we won't be gone long."

"Okay. If you're sure."

"Wouldn't leave her with him if I wasn't."

For reasons I couldn't explain, I trusted Grim, even with my precious daughter, so I agreed, and half an hour later, we were pulling into the bar's parking lot. I put on my best smile as I followed Grim inside. Rosie's was small, with just a few booths along the wall and a couple of tables scattered about. It was a bit rough around the edges, but folks seemed to like it. There wasn't an empty seat in sight, and it wasn't even dark yet.

When we reached the bar, I spotted an elderly man with short gray hair and dark, square glasses. He was wearing a long-sleeved, black t-shirt with washed-out jeans and boots, and he didn't seem to be in any hurry as he shuffled from one end of the bar to the other. From the way Grim had described him, I could only assume that he was Jud—the owner of the bar.

As soon as he spotted Grim, he smiled and started over to us. "Well, I'll be... I didn't expect to see you back here so soon."

"I told you I was coming."

"Yeah, well, you were three sheets to the wind when you told me that."

"Meant it just the same." Grim motioned his head over to me. "This is Jenna. She's the girl I told you about."

"Pretty little thing." He straightened his back and leaned to the side, trying to get a better look at me, then said, "You ever worked in a bar before?"

"No, sir, but I'm a quick learner. Just tell me what you need me to do, and I'll do it."

"Hm-hmm." Jud turned his attention back to Grim. "You think she can handle it?"

"Wouldn't have brought her here if I didn't." Grim cocked his head. "But there's a catch."

"Of course there is."

"She's got a kid." Grim sounded hopeful as he said, "I was thinking Stacie could keep an eye on her while she was working. I'd make it worth her while."

"Wait," I interrupted. "Who's Stacie?"

"She's my granddaughter," Jud answered. "She's been living in the apartment upstairs since the accident, and it doesn't look like she'll be leaving any time soon."

"Still not gettin' out?"

"No." Jud shook his head and sighed. "But we're still working at it, and one day, she'll get her life back."

Grim must've sensed my unease because he leaned over to me and softly said, "Stacie was attacked a few months back. We're still not sure who was behind it, and that's making it harder for her to get back on her feet."

"That's awful. I can't imagine how hard that's been for her."

"It's been rough, but she's gettin' stronger every day."

"So, you think she'd be up for watching Luna?"

"Yeah, I think it'd do her good," Jud answered confidently. "How old's the kid?"

"Almost four," I answered. "She's very well-behaved and won't cause Stacie any trouble."

"Yeah, I think that could work." He looked back at me as he asked, "When can you start?"

"Anytime," I answered excitedly.

"Alright then. Be back here tonight at seven, and we'll see if you can keep up."

"Great! I'll see you then."

We said our goodbyes, and I felt like I was walking on cloud nine as we made our way back to the parking lot. I had a real chance to make good money—the kind of money that could make a real difference in our lives. And I owed it all to Grim. He'd been so wonderful to me and to Luna. It was hard not to have feelings for him —strong feelings. We'd only known him for a short time, but he'd already made such an impact on our lives.

And I couldn't help but wonder if we'd had a similar impact on his.

Grim

※

"How's she doing?"

Jud glanced over his shoulder and watched as Jenna took another order. "It's only been a couple of days, but she's catching on."

"Oh yeah?"

"Don't get me wrong." Jud tugged his long, silver beard. "She's got a lot to learn when it comes to making drinks, but she seems eager to learn and folks seem to really like her."

"So, you think this is gonna work out?"

"I don't see why not." His eyes drifted back over to Jenna as she served a group of rowdy guys at the other end of the bar. "She's got potential if she just sticks with it."

"And Luna?"

"Cute kid." Jud smiled. "I think having her around is gonna do wonders for Stacie."

I was just about to respond when Jenna came up behind Jud and smiled. A sexy smirk crossed her lips as she asked, "Are you checking up on me?"

"Just stopped by for a beer."

"Um-hmm." Damn, she looked good. Her hair was pulled up, and she was wearing a pair of slim-fit jeans that hugged her ass in all the right places. And when she smiled that smile, it nearly knocked me out of my boots. She placed her hand on my shoulder and eased up on her tiptoes, whispering in my ear, "Don't worry. I won't embarrass you."

"Never thought you would." I admired her smile for a moment, then asked, "So, you're making it okay?"

"I've been better than okay. The people are nice, and Jud has been so patient and nice." Jenna motioned her head towards the stairs in the back. "And Luna absolutely adores Stacie. She made her mac-and-cheese for dinner, and that earned her some major brownie points."

"Glad to hear it."

"Well, I better get back to it." She gave my shoulder a pat. "Wouldn't want to upset the boss man."

"You don't gotta worry about that," Jud replied with a wink.

As soon as she was out of earshot, I leaned closer to Jud and said, "Thanks for giving her a chance, Jud. I owe you one."

"I should be the one thanking you. She's a good one."

"I'm glad it's working out." My gaze lingered on Jenna for a moment longer before I stood and announced, "I'll leave you to it. Let me know if you need anything."

"You know I will."

Once he returned his attention back to the bar, I turned and started weaving my way through the crowd. When I reached the door, I looked back, and a sense of pride washed over me as I watched Jenna as she carried a round of beers to a group in the corner. She was doing alright. Hell, she was doing more than alright, and that pleased me in ways I didn't expect.

I left there feeling pretty good, and the feeling stuck with me the following day as I entered the clubhouse. The guys were gathered in the kitchen, talking and enjoying their coffee, and even though it had been a long week, they all seemed to be in good spirits. I poured myself a cup of coffee and made my way to the end of the table where Memphis was sitting. As I sat down beside him, I asked, "How's the hand?"

"It's still attached," Memphis grumbled. "But I gotta tell ya. This cast is a fucking nuisance. Hell, I can barely wipe my damn ass."

"Should've thought of that before you got tanked and tangled up with those Kings," Prez barked from across the room.

"Yeah, yeah. I know." He leaned in closer as he whispered, "Dude had a noggin like a fucking brick. I don't know how he could keep his balance with that damn thing. Had to be heavy as shit."

"I bet he said the same thing about you."

"Hey, I'm a wounded man over here."

"Because you pulled a stunt you never should've pulled." It had been a couple of weeks, and Prez was still pissed about the fight. I couldn't exactly blame him. We'd had issues with the Kings in the past, and none of us were looking forward to another run-in with them, especially Prez. He knew their threat wasn't something to take lightly, and that had him on edge. He was at his breaking point when he told Memphis, "Hell, you should've just broken it yourself and saved us all the trouble."

"Hey, this shit ain't all on me," Memphis argued. "The Kings have been a pain in our asses for months. I just gave them a little taste of what they've got coming."

"And you didn't think we needed a minute to catch our breaths after everything we had going on?"

"He didn't think," Prez interjected. "That's the problem. He was too busy wallowing in his little pity party to think about the consequences of his actions, and now, we're stuck having to deal with the aftermath."

Memphis turned and glared. "It'd be nice to see you doing a little wallowing. You lost a son, remember?"

"You're going through something. I know that 'cause I'm going through it, too. So, I'm gonna let that shit slide, but I'm only gonna let it slide once." Prez's eyes glared with a fury I'd never seen before as he growled,

"You even think about throwing your brother in my face again, and I'll have your ass on a fucking string. You got that?"

"Yes, sir," he muttered with defeat. "I got it."

"Good. Now, pull your head out of your ass and figure out a plan for next week's run."

There was no plan to figure out. We already knew exactly who was going where and when. It was decided days ago. Goose, Memphis, and I were meeting with our handler later in the week. We'd give him the goods, and he'd give us a satchel of money in return—money that we would launder throughout the next month.

Each Fury chapter had a front business—a construction company, a diner, or a bar. The business was used to launder the money we made from running guns and high-grade marijuana.

We had the Vault.

It was a high-end gentleman's club with décor that matched its name. Our women were not only smoking hot but clean and eager. We also had certain VIP amenities that drew in a crowd from miles away, which gave us ample opportunities to move the marijuana we had coming in.

It was a successful venture all around, and we needed to make sure it stayed that way—which was why I turned to Prez and said, "We'll take care of it."

Prez nodded, then turned his focus back to his conversation with Seven and Creed. Memphis looked like someone had pissed in his Cheerios as he grumbled, "I need a fucking drink."

"I tell ya what. Let's ride over and check on things at the Vault." I gave him a nudge. "I'd bet that cast will get ya some extra attention from the girls."

"If it means getting the fuck out of here, I'm all for it."

And with that, we got up and headed out. It was a beautiful day—perfect for riding, but Memphis's broken hand made that difficult. We had no choice but to take the truck. As soon as we got inside, Memphis looked at me with a grimace. "Sorry about having to take the cage. I know it sucks."

"Don't sweat it." I started the engine. "It won't be long before you're back at it."

"Three weeks seems like a lifetime."

"It'll be done in a blink."

"We'll see about that." His smile faded as he said, "Goose mentioned that you've got Clayborn's sister staying over at your place."

"She is."

"Her brother killed Beck."

"She might've been his sister, but there was no love lost when he died. He was a piece of shit, and she knew it."

"But blood is blood."

"Come meet her."

"What?"

"You heard me. Come meet her, and then come at me with the whole blood is blood shit."

"And if I think you should put her out?"

"You won't."

"But if I do?"

The thought brought an unexpected unease, but Memphis was my brother. If he wanted her gone, then I'd have no choice but to put her out. "Then, she goes."

"Alright, then. When do I meet her?"

"Just say the word."

He gave me a nod, then turned his attention back to the road ahead.

Damn.

It was always something.

The club was only a few miles away from the Vault, so it didn't take us long to drive over. It wasn't even dark yet, and the lot was already filling up. Memphis and I parked and then headed inside. As soon as we walked through the door, I started scanning the room, taking note of who was there and what they were doing, while Memphis paid his respects to a couple of our regulars. I gave him a minute, and then we started through the crowd.

"Everything looks to be running smooth."

"So, it seems."

Memphis and I continued towards the back, where several of the dancers were talking among themselves. We had twenty or more girls who worked various shifts throughout the week. They were all good girls, but there were a couple who stood out above all the rest—like Star and Nikki. They'd been working with us for several years and knew all the ins and outs of the club.

They also knew our expectations, so I wasn't surprised when they both stopped talking the second they saw us walking towards them. Their backs straightened, and their expressions were a mix of respect and curiosity as they listened to me say, "Evening, ladies."

"Hey, Grim," Star replied. "How's it going?"

"Can't complain." Star was a pretty redhead with the greenest eyes I'd ever seen and a killer figure. She was wearing a silver getup with a tiny halter and an even smaller skirt, and it looked damn good on her. "You're looking good today."

"Thanks." She smiled. "I borrowed it from Casey Jo."

"It suits you."

Nikki's blue eyes widened as she stepped over to Memphis and gasped, "What happened to your hand?"

And just like I expected, the rest of the girls rushed over and started fretting over him like he'd lost a damn leg or something. They had their hands all over him, doting like he was their man, and Memphis was eating it up. It gave him the distraction he needed, so I just stepped back and let him have his moment.

He played along for a bit but eventually stepped back and said, "Ladies, ladies. I'm good. I just let my temper get the best of me. Consider it a lesson learned."

"Is there anything we can do?"

"Just do what you do." Memphis glanced around before saying, "Looks like we're off to a good night."

"Oh, yeah." Star nodded. "Tuesday nights have become popular ever since you hired Kip."

"I'm not surprised." Kip wasn't any prettier or better figured than any of the other girls, but she had skills when it came to the pole and the guys loved it. "So, no issues?"

"Nothing we couldn't handle."

"And what about the other new recruits? How are they shaping up?"

"They're adjusting." Nikki feigned a smile as she added, "It's just gonna take some time."

"They know what they signed up for." It was cold but true. "Just make sure they understand the rules and stick to them."

"Of course."

"Alright, ladies." Memphis gave them one of his boyish smiles. "We're out. Give us a shout if you need anything."

They were all busy saying their goodbyes when my burner vibrated with a message. I pulled it out of my pocket and was surprised to see that it was from Jenna.

JENNA:

Hey. I'm sorry to bother you, but something's wrong with Luna.

. . .

ME:

Gonna need more than that.

JENNA:

She's really sick.
I've never seen her like this.

ME:

She got fever?

JENNA:

She feels really warm to the touch.
I looked for a thermometer but couldn't find one.

ME:

Doubt I've got one.

JENNA:

I was going to take her to the free clinic, but the doctor isn't there today.

ME:

What do you need me to do?

. . .

JENNA:

Can you come home?

I'm really worried. Something isn't right.

ME:

I'm on my way.

I SHOVED MY PHONE BACK IN MY POCKET, THEN turned to Memphis and said, "Looks like you're gonna meet the sister sooner than later."

"What's going on?"

"Won't know until we get there."

"Then, let's get moving."

I had a bad feeling, and that bad feeling only grew worse as we got in the truck and started towards the house. I had no doubt that Memphis had questions, but he kept quiet and left me in my own world of daunting thoughts. Luna had seemed fine the past couple of nights—not that I'd seen all that much of her.

Jenna had started working at Rosie's, and I was either already in bed or gone when they got home. Jenna hadn't mentioned anything, so I'd just assumed all was well. Clearly, I was wrong.

When we got to the house, I parked right at the

front door and headed inside. As soon as we walked in, I heard Jenna call out, "We're in the living room."

Memphis followed me through the kitchen and into the living room, where we found Jenna sitting on the sofa with Luna's head on her lap. Luna's color was off, and she had rosy-red cheeks. Poor kid wouldn't even look at me as I asked, "How's she doing?"

"She's getting worse." Jenna was normally very composed and strong, but at that moment, she looked like she was on the edge of breaking. "She was complaining of her tummy hurting last night, but I thought it was just something she ate. Now, she doesn't even want to move."

I reached over and placed my hand on Luna's forehead and knew right away we were in trouble. "Damn. She's burning up."

"I know. What am I going to do?"

Luna rolled her head towards me, and my heart sank when she muttered, "I don't feel good."

"I know, kid, but we're gonna get you taken care of." I turned to Memphis as I said, "We gotta get her to the ER."

"We can't," Jenna interrupted. "I don't have insurance."

We had two hospitals in the city. Regional was one of the best around, but they only accepted patients with insurance. Without it, you are forced to go to County—even if you have the money to pay. People died there left and right, and there was no way I was going to take that kind of chance with Luna.

I was trying to decide the best thing to do when Memphis stepped closer and suggested, "We could take her to the clubhouse and let Blade have a look at her?"

Concern marked Jenna's face as she muttered, "Blade?"

"He's the club's doctor."

"Do you think he can help her?"

"Only one way to find out."

Jenna nodded, and her hands shook nervously as she wrapped the blanket tighter around Luna. I reached down and lifted her into my arms, immediately feeling the intense heat radiating off her body. She barely moved, and that shit freaked me out. I held her close and rushed her out to the truck. I messaged Blade to let him know we were coming, and then we were on our way.

Urgency hung in the air as I drove them over to the clubhouse.

When we pulled through the gate, I glanced up at the rearview mirror, and Jenna's focus was totally on Luna. She had no idea that they were about to enter a whole new world—a world where the men inside didn't exactly trust her. Not only that, the clubhouse was rather large and somewhat daunting, especially with the high fences and barbed wire.

But she didn't even notice her surroundings when I opened the door and grabbed Luna from her hands. She and Memphis followed me up to the back door and straight inside. We started down the long, dark hall, and Jenna's focus remained on her daughter as we made our way to the infirmary.

We'd barely stepped inside when Blade appeared and ordered, "Bring her over here."

"She's burning up." I laid her down, and Luna's eyes shifted over to Blade, watching him intently as he started taking her vitals. "She's been complaining that her stomach hurts."

"Any vomiting or diarrhea?"

"A little last night," Jenna answered.

"Eating and drinking?"

"A little juice, but no real food since lunch yesterday."

Blade was steadily checking her stats as he asks, "Has she had any issues like this before?"

"No, she rarely ever gets sick. She always eats well and is pretty healthy."

Blade placed his hand on Luna's side as he whispered calmly, "Alright, kiddo. I'm gonna have to do something that might hurt a little. I just need you to hang in there for me, okay?"

Luna gave him a little nod and watched with a fearful eye as he pressed down on her side. She whimpered a bit, but she handled it just fine. "I don't know, guys. She's too young to be dealing with appendicitis and there's no obtrusions, so I'm pretty sure it's just a bad stomach bug and she's a little dehydrated. You could take her over to the ER and have her checked out just so we're sure."

"No insurance, so just do your thing and we'll see how she does."

"Alright. I'm gonna start with some fluids and an antibiotic. Once I get that going, I'll give her something for the fever and nausea." Blade grabbed an IV bag as he told us, "I can draw some blood and send it over to one of my friends at the lab. That way, we'll know for certain what we're dealing with."

"That would be good. Thanks, brother."

"No problem." Blade turned his focus back to Luna. "Don't worry, doll. We're gonna get you all fixed up."

Relief marked Jenna's face as she said, "Thank you. I don't know how I will ever repay you."

"It's all good." Blade gave her a wink. "Glad I can help."

Jenna and I stepped back and gave Blade some room to do what he needed to do. Memphis hung out for a bit, but when Blade started to put in the IV, he'd had enough. He leaned over to me with a grimace as he said, "Hey, brother. I'm out. I'll catch up with you two later and see how she's doing."

"Sounds good."

"It was nice to meet you, Memphis." Jenna motioned her head towards Luna. "I'm sorry it was under such crazy circumstances."

"Nice meeting you, too. Really do hope she gets better."

"Thank you. I appreciate that."

He gave her a smile, then turned and headed out of the room. Jenna and I turned our attention back to Blade and Luna. He was soft and gentle with her, and Luna looked at him with trust in her eyes as he gave her the medicine she needed. I found myself wondering if she could ever look at me like that. I found it doubtful. And that had me looking away.

That's when I realized Jenna was staring at me, and she had this weird look on her face. Before I realized what she was doing, she'd reached out and wrapped her arms around me, hugging me tightly. Her mouth was at my ear as she whispered, "Thank you, Grim. Thank you. Thank you. Thank you."

I didn't respond. I just sat there, letting her hug me.

I'd made a point not to touch her. I knew it was just asking for trouble. And I was right. It felt good to be in her arms—damn good, and I only wanted more. But she'd been through hell and needed the hug.

So, I did the only thing I could.

I hugged her back.

Jenna

"Her fever broke."

"Really?" I sat up in my chair and stretched, trying in vain to ease my aching muscles. "Does that mean she's better?"

"It's definitely a good sign." Blade was the nicest, smartest doctor I'd ever met, and I couldn't have been more relieved when he said, "I got the test results back, and it looks like she was fighting off some kind of gastrointestinal infection. Nothing major. Just something kids pick up from time to time. The antibiotics I gave her should take care of it."

"That's great." Blade glanced over at the clock, then looked back to me and said, "It's been a long night. Why don't you go down to the kitchen and grab yourself a bite to eat."

"That's okay." Blade had been so wonderful. Not

only had he helped Luna, but he'd done his best to look after me as well. "I'm not all that hungry."

"You're not going to do her any good by wearing yourself out. You've been here all night. You need to eat, and you could use some sleep, too."

"I don't want to..."

Before I could finish my thought, the infirmary door opened and a man I'd never met stepped into the room. He was older with a broad, muscular build, and while he was handsome, he was terrifying. There was no mistaking the patches on his cut. He was the president of Satan's Fury—which meant he was the fiercest of them all.

He had an aura of authority that made it difficult to look away, especially when his eyes were fixed on me and my daughter. His expression hardened into a glare that sent shivers down my spine. He crossed his arms as he asked, "How are things going in here?"

"Pretty good," Blade answered. "Her fever just broke."

"Good."

Blade gave me a reassuring look as he said, "This is Prez."

"You can call me Preacher."

"Okay."

Preacher turned to Blade as he ordered, "Give us a minute."

"Sure thing."

Blade gave me a reassuring nod before slipping out

of the room. My heart started to race when he asked, "So, you're the sister."

"Yes, sir. I'm Jenna."

"I know who you are. We've looked into you."

"Oh, okay."

"It seems you've had a rough go of it."

"Yeah, you could say that."

"In my experience, people with your kind of past tend to either become fierce fighters who keep fighting to the bitter end or they become derelicts who will do anything to get what they want." His voice was low and threatening as he added, "Which one are you?"

"I don't know." I glanced over at my daughter. "I guess, if I'm being honest, I would have to say both. I'm a fighter. It seems I've spent the better part of my life fighting, but when it comes to her, there's nothing I wouldn't do. But let me be clear... *I am not my brother*. He died long before Grim and his brothers killed him."

"Come again."

"Steven was a good guy, a really good guy, but the Assassins changed him." I shook my head. "He quickly became a man I didn't even recognize."

"Men like that do have that effect." He studied me for a moment, then said, "Glad your daughter's doing better."

"Thank you, and thanks for allowing Blade to help us."

He gave me a nod, and without saying anything more, he turned and walked out of the room. I let out a breath of relief, then got up and walked over to Luna. She was still sleeping, but I could tell that her color was improving. I leaned closer as I whispered, "You had your momma worried, little girl. I'm so glad you're doing better."

"You two ready to go home?" Blade asked as he entered the room.

"Do you think she's ready?"

"I don't see why not." He stepped over and glanced up at the almost empty IV bag as he said, "We'll finish this up, and then, I think you two will be ready to go."

Grim had slipped off an hour or so ago, and I hadn't seen him since. I wasn't sure if he was planning on coming back, so I said, "We rode with Grim."

"I'll get word to him and let him know that you're ready."

"Thanks, Blade."

He reached into his pocket and had just started to send Grim a message when Skid came barreling through the infirmary door. Worry marked his face as he rushed over to us and asked, "Is she okay?"

"She's fine. She just gave us a little bit of a scare, but she's much better now."

"What was wrong with her?"

"It was just a bad stomach bug. She was dehydrated and couldn't rebound like she should."

Skid leaned over Luna and placed his hand on her arm as he whispered warmly, "Sorry you were sick, kiddo. I had no idea."

Luna managed a light nod, but she was too tired to do much more. Skid gave her arm a tender squeeze before turning his attention to me. "Are you guys gonna be here for a while?"

"Actually, Blade was just telling us that we could go. I was just waiting for Grim to get back so he could take us."

"I can take you. I was just about to..."

"I'm taking them," Grim interrupted from the doorway.

"Oh, okay. That's cool." Skid and Grim exchanged a look, and Skid seemed a little aggravated as he said, "I'll get going then."

"Okay." I smiled as I said, "Thanks for stopping by."

"No problem. I hope Luna continues to get better." As he walked out the door, he added, "I'll check in with you guys later."

Grim's face was void of expression as he watched Skid walk out of the room. Once he was gone, he walked over to Blade and asked, "You sure she's good to leave?"

"Yeah. I'll swing by your place tomorrow and check on her."

"That would be good. Thanks, brother." Grim looked down at Luna, and there was this gentleness in his eyes that tugged at my heart. "You ready to go home?"

My breath caught when he called his place home. He could've said anything, but he called it home. It was more than likely nothing, but I found it touching, nonetheless. Luna didn't seem to notice his slip of the tongue and simply nodded.

"Then, let's get you outta here."

Grim waited for Blade to remove the IV, and then wrapped Luna up in her blanket and lifted her little body into his arms. Seconds later, we were walking down a long, dark hall with multiple doors on each side. I didn't think much of it until we stepped outside, and I saw just how big the place really was.

It took up at least a full acre, and there was an enormous fence with barbed wire that surrounded the entire compound. There was a large gate at the front with two guards standing at the entrance, making the place seem even more frightening. I was still taking it all in when we got out to Grim's truck. I opened the back door for him as I said, "This place is really something."

"Um-hmm."

He waited for me to get inside next to Luna before he closed the door. He didn't say a word as he got in and started the engine. His silence remained as he whipped through the gate. Something was wrong. I could feel it. Tension literally radiated off him, but he didn't say a word. He just gripped the steering wheel and sped toward his house. It might've just been my imagination, but I got the feeling that something was really bothering him.

I didn't want to make matters worse, so I kept my focus on Luna and left him alone. When we got back to his place, he helped me get Luna inside and settled in our room. I'd barely pulled the covers over her when he turned and walked out. I turned on the TV and got her some juice before asking, "How ya doing?"

"Okay."

"You need anything? Maybe some crackers or some toast?"

I wasn't surprised when she shook her head and mumbled, "No."

"Okay, then drink a little juice and watch your show. I'm going to step into the kitchen for a minute and talk to Grim, but I'll be right back."

"Okay, Momma."

I gave her a quick kiss on the forehead before walking out to find Grim. I didn't have to go far. He was in the kitchen pouring himself a tall glass of vodka. It was early—much too early for such a stiff drink, which made me worry even more that something was wrong.

He looked up and watched me watching him, but again, he didn't say a word. "Is everything okay?"

"No."

"Wanna talk about it?"

"No."

It was clear something was bothering him—more than likely something with the club or one of his brothers, and even though I wanted to push for answers, I let it go.

It was something we both did whenever one of us didn't want to talk. It was an unspoken parameter that we'd created since I'd been staying there. It wasn't the only one. In fact, there had been several—like don't leave the coffee pot empty, and if one loads the dishwasher, then the other empties it.

Those were the easy ones.

The tough ones were things like, don't ask questions you don't want to know the answer to. That one was for me, and I struggled with it, especially on nights like these when Grim wasn't himself. I moved slowly as I continued towards him and said, "I messaged Jud and let him know about Luna and that I wouldn't be able to make it in tonight, but I haven't heard back from him."

"Already talked to him." He lifted his drink and took a sip. "He was cool with it."

"Oh, okay. Well, thanks." His eyes locked on mine, and I felt an unexpected chill down my spine. I tried to look away, but there was something about the look in his eyes that kept drawing me back in. "I'm sorry for this whole thing with Luna. I know you are busy, and..."

"Don't," he interrupted. "You need me, you call."

I nodded and held his gaze as long as I could bear it, then looked away and sighed, hoping the slow release of air might help ease the tension I felt brewing between us. "Well, I guess I'll leave you to it."

I was about to turn around and leave when Grim muttered, "Jenna?"

"Yeah?"

He didn't respond.

Instead, he stepped toward me and placed his hand

on the nape of my neck, pulling my mouth to his, and he kissed me like I'd never been kissed before. There was no hesitation. No second thought. I kissed him right back. I couldn't help myself. His big, strong arms felt so good wrapped around me, and having his mouth on mine had every nerve in my body burning with need.

He dropped his hands to my waist, pulling me closer as he deepened the kiss. Our tongues twisted, tasting each other, and we were on the brink of losing control. I couldn't let that happen. Luna was recovering in the next room, so I placed my hands on his chest and gave him a slight push, breaking our embrace.

The loss of his touch had me feeling an immediate pang of longing. His arms felt like home. It was a feeling I hadn't realized I'd craved until now. Craved or not, I had a daughter to tend to, so I took another step back as I whispered, "Luna."

"Yeah, yeah. I wasn't thinking."

"Grim."

"Don't." His face was void of expression as he reached for his glass and downed the rest of his vodka. "It never should've happened."

He was shutting me out, or at least, he was trying to. There was something about his tone that made me think that he didn't really mean what he'd said, but it still hurt, especially when I'd enjoyed kissing him as much as I had. I didn't want him to know that his comment got to me like it did, so I feigned a smile as I whispered, "I should go see about her."

"Yeah, you should."

"Have a good rest of the day, Grim."

I turned and I'd just started out of the room when I heard him mutter, "Lawson."

"What?"

"Call me Lawson." I turned to face him, and his longing expression tugged at my heart. "When it's just you and me and the kid, it's Lawson."

And just like that, he inched the door open.

Progress.

It was small and I had no idea why it happened, but I took what I could get and said, "Bye, Lawson."

Grim

✿

I don't know what the hell I was thinking.

I had no business kissing Jenna like that.

And I certainly had no business telling her my fucking name.

But she was there when I needed something to cling to—something to keep me from going completely out of my mind. And it worked. The second her lips touched mine, my center of gravity shifted, and for the first time in a very long time, everything felt right in the world.

My timing couldn't have been worse.

Luna was in the next room recovering. I should've been focused on her—just like her mother had been, but after my conversation with Shep, I wasn't thinking straight. I'd gotten a couple of hours of shut-eye and was headed back to the infirmary when I ran into him in the hallway.

That's when he informed me that he'd caught wind of the fact that someone had been asking questions about what had gone down with the Assassins. They wanted to know who'd had beef with them and why. So far, there hadn't been a connection to us, but I feared it was only a matter of time—which is why I ordered Shep to find out who'd been working with the Assassins.

I knew it would take him some time, but I was impatient and wanted answers. So, I grabbed my keys, and without telling Jenna I was leaving, I headed outside to my bike. I kicked my leg over the seat and turned the key. The engine roared to life, drowning out the noise of my inner thoughts.

I backed out of the driveway and started down the street. The wind whipped against my leather, and with each mile I drove, I felt the tension leaving my body. I couldn't explain it. There was just something about being out in the wind in the midst of the busy city streets that always helped clear my head, but sadly, it wasn't long before thoughts of Jenna and that fucking kiss started creeping back in.

Damn.

I needed to pull it together.

There was a possible threat against the club. That's where my head needed to be. Not on some fucking kiss.

The ride was a damn waste. I was even more frustrated when I got to the clubhouse. I was hoping Shep would have news for me, but when I got down to his room, he was still plugging away at his laptop. I knew that wasn't a good sign, but I had to ask, "Find anything?"

"Not yet." He ran his hand over his beard as he shook his head. "I've had some leads, but so far, they've all been dead ends. Prez is making some calls, so hopefully, he'll be able to come up with something."

"Somebody knows something."

"Yeah, it's just a matter of finding them."

"What can I do?"

"Just hang tight and try to be patient."

"I was afraid you were going to say that."

"Just need another hour or so."

"Okay. You got it."

I started out of the room but stopped the second I realized our answer was right there under our fingertips—I'd just been too damn distracted to even think about it. "I'll get the information we need."

"What?"

"I've still got Ruben."

"Ah, damn. I forgot all about that."

"Give me an hour."

Without saying anything more, I charged down the hall and out to the room where I'd been holding Ruben. I'd visited him several times over the past few weeks, and while my methods weren't exactly the same, I'd made sure he'd experienced everything he and his buddies had done to Amy. Needless to say, he wasn't pleased to see my face when I stepped into the room.

"Ah, God. Not again."

He had a place to sit, but considering what he'd been through, I wasn't surprised that he was standing. His hands were bound behind him, and he was covered in bruises and abrasions—but he was still breathing, which meant he was capable of withstanding more. I gave him a sinister smile as I said, "Well, hello to you, too."

"I can't do this shit anymore, man." Ruben was a big fella who tried to play it tough, but in the end, he was a low-life coward. "Please, just end it. I'm begging you."

"I could do that." I walked over and stood directly in front of him. "But I'm gonna need something from you first."

"Anything. Just no more of this shit."

"If you want it done, you're gonna have to tell me who your crew was working with?"

A spark of hope flashed through his eyes as he asked, "You mean our supplier?"

"Suppliers. Distributors. I want to know everyone with ties to your crew."

"Ah, man," he snickered. "You boys got trouble."

I grabbed the broom handle that was leaning against the wall as I warned, *"Answer the fucking question."*

His smile faded as he looked at the broom, then back to me. Knowing what was in store for him if he didn't talk, he let out a sigh and answered, "Marco Delgado."

"Who the fuck is that?"

"He's cartel, and he's our supplier." Ruben couldn't

even look at me as he explained, "He wants his money, and nothing's gonna stop him from gettin' it."

"How much money are we talking about here?"

"'Bout a quarter of a mill. He did a drop a couple of days before you and your boys came after us. That's been at least a couple of weeks, so yeah. He wants his fucking money."

"How can we find this guy?"

"His number's in my phone. Just don't tell him how you got it, or he'll kill everyone I ever cared about." Ruben shook his head. "Dude is one sick motherfucker—even worse than you, and that's saying somethin'."

After I leaned the broom back against the wall, I grabbed Ruben's phone from the counter and started for the door. "Good doing business with you."

"Whoa! Wait!" Ruben screeched. "You said you were gonna finish me off!"

"I lied."

"Come on, man! Don't do me like that."

Without responding, I walked out of the room and let the door slam behind me. I went back and got Shep, and together, we headed to Prez's office. When we walked in, he was sitting at his desk, and Creed was sitting across from him. Prez leaned back in his chair as he said, "I hope this means one of you found something."

"Yeah, you could say that."

I took a minute to tell them everything Ruben had

told me, and once I was done, Prez shook his head and sighed. "This is not the news I wanted to hear today."

"How do you want to play it?"

"As far as I see it, there's nothing to play," Prez answered. "Delgado doesn't know we were involved, and there's nothing out there that will lead him to think otherwise. So, we keep quiet and don't buy trouble we don't need."

"And if he happens to piece something together?"

"Not gonna happen, but if he does, we'll deal with it." Prez immediately turned to Shep and ordered, "Get me everything you can find on this guy. Just so we cover all our bases."

"You got it."

"Let me know what you find."

"Will do."

Shep turned and started out of the room. Once he was gone, I looked over to Prez and said, "My time with Ruben has run its course. I figured you or Memphis might wanna come finish him off, or I can do it myself. It's your call."

"We'll take care of it."

"Good deal. Just let me know if you need anything."

"You made him suffer?"

"In ways you can't imagine."

He gave me a nod, and I took that as my cue to head out. I went back to Shep's room and spent the next few hours helping him collect everything we could possibly need on Delgado. He was true cartel, vicious and powerful, but we'd gone up against men like him before and would again. It was one of the many risks that came with being in a club like ours, especially when you controlled a territory like Little Rock.

Over the next few days, things were pretty quiet. There was no more talk of Delgado and his hunt for the Assassins, and while we were relieved, I knew better than to think we were totally in the clear. Hell, we were never totally in the clear—not with anyone.

But we didn't let it slow us down.

We kept business running as usual, and business was good. The new blood at the Vault was bringing in quite a crowd—even more than usual, and our latest run had gone off without a hitch. For the most part, I'd say things were going pretty well. The same held true for Jenna.

Once she was certain Luna was okay, she went back to work at Rosie's and things seemed to be going really well. She'd learned how to make some of their more popular drinks and was making tips hand over fist. I wanted to see her in action, so I stopped by the bar on my way home. When I walked in, I wasn't pleased to discover that I wasn't the only one who'd decided to stop by.

Skid was sitting at the front bar, talking with Jenna and a nearby customer. Jenna was smiling at him, and she looked so damn beautiful. I found myself wishing it was me she was talking to. I considered going over and joining them but decided against it when Jenna started laughing at something Skid had said.

I should've taken that as my cue and just left. That would've been the smart thing to do, but I let my hard head get the best of me and sat at a table in the back corner. A knot formed in my stomach as I sat there watching them laugh and carry on like a couple of love birds. I was tempted to go over and rip Skid a new one, but I couldn't.

I had no claim to Jenna. She was simply a girl I was helping out.

Nothing more—even if I wanted it to be.

It was just the way it was.

I hadn't been sitting there long when Jud came shuffling over with a cold one in his hand. He placed it in front of me as he said, "You look like you could use one of these."

"As a matter of fact..." I picked it up and took a long pull before saying, "It's been a day."

"Must be something in the air." Jud glanced around the almost empty bar and sighed. "Been the slowest night we've had in weeks."

"I'm sure things will pick up."

"I certainly hope so." He motioned his head toward the front. "Your boy seems a bit smitten."

"I see that."

"You want me to do something about it?"

"Nah, no need in all that." I quickly finished it off,

then stood and dropped a ten on the table. "I'm heading out."

"So soon?"

"I've got shit to do."

I gave him a pat on the shoulder and started for the door. I'd just stepped outside when I heard Jenna call out, "Grim! Hold up!"

I glanced over my shoulder and my eyes met with hers. I held her gaze for a moment, then continued out to my bike and headed home.

The knot in my stomach was still there, and with every mile I drove, it got tighter and tighter. I needed to get a damn grip. I thought a hot shower might help, but no such luck. So, I tried a drink and then another. I was about to pour a third when Jenna walked through the front door, and I couldn't help but notice that she was alone.

"Where's Luna?"

"She's staying with Stacie tonight." She dropped her purse and keys on the table. "I'm going by in the morning to pick her up."

I didn't respond.

Instead, I poured myself that drink and tossed it back.

I didn't miss the hesitation in her step as she made her way over to me. "I saw you at Rosie's tonight."

I gave her a silent nod.

"I called out to you."

"I heard."

"But you left."

"I did."

"Are you going to tell me why?"

I poured another drink as I told her, "You seemed to have enough company for the night."

"Are you talking about Skid?" Her brows furrowed. "He was there for like two seconds. He just wanted to see how Luna was doing."

"That's not what he wanted."

"What's that supposed to mean?"

"You're a smart girl. I'm sure you can figure it out."

"Grim."

"Back to Grim already, huh?"

"What is this?" She crossed her arms. "Are you jealous?

"I don't get jealous."

"Good, because you have no reason to be. I have zero interest in him. He's just a friend."

I cocked my brow and scoffed, "Does he know that?"

"I know he likes me. I'm not a complete idiot." She rolled her eyes and sighed. "Strike that. Actually, I am an idiot. I'm standing here trying to have this conversation with you, and you can't even admit how you feel."

"There's nothing to admit."

"You have feelings for me. You can deny it all you want, but I see the way you look at me... and the way your breath catches anytime I get too close." She took a step forward. "*Oh, and that kiss...* That kiss said it all."

"Jenna..."

"Don't bother. I already know what you're gonna say. *I deserve better. You're not right for me. You're too old. I'm too young. I've got a kid.* And you'd be right, but none of that really matters. Because I know there's something here. I feel it, and I know you feel it, too."

Before she could say anything more, I dropped my mouth to hers, silencing her with a kiss. She was right. I was going to say all of those things. Because they were true. But in the end, I couldn't stop myself from wanting her.

Her mouth was warm and wet, and all her little moans and whimpers made my cock ache with need. I knew right then that there was no going back. She felt too good, too right. The scent of her skin, the warmth of her mouth, got to me in a way that no woman ever had.

Damn.

My hands made their way past the small of her back down to her perfect ass, and I pulled her even closer. As I lowered my mouth to her neck and began trailing kisses along her collarbone, my hands roamed across the curves of her body. Damn, she felt so fucking good. She inched closer with a wanton groan, and it was all I could do to keep myself from bending her over the kitchen counter.

There was no denying that I wanted her.

Hell, I wanted her from the second I first laid eyes on her, and every time I looked at her, I wanted her that much more. When she inched closer, squirming against me with a whimper, I knew one night with her wouldn't be enough.

"I can't make you any promises. You need to know that."

"I'm not asking you to."

"I don't want to hurt you."

"Then don't."

"It's not that easy."

"It can be if you let it." Her eyes locked on mine as she said, "I want this, Lawson. Promises or not."

Without any further hesitation, I lowered my hand to her waist, then slowly trailed along her inner thigh. As I got closer to the hem of her skirt, she widened her stance, giving me access to trail towards her inner thigh. Her breath quickened as the tips of my fingers grazed the lining of her lace panties. My cock throbbed against my zipper, knowing she was already wet.

Fuck.

She shifted her hips forward and rested her head on my chest, closing her eyes as I continued to caress her slowly—teasing her and making her even wetter for me.

"So fucking incredible."

I lifted her up and placed her on the edge of the kitchen counter. She raked her teeth over her bottom lip as she kicked off her boots, letting them drop to the floor. I stepped between her legs, gripped the front of her sweater and slipped it off her shoulder. I lowered the cups of her bra to reveal her perfect round breasts. I trailed kisses down her collarbone to her breast, then began swirling my tongue around her sensitive flesh. "Oh, God."

I nipped and sucked, relishing the sounds of her little moans and whimpers as I teased her with my tongue and teeth. Needing more of her, I took off my cut then quickly removed my shirt. Desire flashed through her eyes as she lowered her gaze and studied my ink.

She reached out and placed the tip of her finger on my tattoo, tracing the lines across my chest. "You're beautiful."

"Nothing beautiful about me, babe." She lifted her hips just long enough for me to take hold of her skirt and panties and ease them down her long, lean legs. "That's all you. Every fucking inch."

I tossed them to the floor and watched as she laid back on the counter. Her eyes never left mine as I lowered my head between her legs. Unable to wait a second longer, I leaned forward, widening her legs. She inhaled a deep breath as soon as my beard brushed the inside of her thighs, and my tongue skimmed across her center.

The second I tasted her, I knew I was in trouble. She was like the most addictive drug on the planet, and one taste of her would never be enough. I teased back and forth in a gentle rhythm against her sensitive flesh, loving the way her body instantly reacted to my touch.

Her breath became uneven and hitched as I thrust

my finger deep inside her, rubbing against her g-spot—slow and steady. She tensed around me, and goosebumps prickled across her skin. I continued to tease her, staying just inches away from that spot that I knew would send her over the edge.

Her hips lifted up from the counter, begging for me to give her more. I instantly drove my fingers deeper inside her while my mouth clamped around her clit and sucked hard, giving her exactly what she needed.

"Lawson!"

And there it was.

The sound of my name on her lips set my soul on fire.

I continued teasing that spot that was driving her to the edge as I taunted, "That's it. Come for me."

She whispered my name over and over as she spasmed around my fingers. While she was still in the throes of her release, I slipped my hands under her ass and lifted her into my arms. I carried her into the bedroom and lowered her down onto the mattress.

She eased up on her elbows with a wanton look in her eyes. She was so unbelievably beautiful—like an angel that had fallen from the sky, and she was about to be mine.

All mine.

My eyes were still fixed on her as I pulled my wallet out of my back pocket and grabbed a condom. I quickly dropped my jeans to the floor, kicking them off along with my boots. I rolled the condom on, then settled between her legs.

Fuck.

I inched towards her, raking my cock across her center. She was warm and wet, and I ached to be inside her. My voice was low and gruff as I told her, "I'm not going to be able to go slow and easy. It's just not in me, especially when you feel as good as you do."

"I can take it."

Clearly unfazed by my warning, she arched her back towards me and moaned while her legs wrapped around my hips to pull me forward. With one swift thrust, I drove deep inside her and froze.

Damn.

She felt too fucking good.

I needed a second to get my act together, or I'd be done before I ever got started. I regained my focus, then worked myself deeper until I'd given her every inch. My tortured growl echoed through the room as I slowly withdrew.

And a light hiss slipped through her teeth as I pulled her up by the waist, so we were chest to chest. I drove into her again and again—each time a bit faster and unforgiving.

Her heels dug into my shoulders, and she shouted, "Oh God, yes!"

Her nails dug into my back.

Her breath became shallow and strained.

Her skin flushed with desire.

Her hips thrust in time with mine.

She was getting close to the edge.

"That's right, baby. Fuck me like you mean it."

I reached up and fisted my hand in her hair at the base of her neck, giving it a gentle tug. She cried out in pleasure when I drove into her again, giving her every fucking inch. I couldn't imagine a better feeling. I held onto her waist with my other hand as I withdrew and plunged deep inside over and over again.

She took everything I had to give and still wanted more.

Her chest rose and fell as she tried to steady her breath, each gasp of air sounding more desperate than the last. "Lawson."

Each time she said my name, I felt my world still on its axis. I didn't get it. No woman had ever affected me like this. She had me in knots and wasn't even trying.

I'd meant it when I told her she was everything. She was that and more.

A soft smile swept across her lips when I muttered, "So fucking beautiful."

I couldn't believe how incredible she felt as I rocked my hips forward. This woman made me burn for her, every inch of her, and as I drove deeper inside her, I only yearned for more.

I could feel her pulsing all around me as her second orgasm started to take hold. Her panting and moaning urged me on, and it wasn't long before I could feel myself getting close. My body grew rigid as I struggled to hold myself back, and it only became more difficult when she clamped down around me as her body writhed in pleasure.

I looked down at her, and I was in complete awe as I watched her gasp for breath. I knew it would be good with her—there was no way it wouldn't be, but I never dreamed it would be this fucking good. It was like her body was made just for me. Unable to control myself, I slowly drew back and slammed into her again and again, giving her everything I had.

"Fuckkk!" I shouted out as my throbbing cock demanded its release too fucking soon. Unable to restrain myself, I continued to drive into her in an unforgiving rhythm until, at last, she twisted the sheets with her hands and let out a tortured groan.

Her body clamped down around me like a vice, and I was done. I recklessly drove into her once more, then finally came deep inside of her. I kept my hands planted on her hips, holding her in place as I relished the last moments of being buried deep inside her.

We were surrounded by darkness as I removed my condom and tossed it in the trash beside the bed, then collapsed on the bed next to her. I stared up at the ceiling as I told her, "That's not how I expected the night to play out."

"But it was good, wasn't it?"

"It was more than good." I reached over and pulled her over to me. "It was incredible."

She rested her head on my shoulder as she whispered, "So, no regrets?"

"No regrets."

I closed my eyes, just for a moment, but it was just enough for me to realize that the noise that usually played in my head was gone. There were no issues lurking in the back of my mind. No list of things I needed to get done. It was just silence and absolute peace—something I hadn't felt in a lifetime.

Jenna

❦

"We were slow tonight, but I still made over a hundred in tips. That's almost six hundred for the week." I rested my head on the crook of his arm, and with the tip of my finger, I traced aimless patterns on his chest. "At this rate, it won't be long before I can afford a place on my own."

"You that ready to get out of here?"

"No, not at all." I looked up at him and smiled. "I like staying here, but I don't want to take advantage."

He leaned over and kissed me on the forehead as he whispered, "Couldn't if you tried."

"How'd you get to be so great?"

"You do know who you're talking to, right?"

"I'm serious," I argued. "You took us in and helped us out for no reason at all. You got me a job, and if that wasn't enough, you took care of Luna when she was sick."

"That was Blade."

"But you're the one who got her to him. You just knew what to do. It's hard to believe you don't have kids of your own."

"Who said I didn't."

"What?" I eased up on my elbow. "You have kids?"

"I have *a kid*." A strange look marked his face as he admitted, "Well, he's not a kid anymore. He's in his twenties now."

"Seriously?"

"Yeah, I probably should've mentioned it sooner." Lawson looked down at me with a blank expression. "Skid's mine."

"What!"

"Yeah, he's mine."

"But he never acted like he was your son." I felt a little betrayed as I told him, "Neither of you did."

"That's because he's prospecting. The whole father/son thing was put on hold. It's what he wanted, so I played along."

"But you could've at least mentioned something about it."

"Yeah, I should've."

My mind was reeling. I'd seen the resemblance. Anybody could see it. They both shared the same dark hair and eyes, and they even walked the same and had some similar personality traits. But I hadn't pieced together the fact that they were father and son. "What about the pictures? I didn't see any of him and you when I was unpacking those boxes."

"You'd have to ask his mother about that."

"Oh." Until that moment, I hadn't even considered Skid's mother. Nor had I considered the fact that Grim had a past wife or a significant other. "Is she still around?"

"Nah, she's long gone. She couldn't handle the club life."

"And what about Skid?"

"She couldn't handle him either." I could hear the anguish in his voice as he explained, "We were just kids when we met. Too young to get tied up like we did, and when Thatch was born, things took a turn. She didn't want to be tied down. Not to me or to Thatch. So, she left."

"How old was he when she left?"

"Just before his ninth birthday."

"Oh, bless his heart. That must've been really hard for him. And hard for you, too."

"Not as hard as you might think. We had the club, and the brothers did what they could to help out where they could."

"That must've been nice."

"It was. I don't know what I would've done without them."

"I wish Steven and I had people like that when we were growing up."

"I do, too, babe. But you're here now, and you're safe

and doing okay."

"Yeah, thanks to you."

"You're a smart girl, Jenna." He leaned over and kissed me on the temple. "You would've figured it out with or without me."

"Maybe so, but I'm glad you came around when you did." I grimaced. "Well, the 'when' and the 'how' was not the best, but you know what I mean."

"I do, and I agree. But things happen for a reason." He rolled over on his side. "Now, do you wanna keep talking, or you wanna go for another round?"

"Another go? Already?" I gave him a playful smirk. "Are you sure you're able at your age? It's only been a couple of minutes."

"You didn't."

"Oh, yeah," I giggled with a nod. "I did."

"I'll show you what this old man can do."

With that, he grabbed a condom from the bedside drawer, then eased on top of me and settled himself between my legs. He looked down at me with desire so intense I could feel the heat of his gaze burn against my skin, and just like that, my entire body tingled with desire. He spent the next hour showing me exactly what he could do, and he did not disappoint.

By the time he was done, I was both satiated and exhausted.

I'd never had sex like I had with him—so possessive and full of desire. It was like Lawson wanted to own my body, and I couldn't get enough of it. And as I lay there listening to his breathing begin to slow, I felt a sense of contentment I hadn't felt before.

He gave me a light squeeze, pulling me from my thoughts.

A sexy grin spread across his face as he said, "Not bad for an old man."

"Nope. Not bad at all."

He sprawled out beside me with a sigh. I eased over next to him and gently laid my head on his shoulder. I closed my eyes, and after a few minutes of listening to the rhythmic sounds of his heartbeat, I drifted off to sleep.

When I woke up the next morning, Lawson was still sleeping soundly. As much as I wanted to stay there in that bed with him all day, I needed to go pick up Luna. I carefully eased the covers back, and being careful not to wake him, I got out of bed and tiptoed out of the room. I took a quick shower and threw on some sweats before heading out to my car.

On the way to Rosie's, I couldn't stop thinking about my night with Lawson.

Spending the night in his arms made me realize just how much I truly liked him. He was good to me and Luna and being with him made me happy. And that was huge. Happy didn't come easy for me, but at that moment, I truly was. In fact, I couldn't remember a time when I was happier.

I wished desperately that my grandmother was still alive. I missed talking to her, telling her all the crazy things that were going on in my life, and listening to her words of wisdom. I knew she'd have plenty to say about Lawson and his brothers, but she'd be able to see how happy I was.

Even though she wasn't there to tell me herself, I already knew what she'd say. She'd smile and tell me to follow my heart, and that was exactly what I planned to do.

When I got to Rosie's, I parked in the side parking lot, and the second I got out of the car, I got a strange feeling that I wasn't alone. I looked around but saw no one unusual. I shook it off and started up the back steps, and the sensation grew even stronger. I stopped and took another good look around, but again, there was no one to be seen.

I figured it was just my imagination playing tricks on me and continued up the steps to Rosie's back entrance. When I reached the door, I knocked and waited for Stacie to answer. After a few moments, the door creaked open, revealing Stacie with sleepy eyes and messy hair. "Oh, man. I woke you up."

"It's okay." She motioned me inside. "Come on. Luna's upstairs getting her stuff together.

I nodded, then followed her up the narrow stairwell to her apartment. I was still feeling a little off, so I glanced over my shoulder and was relieved to find that no one was behind us. When we reached the top of the stairs, Stacie opened the door and called out, "Hey, Luna Bug! Your momma is here!"

"Momma!" Luna raced over to me and jumped into my arms. "Are we going home?"

"Yes, sweetie. We're going home, but I need to stop for some coffee on the way back."

"I want some."

"We'll see. Now, do you have everything?"

"My bag."

"I'll get it." Stacie shuffled over to the sofa and grabbed Luna's pink backpack, then carried it over to us. "Here ya go."

"Thanks, Stacie. I really appreciate you letting her stay with you last night."

"Any time. I loved having her." Stacie gave Luna a wink. "I'll see you next time, cutie patootie."

"Bye, Stacie."

Luna waved as we started our descent down the stairs. As soon as we were back outside, I got that weird feeling again that I was being watched. I looked behind us, and my heart started to race when I spotted a shadowy figure dart out of sight.

I tightened my grip on Luna and raced for the car. I got inside and locked the doors, then scanned the parking lot, looking for any signs of the person who'd been watching me. I had no idea if it was just some homeless guy looking for a handout or someone with bad intentions, but I wasn't going to take any chances, especially with Luna there with me.

I got her in the car seat and buckled up before rushing back to the house. I was a nervous wreck when

I pulled into the drive. I had every intention of telling Lawson all about my encounter, but the second I opened the front door, I was hit with the delicious scent of pancakes and freshly cooked bacon. Luna's eyes widened with excitement. "What's that?"

"I think someone cooked breakfast."

We made our way into the kitchen, and my heart skipped a beat when I spotted Lawson standing by the stove with no shirt on and a pair of loose-fit jeans. He glanced over his shoulder with a smile. "Just in time."

"What's all this?"

"This is my sad attempt at building my resources." He gave me a sexy smirk. "Apparently, something I need to do at my age."

"I see." I carried Luna over to the counter and sat her on one of the stools. "It smells so good. Can I help with anything?"

"Get us a drink and the syrup from the cabinet."

"You got it."

I took the juice from the fridge and poured us each a glass. As I placed it on the table, I couldn't help but notice that Luna was staring at Lawson with a mystified expression on her face. I walked over and placed my hand on her back. "Is everything okay?"

"Grim's got booboos."

"Those are tattoos, not booboos, sweetheart."

"Nuh-uh." She pointed to his lower back. "Dat's a booboo, and there's another on his front."

"Oh?"

I turned to take a look and was surprised to see that Luna was right. There was a gnarly scar on his back and another on his chest, both of which were hidden in the mix of all his tattoos. I couldn't believe I hadn't noticed them before, especially last night. I stepped over to him and placed the tips of my fingers on the rough ridges of his scar.

"It's nothing, babe."

"It doesn't feel like nothing."

"It happened a long time ago. Nothing to worry about." He gave Luna a wink. "Takes more than some little booboo to get me down."

"That's cause you got muscles."

"That's right," Lawson chuckled. "Now, are you girls hungry or what?"

"I'm hungry."

"Then, let's fix you a plate."

He took a couple of slices of cooled bacon and put them on a plate. My heart swelled as I watched Lawson interact with Luna. His tattoos and scars were all but forgotten as she watched him fill her plate with pancakes. As soon as he finished with hers, he got to work on ours.

Once everything was ready, we gathered around the table and started eating. I considered using the opportunity to tell him about what happened when I went to pick up Luna but decided against it. I wanted to enjoy the moment.

That would be a decision I would soon regret.

Grim

❧

"We have a lead on the situation with Kings." The room fell silent as Creed continued, "They had a big run-in with the Saints last night and lost over half their crew."

"No shit?" Memphis asked, sounding relieved.

"Looks like we won't have to worry about those assholes anymore."

"What the fuck happened?"

"One of them tangled up with the wrong chick, and it bit them in the ass. The Saints nearly wiped them all out."

"That fuck-up couldn't have come at a better time."

I wasn't all that worried about the Kings. They could've caused us some trouble, but nothing we couldn't handle. But we already had enough on our plate and didn't need any more bullshit. Clearly feeling the same, Prez shook his head and grumbled, "Ain't that the fucking truth."

"Any more talk from Delgado?"

"There's been some chatter here and there, but it's slowly dying out," Shep answered.

Prez looked reassured as he said, "That's good. Maybe this thing with him will just pass us by."

"I don't know, Prez." I shook my head. "I hope I'm wrong, but I don't have a good feeling about this guy."

"Then, we will remain diligent, and if anything comes up, we will be ready."

"While we are being diligent and all that..." Ghost winced. "We ran into some trouble at the Vault last night."

"What kind of trouble?"

"A couple of assholes tried to swipe Cherry's bag of goods last night." There was no missing the apprehension in his voice as he went on to explain, "It was her fault. She wasn't being careful, and they snatched that shit. She tried to stop them, and they roughed her up a bit."

I straightened my back and cocked my chin as I snarled, "Why am I just hearing about this?"

"'Cause we took care of it," Ghost answered quickly. "Goose and I got the goods back and beat the fuck out of those guys. Told them they were banned and to never try and step foot in there again."

"And Cherry?"

"She's okay. Just a little shaken."

"Not what I meant." I tried to hold back my anger

as I asked, "What did you do to make sure that shit didn't happen again?"

"I told her to be careful."

"That's not enough. These girls clearly need better training. I'll go by there and set it up with Star and Nikki. A couple of us need to be there to make sure they get it done right this time."

"I'll go," Rusty volunteered. "I've got a shift tonight. I can either go in early or stay late. Whatever works best."

"Me, too," Memphis offered. "I'll be there all night."

"I'll call and set it up."

"Keep us updated on how things play out," Prez ordered. "I don't want this thing getting out of hand."

"Agreed."

We talked a few moments longer, and then Prez slammed the gavel on the table, dismissing church. The guys quickly started to disperse, and I decided to use the opportunity to have a word with Memphis. I followed him out into the hall and down to the bar. When I finally made my way up to him, I said, "Hey, brother. You got a minute>"

"Yeah?" Concern marked his face as he asked, "What's up?"

"I'm not gonna be able to do it." I walked over to him as I continued, "Even if you wanted me to. I just can't."

"Whatcha talking about, brother?"

"Jenna and Luna... I can't put them out on the street. I won't."

"Already knew that."

"Oh?"

"Well, yeah? We all knew it." He chuckled. "You think we haven't noticed that you stopped sleeping at the clubhouse? The question is, are you gonna do anything about it?"

"That depends."

"You ain't gotta worry about me, brother. She's cool. The kid is, too."

"So, we're good?"

"Yeah, brother. We're good. Now, quit with the bullshit and go get your girls."

He gave me a pat on the shoulder and then continued over to the cooler and grabbed a beer. I, on the other hand, didn't move. I was still taking in the fact that he'd called Jenna and Luna 'my girls'. I liked the idea, but it also rattled me—and nothing rattled me. But it wasn't enough for me to walk away. At this point, I wasn't sure anything would do that.

That thought had me reaching for my phone.

Me:

Got plans tonight?

Jenna:

No. Not that I can think of.

Me:

You think Stacie could watch Luna?

Jenna:

I could call and see.
Why?

Me:

Thought I'd take you over to the Vault tonight.
Let you meet some of the girls.

Jenna:

The strip club?

Me:

It'll be good.

Jenna:

It's a strip club.

. . .

ME:

A strip club that Fury owns and runs.

JENNA:

Not sure that makes a difference.

ME:

It does.
Trust me.

JENNA:

Okay. I'll call Stacie.

ME:

That's my girl.
I'll pick you up at 7.

JENNA:

What do I wear?

ME:

Sweats for all I care.

. . .

Jenna:

I'm not wearing sweats!

Me:

Then jeans.
Doesn't matter what you wear.

Jenna:

You're not helping.

Me:

Jeans will be fine.

Jenna:

That's more like it.
I'll see you at 7.

I wasn't ready for our conversation to end, but sadly, I had shit to do. So, I shoved my phone in my pocket and went to track down Shep. We spent the better part of the day discussing some possible changes to the security at Vault. Things were already pretty tight, but with so much at stake, I didn't want to take any unnecessary chances.

When we were done, I stopped by my room, and after a quick shower, I threw on some fresh clothes and headed out to my bike. We were still in the middle of a warm spout, so I figured I would use the opportunity to take Jenna for a ride. It was getting close to 7, so I wasted no time getting over to the house.

I pulled up into the drive and was about to head inside when Jenna stepped outside. She gave me a warm smile, and the sight of her nearly took my breath. Her dark hair was down with loose waves cascading around her shoulders. She had on a pair of distressed black jeans with a red top that accentuated her curves and a pair of cowboy boots. "Hey there, beautiful."

"Hey, yourself." She stepped out onto the porch as she asked, "You ready to go?"

"Ready when you are." I felt a sense of pride knowing that she was mine for the night. I was getting into dangerous territory, but I couldn't help but wonder if she was beginning to feel the same. "You look incredible."

"You don't look too shabby yourself." She motioned her head over to my Harley. "We taking the bike tonight?"

"If it's cool with you."

"It's fine, but it's been a long time since I've ridden."

"You'll do fine." I offered her my spare helmet, and once she had it on, I offered her my hand and helped her onto the back. "Hold on tight."

She nodded, then positioned her hands at my waist.

Her grip tightened as I eased out of the drive, and it tightened even more as we started down the main road. After a few miles, she started to relax and eased back, signaling that she was starting to enjoy the ride—which made me enjoy it even more.

I liked having her on my bike. It had been a long time since I'd ridden with someone, mainly because chicks always tried to read something into it, especially the hang arounds. It was just a damn ride, but this was different. This meant something to me, and I hoped it meant something to her. Hell, I never expected to feel this when I rescued her and Luna from the streets, but the more time I spent with her, the more I realized how much I cared about her.

When we got to the Vault, I wasn't surprised that the parking lot wasn't full. Wednesdays were usually slow, so I hoped Jenna would have some time to get to know the girls. Once we were parked, Jenna got off and removed her helmet before looking up at the big neon sign overhead. "Cool name, by the way."

"I thought so."

"You came up with it?"

"I might've mentioned it."

"That's really cool."

"Come on. I'll show you inside."

I reached over and took her hand in mine, leading her to the front door. When we walked in, we were both hit with the usual scent of smoke and alcohol, and the music was blaring. The lights flickered to the rhythm of the pulsating beat, and the girls on the different stages were giving it all they had.

Jenna's eyes widened as we made our way further inside. I led her towards a table near the back and ordered us a couple of drinks. Jenna sat down, and her eyes immediately started darting around as she took in everything around us. It was a sight for a newcomer. Not only were there various dancers on stage, but scantily clad waitresses moved through the floor, taking drink orders. Jenna looked tense as she leaned over to me and whispered, "They're all so beautiful."

"They don't got nothing on you, babe."

"Oh, come on," she huffed. "These girls clearly work out every day. They don't have an inch of fat anywhere, and their boobs are perky and bouncy and perfect. Just looking at them makes me insecure."

"You have no reason to feel insecure." I leaned back and let my eyes slowly skirt over her. "Not when you're sitting here looking like that."

"You're sweet but full of shit."

"They're good girls, Jen. You'll see once you meet 'em."

"I'm meeting them?"

"It's why we're here."

I spotted Star over at the bar and motioned her over. She was wearing her usual getup—tiny skirt and even tinier halter, and she was all smiles as she sauntered over to the table. "Hey, Grim. How's it hanging?"

"Can't complain. How'd the meet go this afternoon with the girls?"

"Pretty good. There still needs to be more training, but we'll get it done."

"Need anything from me?"

"No, I think we've got it."

"Good deal. While I've got ya, I'd like you to meet Jenna. I thought you and the girls could show her a good time."

"Yeah, we could definitely do that." She smiled. "She's with you?"

"You could say that."

"Seriously?" Star's smile grew even wider. "You've never brought a lady friend in here before."

"First time for everything."

"This is so awesome." Star looked like she was about to bust as she motioned over to Nikki and the others to come over to join us. She sat down next to Jenna and said, "You've gotta give us all the tea."

"About?"

"Grim, of course." Star turned her attention to me as she said, "Could you grab us some drinks?"

"Yeah, I can do that."

As soon as I stood, Nikki and several of the others came over and sat down. They immediately started in with their girl talk, and I knew then that Jenna was about to have one hell of a night.

Jenna

I was just about to grab my drink when Lawson came up behind me and wrapped his arms around my waist. The warmth of his breath sent goosebumps down my spine when he whispered, "You know if you have many more of those, I'll be carrying you out of here over my shoulder."

I leaned into him, resting myself against his chest with the back of my head on his shoulder, and teased, "Is that a bad thing?"

"Not at all." The bristles of his beard tickled against my neck when he said, "Looking forward to it."

"Well, that's good because I stopped counting after the third shot," I laughed.

"She's a total lightweight," Nikki chuckled, barely able to keep her eyes open. "She's only had three. I'm on number six."

"I wouldn't brag," Star scolded. "Danny is going to have your ass when he picks you up tonight."

"A girl can hope," Nikki giggled.

Star looked up at Lawson with a big smile and slurred, "Just so you know, I approve."

"Of?" he asked.

"Your girl. She's the best," Star giggled with a slur. "She doesn't hold anything back."

"Is that right?"

"Um-hmm." Star gave him a goofy smirk. "She told us all about how hot you look without a shirt on. I think you should show us."

"I think not."

"Why not?" Nikki pouted. "You see ours all the time."

"She's right," I interjected. "It's only fair."

"I think it's time for us to call it a night."

"Such a Debbie Downer." Jenna stood with a sway and said, "Thanks for an awesome night, y'all. I had a great time."

"We did, too," Nikki replied with a giggle. "You've gotta come back and hang with us."

"You've gotta come back and do amateur hour!" Star gasped. "You would be incredible."

"Not a chance," Jenna scoffed as she motioned her hand over her hips. "Besides, nobody wants to see all this."

"You're crazy. The guys would flip over you." Star turned to Lawson as she pushed, "Wouldn't they?"

"We'll never know." He gave Star a look, signaling her to let it go, then added, "You ladies enjoy the rest of your night."

"You, too!"

Lawson took my hand in his and led me outside. When we got to the parking lot, I was surprised to see that his bike was gone and had been replaced with his truck. "Whoa. Where's your Harley?"

"Not safe for you to ride when you've been drinking."

"But how'd this get here?"

"I had a prospect bring it over."

"And they all just do whatever you tell them to?"

He opened the door and waited for me to get inside as he answered, "Pretty much."

"That would be kind of nice."

"It has its moments."

Once I was settled and buckled in, he closed the door, walked over, and got in next to me. I leaned my head back and closed my eyes for just a second, and the next thing I knew, I was in Lawson's arms as he was carrying me up the front steps of his house. I let out a little sigh and rolled my head to his shoulder. "You're so strong and handsome. Why did it have to take so long for me to find you?"

"I've asked myself the same about you."

I would've pushed him to tell me more, but the alcohol had blurred my thoughts, and I was fighting to keep myself from passing back out. He carried me into his bedroom and laid me down on the mattress. I was barely hanging on as I kicked off my boots and rolled to my side. "Hold on. Need to get those jeans off ya."

"Are you trying to take advantage of me?"

"No, afraid not." He placed his hands on my hips and rolled me to my back. He started unfastening the buttons as he said, "But tomorrow morning is gonna be a different story."

"Mmmm, I like the sound of that."

"I'm gonna get you some water and a couple of Tylenol." I sat up and lifted my hips as he slipped off my pants. "You need to take them before you go to sleep."

"You're always soooo serious."

"Just looking out for you, babe."

"Babe, hmmm... I like it when you call me that." I giggled. "It's sex-xy."

"Is that right?"

"Um-hmm. You're sexy when you cook breakfast, too."

He stepped over to his dresser and grabbed a fresh t-shirt, then brought it over to me as he said, "You're a goofy drunk."

"I'm not drunk." I pulled off my top and bra, then waited as Lawson slipped it over my head. "I'm just a little tipsy."

"You were tipsy about four shots ago. Now, you're toast."

"Mm. Toast sounds gooood." I grabbed the edge of the covers and pulled them over my legs before falling back on my pillow. "With some butter and some grape jelly."

"I'm gonna go get that water and Tylenol."

"The girls said you're scary. I mean... I get it. You can be." I rambled when I drank, and my words were barely even words as I muttered, "But they don't see what I see."

"Oh? And what's that?"

"You're a good man." I curled into the pillow. "You can deny it all you want, but I see it. I know."

"Yeah, you're definitely toasted." He chuckled softly. "Hang tight. I'll be back in a sec with that water."

I didn't respond.

I was too out of it. A few minutes later, Lawson returned with some water and Tylenol. I quickly took them and laid back down on my pillow. I let out a comforted breath and gave in to my drunken state.

The next morning, I woke to the feeling of Lawson's body hovering over me. I started to stir, and he used the opportunity to drop his hands to the hem of my t-shirt and ease it up, slipping it over my head. "Good morning, beautiful."

"Mm-mm."

"How you feeling?"

His warm tongue raked over my nipple, and I arched my back towards him as I answered, "Better now."

"You sure?"

"Absolutely."

I loved how his touch made my entire body tingle.

The man had a skill for turning me on in a way no one ever had before, and just a simple flick of his tongue had pleasure surging through me. Ever so slowly, he started to work his way down my abdomen, kissing and nipping along the way, making me gasp with anticipation.

As he got closer, I let my legs fall open, giving him access to everything he wanted. I ran my fingers through his hair and closed my eyes as I waited for him to touch me. My muscles tensed and my breathing quickened as he hovered over me, using only the heat of his breath to caress me. His fingers softly swept across my inner thighs, teasing me as they drifted closer. I tried to contain myself, but it was all too much.

"Lawson," I muttered as I inched my hips forward, urging him on.

He took the hint, and a shock of pleasure rushed through me as the flat of his tongue brushed hard against my clit. His touch was firm and demanding like a man possessed, and it felt so damn good—better than I remembered.

As his warm, wet mouth clamped down around me, jolts of pleasure surged through me. I was barely able to take a breath when two of his fingers drove inside me, twisting and turning as he dragged them across my G-spot. With each swirl of his tongue and flick of his finger, he brought me closer and closer to the edge, and it wouldn't be long before those euphoric, tingling sensations took over my body.

"Oh, God," I panted as his tongue raked against me,

I felt the storm of pleasure brewing inside of me. My hips jerked forward as my body clenched tightly around his fingers. After a few more grazes of his tongue, my orgasm took hold. My fingers tangled in his hair as I held his head shamelessly in place while he continued to tease me relentlessly, intensifying my orgasm.

I was still fighting to catch my breath when suddenly Lawson stood up and removed the rest of his clothes, grabbed a condom, and slipped it on. Gazing at his perfectly sculpted body made me writhe with anticipation. I wanted him, all of him, and I didn't want to wait a moment longer. My voice was filled with angst as I pleaded, "*Lawson.*"

His eyes never left mine as he eased back onto the bed and centered himself at my entrance. I wrapped my legs around his waist, pulling him to me, and wound my arms around his neck. His body felt so good against mine, and I shuddered when his cock brushed against my clit. Every touch was like a spark igniting a flame, causing my entire body to burn with desire.

I needed him and gasped with relief as he finally slid inside me. I was in absolute heaven, and he was just getting started. Each and every move was meticulously slow but forceful, making every nerve in my body tingle in ecstasy. Inch by inch, he drove deeper, claiming me in the most primal way.

"Fuck," he groaned as I tightened around him. He ground his hips against me until he found that steady, hard pace. I met his every thrust with an eager jolt of my hips. Like poetry in motion, we moved together in perfect rhythm. He quickly began to drive faster, harder, slamming into me even more forcefully than he had before. With my head arched back against the pillow and my nails digging into his lower back, I could feel the pressure building.

"Yes! Don't stop!" I moaned and writhed beneath him as wave after wave of pleasure crashed over me.

"Fuck," he growled as he watched me fall apart. "Nothing better than making you come."

The sound of his body pounding against mine echoed throughout the room as his muscles tensed. With one final thrust, he came deep inside me. Exhausted, Lawson collapsed on top of me. He lay there for a moment, and I couldn't get enough. I loved the feel of his weight covering my body.

He took a deep breath, releasing it slowly as he pulled away from me, tossed the condom in the trash, and lowered himself down onto the bed. I placed my hand on his chest and felt the rapid beating of his heart against my palm.

We lay there in silence, catching our breaths for several minutes before he finally turned to me and said, "You're really something."

"I was going to say the same about you."

I nestled myself in the crook of his arm, and as I laid there relishing in the haze of my orgasmic release, I drifted back off to sleep. I don't know how long I was out when I awoke to the sun shining directly into my eyes. I rolled over with a groan and was surprised to find that I was in the bed alone.

I was about to get up and go look for Lawson when I noticed there was a note on his pillow. I picked it up, and a smile crossed my face as I read:

Morning,
    I've gone to pick up Luna.
    Drink your water. Take Tylenol.
    We'll be back soon with coffee and a bite to eat.
    ~Lawson

I looked over to the table, and there was a new bottle of water and two more Tylenol. I did as he'd said and took the medicine and drank the water. Then, I curled back up into the covers and closed my eyes. I didn't sleep. My head was pounding too hard for that, but I was able to rest a bit longer and that did me a world of good, especially with the Tylenol.

I was just starting to feel more like myself when I heard the front door open, followed by Luna's little feet trotting across the kitchen floor. The front door closed just as Lawson warned, "Easy there, kid. You don't wanna dump all the donuts on the floor."

There was some shuffling around, and from the sounds of it, they'd bought all kinds of goodies. After a few minutes, Lawson asked, "You want a glazed or a chocolate one?"

"I want sprinkles."

"You got it."

Luna whispered, "What about Momma?"

"She's still sleepin'."

She didn't say anything more. I knew then that she'd already dove into her donut. It wouldn't be long before she was done and ready to move on to the next thing, so I forced myself out of bed. I grabbed some fresh clothes before slipping into the bathroom. I took a long shower, and once I was done, I got dressed and went to check on Luna.

When I got to the kitchen, there was a big box of donuts sitting on the counter with a large mocha and a large vanilla latte. Like his son, Lawson wasn't sure what kind of coffee I liked, so he bought extra. I put the mocha in the fridge before slipping the latte into the microwave. I warmed it up a bit before making my way into the living room.

A smile tugged at the corner of my lips when I walked in and found Lawson sprawled out in his recliner with Luna lying back on his chest. She was completely engrossed in her TV show while he was taking a snooze.

Luna looked perfectly content like she didn't have a care in the world and seeing her so happy made my heart swell. I didn't want to disturb them, so I stood still and watched as Luna shifted slightly, snuggling even closer to Lawson. He instinctively slipped his arm beneath her, making sure she wasn't going to fall.

I tried to be still, but after a couple of minutes, Luna spotted me and announced, "Momma."

"Good morning, sweet girl." I stepped over and kissed her on the forehead. "Did you have fun with Stacie?"

"Um-hmm. We made cookies."

"That sounds like fun."

"Um-hmm."

She nestled back in the crook of Lawson's arm and glanced back at the TV, signaling that she was done talking. I kissed her once more before heading over to the sofa. I'd just sat down when Lawson muttered, "I thought you'd still be sleeping."

"You would think."

"How ya feeling?"

"Not too bad."

A lazy smile crept over his face as he whispered, "I thought that last shot was gonna get ya."

"It did." I pulled the Afghan over me as I motioned my head over to Luna. "Looks like you two have had a nice morning."

"We're trying." He chuckled. "Your girl loves her some sprinkle donuts."

"That she does, and it was really sweet of you to get her some."

"Glad to do it."

"And thanks for picking her up and letting me

sleep in."

"No problem." His gaze lingered on me before he closed his eyes once again. "But you owe me."

"Oh, okay. Did you have something in mind?"

"Oh, yeah." He turned to me with a smirk. "But we'll talk about that later."

"I'll look forward to it."

I took a sip of my coffee before leaning back and making myself comfortable. We spent the better part of the day just hanging out, and it was really nice. I hated for it to end, but unfortunately, Lawson had to get to the clubhouse, and I had to go to work.

I was putting a bag together for Luna when he stepped into the doorway and asked, "What time do you get off tonight?"

"Around ten unless we're having a busy night. Then, it might be closer to eleven."

"Okay. I've got some stuff I've gotta take care of, so I might not be here when you get home."

"Oh, okay." He'd left us there alone many times before, but this was the first time he'd actually given me a heads-up that he wouldn't be around. I couldn't help but wonder if that meant things were changing between us and that Luna and I meant something to him. "I guess I'll see you sometime tomorrow?"

"You can count on it."

With one quick swoop, he reached for me, placed his hands on my waist, and pulled me towards him. Before I had time to think, he lowered his mouth to mine and kissed me in a way that made my entire body hum.

His arms wound tight around me, inching me even closer as his tongue found its way into my mouth. He was rough, tough, and sexy as hell—and my God, he could kiss like it was nobody's business. I was holding on by a thread, and just as I was becoming completely lost in his touch, he pulled back, quickly breaking our embrace. "I gotta get going. You call me if you need anything."

I nodded, then watched as he started for the door.

Before he stepped outside, Lawson turned and glanced back at me, and there was a strange, almost longing, look in his eye as he said, "I'll see ya soon."

"You can count on it."

With that, he closed the door and was gone. I finished getting our things together, and after I locked up, Luna and I were on our way. Twenty minutes later, we were walking up the stairs to Stacie's apartment. When we reached the top, I knocked, and it wasn't long before the door opened, and Stacie appeared with a smile. "Hey, guys. Come on in."

"Thanks." I placed Luna's bag on the table. "I wanted to thank you again for watching Luna last night. You've been a real lifesaver."

"It's my pleasure. I love having her." Stacie looked over to Luna as she said, "In fact, I was wondering if you and Luna might want to go to the zoo with me one day this week?"

"Really?"

Stacie didn't leave her apartment. She'd become a severe introvert after her attack and was rarely around anyone. She worked from home and had her groceries and prescriptions delivered, and that was it. I had no idea what had inspired her to suggest an outing together, but I was thrilled by the idea. And from the expression on her face, she was, too. "I thought we could pack a picnic and make a day of it."

Luna's eyes widened with excitement. "Can we, Momma?"

"Absolutely. I think it's a great idea."

"Yay!" Luna jumped up and down with excitement.

"Which day would you like to go?"

"I don't know." She bit her bottom lip. "I didn't really think that far ahead."

"That's okay." It was a huge deal that she wanted to go, so I didn't want to push her. "We'll figure it out."

"Great. I'll look forward to it."

"Us, too." I knelt in front of Luna and took hold of her hands. "Momma has to go downstairs to work. You be good for Stacie until I get back."

"Okay, Momma."

"I love you, sweet girl."

"Love you, too."

I gave her a quick kiss, then stood and told Stacie, "I'm supposed to be off by ten. I put some snacks and her PJs in her bag."

"Okay. Sounds good. We'll see you in a bit."

Luna was already breaking out her coloring books when I made my way to the door, so I left her to it and headed downstairs. I rushed over to Jud, and I couldn't contain my excitement when I told him, "I have good news."

"Oh?"

"Stacie asked me and Luna to go to the zoo with her this week."

"The zoo?" His brows furrowed. "It's a bit cold for that."

"A little, but that's not the point." I gave him a little nudge. "She's talking about getting out of the house. That's huge, don't ya think?"

"Yeah, it's incredible." I liked Jud. He was a good guy who absolutely adored his daughter. You could see it any time he talked about her. We all knew it pained him that she'd been attacked, and he worked so hard to help her get past it. It wasn't easy. She'd been through quite an ordeal, but he sounded truly hopeful as he said, "It's been months since she's been out for any length of time."

"Maybe she's finally coming around."

"That would be something." He shook his head and smiled proudly. "It's the kid. She's what's done it."

"I don't know. Maybe so. I guess we'll just have to wait and see if she follows through with us going, but the fact that she suggested it is a big step."

"Yeah, it is. It really is."

There was a rumble of impatient customers in the

back of the bar, so I grabbed my apron and said, "I better get to it."

"Careful with the table in the back. They're a little rowdy tonight."

"Will do."

For an old bar, Rosie's was always jumping, and I spent most of my nights on my feet, weaving between tables. Tonight was no different. I got a rush of adrenaline as I raced to keep up with all the orders. Trying to keep everyone happy and the drinks flowing was a juggling act, but I loved it. There was something exhilarating about wrangling the chaos.

By the end of the night, my feet were throbbing, and I was ready to get home and into bed. I helped Jud clean up, and then I headed upstairs to get Luna. She'd already dozed off on the sofa, so I wrapped her in her favorite blanket and carefully carried her down the stairs.

I was just about to reach the parking lot when I felt it again—someone was watching me, and it sent a chill down my spine. I stopped and quickly scanned the area but saw no one. I continued towards the car, but I didn't get far before a figure emerged from the shadows.

A man dressed in a sleek black suit stepped between me and my car, causing me to stop dead in my tracks. My heart lurched with fear when the man sneered, "Hello, Jenna."

I took a step back and tightened my grip on Luna as I asked, "Who are you?"

"Oh, come now. Don't tell me you've already forgotten me."

He took a step forward, and my blood ran cold when I finally caught a glimpse of his sinister face. He was a drug boss or dealer. I wasn't sure what he considered himself. I just knew that he was the man who Steven and his gang worked for. I'd caught a glimpse of him when Steven sent me to the warehouse to pick up the monthly take.

It wasn't something he would normally do, but the police had been watching him and he had no other choice but to send me. The guards didn't like that he'd sent a woman, but they let me in and allowed the exchange. I was walking out when I glanced up at the office upstairs, and there was a man standing at the window, staring down at me.

Even from a distance, the look in his eye sent a chill down my spine.

"There it is." A sinister smile crept across his face. "She knows. You can call me Delgado."

"Why are you here? What do you want?"

"I came for my money."

"What money?"

"Don't play with me, girl. You know exactly what I'm talking about." He motioned his head towards Rosie's. "You've hidden yourself well, but unlike your brother, not quite well enough."

"Jimmy and Steven are gone. They're both dead."

"That's unfortunate, but it doesn't change the fact

that I don't have my money, and you were the last one seen with my goods."

"I gave it to Jimmy, just like I always did. I have no idea what he did with it. They didn't tell me anything."

"You best get to figuring it out. You're a smart girl. I'm sure you will come up with something." He took a menacing step forward as he announced, "And just to make sure you don't try to pull a fast one like your brother, the kid's coming with me."

"What!" My breath caught in my throat as I clutched Luna protectively to my chest. "NO! You can't!"

"We'll see about that."

Before I had a chance to react, two men stepped out of the shadows, and both were armed and had their weapons aimed right at me. Delgado reached over and wrenched Luna from my arms. She immediately woke and cried out, "Momma?"

Out of pure instinct, I lunged for her, but he raised his hand into a fist and slammed it into my face, knocking me back. My cheek felt like it was on fire, but I didn't care. I wanted my daughter back. I was about to try again when he warned, "Don't even think about it."

"Please, don't do this!" I felt like a cat who'd been cornered. I wanted to lash out and claw at him again, force him to give me my daughter back, but I couldn't take a chance on his men hurting Luna. My only hope was to plead for his mercy. "I'll do anything!"

"Get me my money." The words had barely left his

mouth when a black SUV pulled up. "Then, and only then, will you get your daughter back."

"Momma," Luna cried. "I want my momma!"

"Hush!" Delgado snapped. "I don't want to hear any of that shit."

Luna immediately stopped and looked over to me with panic in her eyes. "It's okay, sweetie. Everything's going to be okay."

I felt gutted, completely gutted, as I watched one of Delgado's men open the back door to the SUV and wait for him to get inside. Before closing the door, he leaned forward and warned, "Don't call the police. That would be a deadly mistake for both you and your daughter."

"I won't tell anyone."

"You have twenty-four hours. You know where to find me."

And with that, the men got in the truck with him, and they drove away, leaving me feeling utterly destroyed. I collapsed to my knees and broke down right there in the parking lot. I cried for a good bit, but then it hit me. Luna was counting on me. I was all she had, and me sitting in that stupid parking lot crying wasn't helping her.

So, I got up, wiped away my tears, and got in my car.

I had no idea where I was going or what I was going to do, but come hell or high water, I was going to get my daughter back—no matter what the cost.

Grim

I keep my circle small and my walls high. Only a few have ever managed to get close, and even then, there were limits. I didn't share my deep, dark secrets or divulge my past. I certainly never told anyone about the memories that haunted me in the stillness of the night.

There were so many, like barely being able to talk when my ol' man started beating me senseless, breaking arms and teeth, or the years we spent living out on the streets, and it was so damn cold I thought we'd freeze to fucking death. I shook so hard I prayed for death to come. It was a constant fight for survival, and there were many, many days when we barely skirted by.

Those were memories I kept locked away.

I saved them for moments when I needed them—moments when I needed to do the unthinkable. As I sat there in Prez's office with him and Creed, I had this gnawing feeling in my gut that I would be calling on them soon. I just had no idea why. Things seemed to be going well.

I'd had a good night and even better morning with Jenna. I hadn't run into any major hiccups at the clubhouse, and things at the Vault seemed to be running smoothly. And our run to Memphis had gone off without a hitch. But something was coming.

I could feel it in my bones, so I turned to Creed and asked, "Any more talk about the Kings?"

"Not much," he answered. "Just that they're scrambling to keep things going. They'd burned a lot of bridges, so I wouldn't be surprised if they disbanded altogether."

"If only we could be so lucky," Prez scoffed. "But assholes like them tend to repopulate like fucking rabbits. It's best to keep an eye on them and make sure they don't sneak up on us."

"Agreed, and we should do the same for Delgado. Talk may be down, but he's still out there, and he can't be happy about losing such a large source of income."

"Already on it," Creed replied. "We have sources monitoring the situation, and if there's a change of any kind, they'll let us know."

"Anything recent?"

"No, nothing new." Creed gave me a look. "But if you're feeling an itch, you could always pay a visit to Tyrone."

"Awe, hell. What is it now?"

"He's asking to push back the drop day again."

"The one for tomorrow?"

"Yeah, he said there's something going on with his guy, and he can't get his hands on the goods until next week."

"You think he'll pull through?"

"Don't have a reason to think he won't." Creed chuckled as he glanced over at Prez. "We've been working with him for years. We all know he's a fuck-up, but he always managed to pull through. But lately, he's been off his game, and it might be time to give him a little direction or cut him loose entirely."

"Yeah, it's not like we don't have options." Creed leaned back in his chair. "Gus mentioned that their chapter has a new supplier who's got some really good shit. Said it was a game changer."

"Who they buying from?"

"Some club out of Nashville. Pretty sure they're growing it themselves."

"Might be worth looking into, until then, you good with me going over and having a word with him?"

"Absolutely. Do your thing," Prez answered. "Let us know how it goes."

"You know I will."

Tyrone wasn't the issue. He had a guy who had a guy, and Tyrone was at their mercy. But that didn't stop me from getting up and heading out of the room. I needed to dot all my i's and cross all my t's, and this was just a start.

I was on my way to my bike when I spotted Skid

hunched over Creed's Harley, and he appeared to be struggling. I walked over and asked, "What have you gotten into now?"

"Changing Creed's oil, but he's got a stripped bolt that's refusing to give." The muscles in his arms tensed with exertion, beads of sweat glistening on his brow as he complained, "Whoever did it last over torqued it."

"You need a hand?"

"Nah, I got it."

"You sure?"

"I said I got it, Dad," he huffed. "I got it."

It had been months since he'd called me dad, and while it was out of anger that he'd let it slip, it still meant something to me. He was my son, through and through, and while I wasn't always that great at showing it, I loved him. Nothing I wouldn't do for him—even if it meant giving up my role as his father while he prospected. He wanted to earn his patch on his own, and I got it. I would've felt the same if I was in his shoes, so I played along.

I continued to play along as I told him, "Spray some 40 on it and let it sit. It'll help lubricate the threads."

Skid looked up at me with a soured expression and disgruntled breath. He dropped the wrench and reached into his toolbox for the WD-40. When he started spraying, I turned and started for my bike. "A dab will do ya!"

"I said I've got it!"

"You do now." I chuckled under my breath as I called out to him, "See ya when I see ya."

"Where ya headed?"

"Got something I need to take care of."

"Need a hand?"

"No." Using his own words against him, I shouted, "*I've got it.*"

I kicked my leg over the seat of my Harley, and minutes later, I was whipping through the clubhouse gate. It was cold out—too cold to take my bike, but I didn't fucking care. I needed some wind therapy to clear my mind. I had a million thoughts trampling through my head, and I just needed them all to stop—even if it was only momentarily.

My leather jacket and gloves did little to help with the bite of the cold night air, but it did as I'd hoped and got my mind off of things. As I drove further into the city, the surroundings quickly started to change. The buildings went from newly remodeled storefront to dilapidated shells that were marked with various gang graffiti.

It was a place where the line between right and wrong blurred. Crime was prevalent, and danger lurked in every dark corner. The air was thick with the scent of decay and utter desperation, and it became even thicker when I pulled up to Tyrone's place.

It was a shotgun house that was long and narrow with peeling paint and had old, rusted cars parked in the back. It wasn't as bad as some, but it was in a rough state. I wasn't exactly surprised. It's hard to get a mortgage for a decent house when you've got no proof of employment, but it was more than that. This was the life he knew, and he wasn't looking to change that any time soon.

It was already dark by the time I parked and started up to his front porch. There were no lights on, and even though it didn't look like anyone was home, I pounded on the door. I waited, then knocked again.

I could hear some kind of music playing inside, so I knew someone was there. I knocked again but quickly grew impatient. I tried the door, and when I found that it was unlocked, I stepped inside. Tyrone was laid back on the sofa, watching TV in a haze of smoke. His eyes were glazed over, and he looked completely out of it. The chick next to him didn't look much better.

I walked over to the TV and ripped the plug from the wall, and the room fell silent. "What the fuck!"

Tyrone shot up and started over to me but stopped the second he realized who was standing in front of him. "Hello, Tyrone."

"Aw, shit." He took a quick step back. "I don't want no trouble, Grim."

"Who said there was going to be trouble?" I motioned my head over to his friend. "You need to get rid of her."

"Yeah, yeah. Okay." He rushed over and gave the chick a hard tug. "Come on, baby. You gotta get outta here."

"I don't wanna go," she pouted. "My show ain't over."

"I don't give a fuck about your show. You gotta get out of here, and you gotta get out of here now! Get on home, and I'll be over later."

"Fine, I'll go." She stood with a wobble. "Your friend looks mad."

"It's okay. He always looks like that. Now, git."

She grumbled something under her breath as she swayed over to the door. Seconds later, she was gone, and it was just me and Tyrone. I kept my voice low and steady as I told him, "I hear you've run into some trouble with this month's take."

"It's coming. It's coming. There's just a little delay."

Tyrone wasn't a small guy. He was at least six-two and had a heavy set with a thick neck and thicker biceps. On the regular day-to-day, he could hold his own, but at that moment, he was high, and I was pissed. That wasn't a good combination—at least, not for him. I charged toward him, grabbed hold of his throat, and slammed him against the wall. "I don't like gettin' dicked around, Tyrone."

"It ain't on me. I swear it. My handler has had some issues. I don't even know what they are, but it ain't because of me. I'm here and sitting on go."

"Who's your handler?"

"You know I ain't got a name. My guy has a guy who has a guy."

"I want names!" I tightened my grip on his throat.

"You've got twenty-four hours to get them to me, or our partnership is done!"

He didn't argue. He simply nodded and said, "I'll get it."

"That's what I wanted to hear."

I stepped back as I released my hold on his throat. As soon as I got back out to my bike, I messaged Prez and told him about my conversation with Tyrone. I had a shift at the Vault that started in less than an hour, so I decided to skip going back to the clubhouse and headed to work.

When I arrived, Ghost and Goose were already there and standing at their posts. I walked over, and as soon as he spotted me, Ghost shook his head and said, "We could've used you a few minutes ago."

"Oh? What was going on?"

"A couple of drunk assholes thought it would be a good idea to start throwing punches."

I was a little disappointed that I'd missed it. I was still on edge after my conversation with Tyrone and could've used a chance to let off some steam. But it was only a matter of time before something else came up. On nights like these, when it wasn't all that crowded, folks tended to lose their shit and start bullshit they had no business starting.

I stood at my post, waiting and watching for any potential issues, and just as I'd expected, it wasn't long before I spotted a familiar face at the bar—a face I shouldn't be seeing. Enraged by his fucking nerve, I charged over to him and placed my hand on his shoulder, whipping him around as I snarled, "Wanna tell me what the fuck you're doing here?"

"Nothing, man. I was just having a drink."

"Is that right?" I grabbed a fistful of his collar and gave him a hard tug, pulling him off the stool and onto the floor. "And why would you come in here for a drink when you know you're fucking banned, Barry?"

I started dragging him towards the front door as I growled, "Or did you think I forgot that you'd tried to fuck with one of our girls?"

"It was just a misunderstanding, man," Barry shouted as his feet drug across the floor, knocking over chairs and one of the tables. "I didn't touch that girl. Besides, it was months ago."

"Banned is banned, asshole."

I stopped just long enough to punch him in the gut, then continued on towards the door. Once I got him outside, I pulled him to his feet and slammed his back against the wall as I snarled, "You show your face around here again, and it'll be the last fucking thing you do."

I gave him one last shove, sending him stumbling into the parking lot. As soon as he made it to his car, I went back inside and reclaimed my spot by the door. Ghost was a bit hesitant, but eventually, leaned towards me and whispered, "You good?"

"Yep," I lied.

"It's gonna be a long one."

"No doubt."

My bad mood only got worse when, moments later, a fight broke out next to the main stage. "Fuck. Here we go."

Without hesitation, we made our way over to the three men who were quickly losing control. I slipped my arm around one of the bigger guys' throat and gave him a hard tug, lifting his feet from the floor as I jerked him away from the others. I threw him down on the ground and started punching him.

I hit him again and again.

The guy wasn't even fighting back, but I kept hitting.

As soon as his buddies spotted us on the floor, they took a swing at Ghost. That was a mistake. Ghost plowed his fist into the smaller one's gut, then immediately turned his attention to the other. He punched him in the jaw, and the dude toppled like a fucking tree.

I reached down and grabbed a fistful of my guy's shirt, jerking him up on his feet. I took hold of his bicep, then grabbed his buddy before starting towards the front door. Ghost followed behind with the third guy, and once we had them outside, I gave the bigger one a hard shove. "Get the fuck out of here."

"Come on, man. We weren't doing nothin'."

"You heard the man," Ghost roared. "Get the fuck out of here."

The three stumbled out into the parking lot and climbed into their truck. A few moments later, they were pulling out of the lot. I was watching their taillights head out into the street when I heard Star's voice ask, "You guys okay?"

"Grim could use some ice for that hand."

Even though it was throbbing like a motherfucker, I shook it off and started back inside. "I'm fine."

Moments later, Ghost came back in, and after a quick word with Star, he came back over to his spot at the door. We both stood on go for the next two hours. Thankfully, our altercation with the three assholes seemed to deter any other disputes, and to all of our surprises, the rest of the night was pretty quiet.

Goose and I stuck around after closing and helped the girls shut everything down. I put the night's take in the safe, and then, we were on our way. When we got out to the parking lot, Goose got in his truck and said, "Another day, another dollar."

"We worked hard for that dollar tonight."

"That we did." Before closing his door, Goose smiled and said, "I'll catch you on the flipside."

"Night, brother."

Once I was sure the last of the girls had gone, I got on my bike and started home. I'd planned to stay at the clubhouse for the night, but after the night I'd had, I was in a shitty mood and needed to lay my eyes on Jenna. It was late. I didn't want to wake them, so I killed the engine at the end of the drive and went up to the front door instead of the back.

I'd been living there for years and never once had I

been so glad to be home. But the feeling quickly faded when I stepped inside and was engulfed by an eerie silence. I knew right away something wasn't right, so I went straight to the bedroom, and a sinking feeling settled in my stomach when I found the bed empty.

I rushed and checked the other rooms, and there was no sign of Jenna or Luna. Thinking they had to be there, I called out, "Jenna? Luna?"

But the only response I got was the hollow echo of my own voice.

Damn.

I stepped over to the window and glanced outside. My chest tightened when I realized Jenna's car wasn't in the driveway. I was so fixated on getting inside to her that I hadn't even noticed. It was almost midnight. She should've been home hours ago. I grabbed my phone from my pocket and quickly glanced down at the screen. I had no missed calls or texts, so I dialed Jenna's number.

When I got no answer, I called again and again. I sent message after message, and still no response. So, I did the only thing I knew to do. I dialed Jud's number. After several rings, he finally answered, "Yeah?"

"Hey, Jud. It's Grim."

"Hey, man. You got any idea what time it is?"

"Yeah, I know it's late, but I was wondering if Jenna was still around?"

"Jenna?" he asked with surprise. "Nah, she left out of here a couple of hours ago."

"You sure?"

"Yeah, I saw her myself. She and the kid left right after we closed."

"Damn."

"Something wrong?"

"Won't know until I find her."

"Well, let me know what you find out."

"Will do."

I hung up the phone and tried Jenna again. When she didn't answer, I nearly lost it. I had to do something, so I grabbed the keys and drove over to Rosie's. As I feared, there was no sign of Jenna or her car, but that didn't stop me from getting out and calling out to her. "Jenna! Luna!"

I called again and again, but neither of them answered.

It didn't make any sense. They should've been there. I looked around once more, and that's when I spotted it —Luna's little tennis shoe. I walked over and picked it up, and as I held it in my hand, every instinct I had told me they were in danger.

I knew it without a doubt in my mind.

I also knew I'd burn the world to the ground to get them back.

Jenna

It felt like my heart was going to pound right out of my chest. I was petrified and wanted nothing more than to get the hell out of there, but I couldn't leave without at least looking for that stupid bag. It had been months since I'd dropped it off at Jimmy's house, and the chances of it still being there were slim, but it was my only hope of getting Luna back. I had to see if it was still there.

I parked on the side of the house and crept over to the back window. I pushed it open, then heaved myself up and wiggled my way inside. That's when I realized I had to be quiet. Jimmy's brother, Brandon, was in the living room with one of his buddies. They were watching TV and smoking a joint.

So far, neither of them had a clue that I was there, and if they heard me, I would never get out of there alive. I prayed that TV and marijuana would be enough to distract them while I made my way down to Jimmy's room.

The entire house was dark, and the shadows seemed to swallow the small light coming from my phone. Every rustle, every creak, felt like a nail going in my coffin, but I kept inching down the hall until I eventually found his room. With trembling hands, I eased his door open, and its hinges creaked with a warning to stop and turn back.

I didn't listen.

Instead, I continued inside and closed it behind me.

I quickly scanned the room but saw no sign of the duffle bag.

I tiptoed over and checked the closet but only found a pile of dirty clothes. It wasn't on the dresser or on the floor. I was starting to lose hope when I spotted a black strap at the foot of the bed. I rushed over and grabbed it, and relief washed over me when I saw that it was the same bag I'd given Jimmy months ago.

I quickly opened it, and when I saw the plastic bags of marijuana, I thought everything was going to be okay.

I was wrong.

So, so wrong.

I hadn't even had the chance to zip it closed when the bedroom lights flicked on, and Jimmy's brother and friend appeared in the doorway. Brandon crossed his arms and snickered, "Well, lookie lookie. We got ourselves some company, and she is fine as hell."

"You ain't lying." The friend gave me the once over as he asked, "Is that little Stevie's sister?"

"Yeah, that's her." Brandon's lips curled into a sinister smile. "Jimmy always had a thing for her, and now, she's right here for the taking."

I stood and held up my hands in surrender. "Look, guys. I don't want any trouble."

"Oh, I don't know." Brandon glanced over at his buddy. "I think trouble was exactly what you were looking for, and baby, you just found it."

"Wait. Stop." I took a step back. "It's not like that."

"Oh, but it is." He took another step towards me, and that's when he spotted the duffle bag at my feet. "What's with the bag?"

"It's nothing." I reached down and grabbed the straps, pulling it toward me. "It doesn't belong to you."

"Don't belong to you neither."

"I gotta have it." I hoped if I was honest with them, they might cut me some slack, so I explained, "The man it belongs to has my daughter, and he won't give her back without it."

"Sounds like a personal problem to me." Brandon looked at his friend. "What do you think, Derek?"

"Sure sounds that way."

"You don't understand. This guy is ruthless! If he doesn't get this back, he's going to kill us all."

"I don't see no guy." Brandon looked around the room before turning to his friend. "You see a guy?"

"Nope, no guy. Just a fine-assed chick who's got a shit-ton of pot. Damn. Is this our night or what?"

Damn.

These guys were numbskulls. They were going to ruin everything. I had to get the hell out of there, but there was no escape. They were closing in on me. I tried to take another step back, but Brandon lunged forward, grabbing me by the arm and pinning me against the wall.

When I tried to break free, Derek moved in to help. "Let me go!"

I tried twisting and turning—anything that might help me get away, but they were too strong. I tried to fight them, but they forced me to the ground, pinning me beneath their weight. A wave of fear and helplessness washed over me when I realized I couldn't get away from them.

As I lay there, helpless and defeated, my mind raced with regret. I'd made a terrible mistake by coming here. I'd just made matters worse, and now, I'd never get Luna back. The thought had me feeling utterly defeated. I stopped fighting and just let my body fall limp. I would let them do what they were going to do, and then maybe, just maybe, I could get the hell out of there.

Brandon was still on top of me when he turned to Derek and rasped, "Hold her hands."

With Derek's hands wrapped firmly around mine, Brandon eased off me and dropped his hands to my waist. "Tonight is your lucky night, sweetheart. We're gonna show you a real good time."

I didn't respond.

I just lay there as he started to unbutton my jeans. I didn't know what it was about these men and their need to overpower a woman. They were just like Jimmy and my stupid brother. It was sickening.

I closed my eyes and tried to shut it all out, but then I thought about Luna. I remembered the fear in her eyes when Delgado put her in the back of that SUV, and I was hit with a sudden urge to fight. I opened my eyes, and when I saw that Brandon was looking down, I slung my head forward and slammed it into the bridge of his nose.

He flailed back, clutching his face as he roared, "You stupid cunt!"

Not ready to give in, Derek tried to worm his way on top of me. But the second he tried to kick his leg over my waist, I lifted my knee and plowed it into his crotch, sending him into a fit of moans and groans. I used the opportunity to scramble to my feet. I quickly grabbed the bag and was about to rush for the door when Brandon reached out and grabbed my foot, tripping me.

"Where ya thinking you're going, you stupid bitch!"

I was face down, clawing my way across the floor, when I felt a sudden shift in the room. Everything stilled as Brandon muttered, "What the fuck?"

The words had barely left his mouth when a gunshot

rang out. Seconds later, he dropped to the floor with a hard thud. Derek immediately started scooting back as he pleaded, "Wait! Stop!"

There was a second gunshot, and Derek fell dead right next to me.

I couldn't move.

I couldn't breathe.

I was absolutely petrified as I lay there listening to the sound of footsteps coming towards me. I braced myself as I awaited my fate, and just when I thought my end had come, I felt his hand on my shoulder, "Baby, it's me."

"Lawson?" I glanced over my shoulder, and my heart nearly leapt out of my chest when I saw his handsome face. "Oh, my God. It's really you."

"Yeah, baby. It's really me." I sat up and wrapped my arms around him, hugging him tightly. "It's okay. I've got ya."

I couldn't hold back my tears as I muttered, "You killed them."

"Yeah, I did." He showed little emotion as he added, "They were trying to hurt you, and there's no way I was gonna let that happen."

He looked down at me with worry in his eyes. "You're gonna have to tell me what the hell is going on. What are you doing here?"

"I came to get the bag."

"I'm gonna need more than that, babe."

He stood there waiting for me to explain, but I was

having a hard time forming the words. The past few hours had been the worst of my life, and just thinking about the moment Delgado ripped Luna from my arms brought tears to my eyes. "He's got Luna, and it's the only way I can get her back."

"Who's got Luna?" Just thinking about her out there alone, crying for me to come and save her broke my heart. I was overcome with guilt and struggled to keep it together. "What the hell are you talking about?"

I had to fight to keep myself from breaking down as I explained everything that had happened and why I'd come to Jimmy's. When I'd told him everything, I added, "I know it sounds crazy, but it was the only thing I knew to do."

"You could've come to me."

"I thought I could handle it, but clearly, I thought wrong."

He brought his hand up to my chin, forcing me to look up at him. "Do I mean something to you?"

"Yes, of course you do."

"*Then, you come to me.* No matter what."

I nodded, and then we both got to our feet. Lawson leaned down and kissed me on the forehead as he whispered, "We're gonna get her back. You have my word on it."

He grabbed the duffle bag and led me out of the room. As we started down the hall, I glanced behind me and asked, "What about them?"

"I'll take care of it."

I thought back to the day he and his brothers killed Jimmy and Steven. They'd torched Steven's entire house, and I hoped they would do the same with Jimmy's. I'd always hated this house, and I hated the men inside even more. Seeing it burned to the ground would be nothing more than a relief.

When we got out to his truck, Lawson opened the door and waited as I got inside. I paused and studied him for a moment, then asked a question that I doubted he would answer. "How did you know I was here?"

"Best you didn't know."

"You tracked my phone or something, right?" When he didn't answer, I let it go and asked, "So, what are we going to do now?"

"I'm taking you to the clubhouse." He tossed the duffle bag in the back seat, then walked around and got inside next to me. "I'm gonna need you to tell Prez and Creed everything you told me. Can you handle that?"

"I'll do anything if it means getting Luna back."

"That's what I needed to hear."

Lawson grabbed his phone from his pocket, and after he sent a couple of texts, we were on our way. With each mile we drove, Lawson became more and more on edge. I could almost feel the rage radiating off of him, and it wasn't long before he was no longer the Lawson I'd come to know and love. He'd shed that skin, becoming Grim and nothing but Grim.

I didn't mind.

Grim was who we needed. He was the one who'd bring my Luna back to me, so I welcomed him by not saying a word. I just sat there and let him stew in his own fury. He would need it to face what was ahead. We both would—more than I even realized.

When we got to the clubhouse, it was well after midnight, but that didn't stop Preacher and Creed from meeting Lawson at the front door. We followed them into the bar, and together, we told them everything that had taken place. Preacher listened with a blank expression. I feared he might refuse to help me, but then, he turned to Lawson and asked, "Have you claimed her?"

"In every way that counts."

"And she knows what that means?"

"She knows enough."

"Then, how do you want to play this?"

"We gotta get the kid back, and once she's safe, I'm gonna make him pay for ever touching her."

"Then, that's what we'll do." Preacher turned his attention to me as he said, "You mentioned that you did a pick-up for your brother."

"Yes, sir. I did.'

"Do you remember where that was?"

"Yes, sir."

"What can you tell us about it?"

"He was set up in an old plant down by the river. It was right next to the lumber yard. I'm not sure what it was, but the building itself was in rough shape. If I didn't know better, I'd say it should've been condemned.

The bricks were crumbling, and lots of the windows were shattered. But it's completely different on the inside."

"How so?"

"As soon as you walk in, you see polished floors, fresh paint, and bright lights. The whole place is fixed up. And there were lots of guards. They were pretty much everywhere, especially at the doors. They pat you down and send you forward down this long hall that opens up, and you see the different levels above. His office was on the second floor, and it has all these windows so he can keep an eye on what's going on."

"You think that's where he took Luna?"

My throat tightened as I said, "He said *you know where to find me* and that's the only place I know, so I guess. But honestly, I don't know."

"Okay, that's a good start." Preacher turned to Lawson as he announced, "It's time to call in the guys."

Creed took out his phone and stepped away from us as he said, "On it."

"We have things to discuss." Preacher motioned his head towards me. "I think she could use a break."

"I'm fine," I argued. "I want to help."

"And you will. But we have a way of doing things."

"Okay. Whatever you say."

"I'll take her to my room."

With that, Lawson took hold of my hand and led me out of the bar. As we headed down the long, narrow hall, I expected him to say something, but he didn't say a word. He wouldn't even look at me. I was already unnerved, and his silence wasn't helping matters. I didn't know what to do or say, so I just followed along until he stopped in front of a door.

When I was there before, I'd seen all the doors, but I'd never actually been inside one of the rooms. He opened it and as I stepped inside, I was surprised to find that it was much like a small hotel room. There was a bed and a desk in the corner, and there was a flat-screen TV mounted on the wall. It even had its own bathroom with a shower. It was nice, but I wasn't looking forward to being in there alone—especially when my sweet girl was off with some monster.

I turned to Lawson for some kind of consolation, but his stone-cold expression made me wonder if he was upset with me. "I'm really sorry about all this. I know it's a lot, and..."

"You have nothing to be sorry about. You did nothing wrong."

"Maybe not, but it's a lot. And you didn't ask for any of it."

"And neither did you, and the same goes for Luna. Poor kid should've never been pulled into this. But don't worry." Lawson slipped his arm around my waist and pulled me close. "We're going to get her back."

Hearing those words from him moved me in a way I didn't expect. Lawson had shown me compassion and understanding like no other man had, and I truly believed him when he said that he would bring Luna back to me. With tears streaming down my face, I wrapped my arms around his neck and hugged him. "I'm going to hold you to that."

"I better get to it." He released me and then stepped over to the desk. He grabbed a notepad and pen off the table and offered them to me. "If you think of anything we might need to know, just jot it down."

"Okay."

"I'll be back when I can."

He kissed me on the cheek, and then he was gone.

I walked over to the bed, and as I lay down, I was engulfed in a whirlwind of anguish and uncertainty. I had no idea where my precious daughter was or what was happening to her. Delgado was an evil, evil man, and even though I tried to fight it, I couldn't stop my mind from wandering to the darkest corners of possibility. It was killing me.

I was in an impossible spot.

Lawson and his brothers were fierce men who would have no trouble handling a man like Delgado, but they weren't just dealing with Delgado. They were dealing with my daughter, too. They couldn't get to her without going through him, and they couldn't go through him without putting her at risk.

I was the only chance they had of getting close to him without hurting her.

I just had to make them see that, but that would mean interrupting their meeting—a meeting they clearly didn't want me to be a part of. But I didn't have a choice. I had to say my piece, and like they say—*desperate people do desperate things.* So, I got up and looked out the door, searching in vain for someone who might be able to tell me where to find Lawson and the rest of the guys.

Sadly, there was no one in sight.

I was on my own.

I shook off my nerves and started down the hall. It wasn't long before I heard voices coming from a room around the bend. As I got closer, I heard one of them say, "A man like this isn't gonna give the kid up without a fight."

"Then, we fight."

"I'm all for it, but we gotta figure out how we're gonna do it without putting the girl in danger."

I took that as my opportunity to push the door open and step inside. It was a fairly large room with long wooden table, and Lawson and Preacher were sitting there with several other brothers. They all turned and glared at me when I said, "I have an idea."

The room fell completely silent—eerily so, and I knew I'd fucked up. "I'm sorry. I don't mean to intrude, but I..."

"I told you to stay in the room," Lawson interrupted.

"I know, but..." I could see that he was angry with me. They all were, but I didn't let that stop me from saying, "Delgado will never let you get close to Luna. He'd kill her before he let that happen."

Their fierce expressions slowly softened as my words sank in.

I hoped that meant they would listen when I said, "You have to let me go in there. I can take the bag I got from Jimmy's and use it to buy my daughter back. Once I have her, you guys can come and do whatever it is you do."

"Absolutely the fuck not."

"But it's the safest way," I pushed. "You can't just barge in there and start shooting. Luna is in there with him."

"She's got a point there," Memphis interjected. "We got no idea where he's put the kid, and without eyes on the inside, we have no way of finding out where she is."

"But sending her in there doesn't fix anything,"

"I don't know. I think it might," Shep disagreed. "She's been there before, so she'll know the lay of the land. We could put a camera on her. Then once she's inside, we can see what we need to see and make a move from there."

"And what if he gets the bag and kills her right there on the spot."

I looked Lawson directly in the eye as I told him, "I'm willing to take that chance."

"The hell you are!"

"Hold up. I might have an idea." Shep turned to me and gave me a look, letting me know that he wasn't going to say anything with me in the room. "Okay. I got it. I'll go. I said what I had to say. Just, please, think about it."

I started back down the hall, and I hadn't gotten far when I heard Lawson call out, "Jenna!"

"I'm sorry." I turned to face him. "I'm just so worried about Luna, and I just want her back."

He didn't respond.

Instead, he charged over to me and brought his hands up to my face, pulling my mouth to his. He kissed me for only a moment, but it was just enough to let me know that he was still on my side and there for me. And that was exactly what I needed.

Grim

I'd dealt with men like Delgado before. I knew the risks. We all did. Going up against a man like him could be catastrophic which was why we were searching for the path of least resistance. Deep down, I knew that path included Jenna, but the mere thought of putting her in harm's way had me tied up in knots. It was all I could do to keep my head in the game when I asked Shep, "So, what's this idea of yours?"

"I know you weren't keen on the idea, but we do like Jenna suggested and send her in with the bag. But deep inside it, we hide a device with somnolixir that can be discharged with a detonator."

"What the fuck is somnon-whatever?"

"It's a hypnotic that's similar to what you'd find in basic anesthesia but doesn't have the risks."

"So, we're gonna knock 'em out?"

"Basically, but it keeps Delgado from having time to

warn anyone that he's under attack, and it keeps him alive for you. But there's one problem." Shep grimaced as he continued, "The radial distance of exposure isn't exactly ideal."

"In English, brother."

"Once detonated, the gas will only reach about twenty to twenty-five feet, so it's only gonna really affect those who are close to it." Shep must've picked up on my unease and added, "But with the cameras, we can wait to detonate until she's face to face with Delgado. Then, we can ensure that he gets exposed, and that could give us a real advantage."

"He's right." Prez interjected. "We get her inside and let Shep's contraption take out who it can, and we deal with the rest."

"But Jenna's gonna be knocked out right along with them."

"Yeah, and all things considered, that might be for the best."

Fuck.

I hated this.

I hated every fucking bit of it.

Luna was already in danger, and soon, Jenna would be, too. Normally, something like this wouldn't phase me, but Luna and Jenna meant something to me. I didn't mean for it to happen. But they'd wedged their way in and had me feeling things I no longer thought I could feel. Now, they felt like they were part of me. They were mine.

Both of them—in every way that mattered.

And I would do whatever it took to get them home safe and sound. I thought about everything Shep had said, and while I wasn't thrilled with the idea of putting Jenna in harm's way, I figured it was our best option. "If we do this, I want Seven on post and want him aimed and ready to take out the guards at the front and Goose doing the same at the back."

Seven had earned his name while in the military. He was a sniper and had taken out seven men in seven seconds. At the time, it was the fastest on record, and the skill had come in handy on more than one occasion. He'd taught Goose everything he knew, and while he wasn't as good as Seven, he was close. Knowing what they could do, Prez nodded and said, "Absolutely."

"Everyone needs to be sitting on go when she walks through that door."

"Wouldn't have it any other way." Prez gave me a look as he asked, "That mean you're on board with Shep's plan?"

"I don't like it, but I think it's our best option."

"I agree." Prez grimaced as he added, "Now, we just need to make sure Jenna's really up for it."

I got up, and Prez and Shep followed me down the hall to my room. I opened the door expecting Jenna to be asleep, but she was sitting on the edge of the bed with an eager look in her eye. She sprang up and stepped over to us as she asked, "Well?"

"It's a decent idea." I glanced over at Shep as I told her, "We just need to make sure you're up for it."

"Okay. Let's hear it."

I inhaled a deep breath, then laid out the plan for her. She didn't interrupt or ask any questions. She just waited for me to say everything I had to say, and then, she announced, "I'll do it."

"Are you sure about this?" I pushed. "There's a lot that could go wrong."

"He's got my daughter, Lawson. He's had her for hours, and I have no way of knowing if she's okay or if he's hurt her. So, yeah. I'll do whatever I need to do to get to her. I just have one question."

"Okay. Let's hear it."

"When do we go?"

"Soon," Prez answered. "We have some things to cover, but we should be ready to head out within the hour."

"I'm ready when you are."

Jenna followed us back to the conference room, where Shep went over everything with her one more time. He wanted to make sure that she knew exactly what she needed to do once she got inside the building. Jenna listened and even repeated the important details back to him.

When I felt like she was getting the hang of things, I got with Seven, and we went out to the artillery room. We started gathering all the weapons and ammo we'd need, and I started searching for the device he'd asked me to grab for him. He didn't have to tell me. I knew exactly what it was for.

I wanted nothing more than to toss the fucking thing in the trash.

It was bad enough that Jenna was going into the building alone, but I wasn't exactly thrilled about the idea of her being exposed to some gas that was going to render her helpless. The only solace I had was knowing that we would be going in there right after her and would take out Delgado and everyone connected to him.

As soon as we had everything together, Prez called us all back together to go over all the final details. Once he was done, Seven and Goose left and headed over to the mill so they could find the perfect spot to set up. The rest of us headed out to the parking lot.

The guys were busy loading everything into the SUVs, so I took the opportunity to talk to Jenna alone. She was standing by her car and looked notably worried. I walked over, and as much as I wanted to pull her into my arms, I couldn't. I knew if I touched her, I would struggle to let her go. "You don't have to do this."

"Yes, I do, and you know it."

Jenna's eyes were full of worry as she listened to me say, "I need you to understand how dangerous this thing is. There's no way to predict how things will play out."

"I know." Jenna met my gaze with unwavering determination, just like the fire that burned within her. "You don't have to worry. I'm going to do exactly what Shep told me to, and hopefully, everything else will play out like it's supposed to."

I stepped closer as I whispered, "Just don't take any unnecessary chances... I don't know what I'll do if..."

"Don't." She placed her hand on my chest. "We're not going to do the whole '*what if*' thing. We're just gonna face this thing head-on and do what we gotta do to get our Luna back."

"Okay, just promise me you'll be careful."

"I will." Jenna gave me a soft smile. "I promise. But I have one favor I need to ask."

"Oh, yeah? What's that?"

"When you get there, don't worry about me or anything else. I want you to promise that you'll go and find Luna." When I didn't immediately respond, she pushed, "I mean it, Lawson. I need you to promise me."

"I'll do what I can."

Before either of us could say anything more, Shep walked up to us and asked, "We good?"

"Yeah, we're good." After a quick kiss on the forehead, I released Jenna and asked, "Is everyone ready?"

"Yeah, just waiting on you two." Shep turned to Jenna as he asked, "How you feeling about things?"

"Okay. Just a little nervous."

"It's good to be nervous. It'll keep you on your toes." Shep motioned his hand to the camera hidden in her hair clip. "Just know that we'll be right there watching you every step of the way."

"Good deal."

Shep opened Jeanna's car and put the duffle bag in her front seat as he said, "She's all set."

"Then, it looks like we're ready to roll."

"Alright then, let's do this."

Jenna held my gaze for a moment, then turned and got in her car. I didn't feel good about any of this and hesitated briefly before following Shep over to my SUV. We got in with Ghost, Little Nix, and Rusty, while Prez and Creed got in with Skid, Memphis, and the others. I was the first to pull through the gate with Jenna following close behind.

It took us less than half an hour to get over to the mill. The processing plant where Delgado was holed up was just across the street, so we dispersed and approached the building from various directions. Memphis parked at the side of the lumber yard between two semi-trucks while Prez parked directly across from where they had a clear view of the back.

Once everyone was in place, Shep pulled out his laptop. With the help of the hidden cameras and microphone, we were able to watch as Jenna pulled up to the front of the building and got out of her car. She paused for a moment, then let out a breath and whispered, "Okay, guys. I'm heading inside."

With the duffle bag in tow, she started towards the front door. She didn't make it far before she was greeted by one of the guards. It was dark, but with the security light overhead, I was able to watch as he patted her down. Once he was certain that she wasn't packing, he reached for the bag and took a quick look inside before he led her through the entrance.

"Looks like we're in," Shep announced proudly.

When he turned up the sound on her microphone, we heard the guard say, "Stay put, and I'll let Delgado know you're here."

"Why do I have to wait?" Jenna pushed. "He knows I'm coming. I have what he asked me to bring. I don't get the holdup."

I wanted to warn her not to act so fucking suspicious, but there was nothing any of us could do. We could only sit there and watch as the guy answered, "You show up here at almost three in the morning and don't expect to wait? Fuck off."

"I'm just anxious to get my daughter."

"Don't give a fuck. Now, stay put like I fucking told ya."

He stepped inside and closed the door behind him, leaving Jenna outside, waiting alone—which I didn't like. I didn't like it at all. "What the fuck is going on?"

"Just give it a minute," Shep whispered. "She hasn't been waiting up there long."

Patience had never been one of my strong suits, so sitting here like a fucking duck had me on edge. I was growing more impatient by the second and was on the verge of losing my resolve when the guard returned.

He eased the door open and announced, "He's ready for you."

She nodded, then stepped through the door. We

could see every step she took, and his place was just as she described. Outside, it looked to be in shambles, but the inside looked like an upscale office you'd find uptown. When she reached the end of the hall, there was a man waiting for her. He was dressed in black dress pants and a blue dress shirt, but his hair was disheveled like he'd just woken up.

"Ah, there she is." A sinister smile crossed his face as he said, "I knew you would come through for me."

"I couldn't come up with the money." As she handed him the duffle bag, we heard her say, "But I'm hoping this will do."

Delgado took the bag from her hand and placed it on the table. He unzipped it, and once he saw what was inside, he looked back to Jenna. "Is it all here?"

"I can't say for sure, but I think so."

"For your sake, I hope you're right."

"Where's my daughter?"

"She's asleep in my office. You can have her as soon as I see that everything's here."

When he started pulling the bags of dope out of the duffle, I knew it was time to move. I didn't want to take a chance on him spotting the hidden device, so I gave everyone a moment to get into position, then I turned to Shep and gave him the nod, giving him the go-ahead to proceed. He took out the detonator and then looked back at the screen.

Delgado was reaching inside when Shep pressed the button on the detonator, triggering the device. The gas was invisible and had no scent, so none of them knew what was coming until Jenna's camera started to sway. Seconds later, she collapsed to the ground, and Delgado gasped, "What the fuck..."

Before he could finish his sentence, he was on the ground next to her. When the other guards quickly started dropping, I ordered, "Let's move."

We all got out of the truck. Prez and Creed led their group up the back while me, Ghost, and Rusty started toward the front. Just as we started our approach, Seven took out the two men standing guard, giving us full access to the door. With weapons drawn, we opened the door and charged inside. It was eerily quiet as we started down the long, narrow hall.

Ghost and I were just about to round the corner when the place erupted in gunfire.

He, Rusty, and I scattered, each of us ducking for cover, but I was a bit too slow.

I'd just stepped into a doorway when I felt a searing pain rip through my side. A bullet found its mark and sliced through my side, sending me crashing into the wall. I was stuck in a momentary haze of piercing pain, but it wasn't enough to stop me from getting to Jenna. I pushed through, and when I spotted the guy who'd shot me, I aimed my gun at his head and squeezed the trigger, sending a bullet right between his eyes.

Prez and Creed had made their way in through the back, and more shots rang out. And more fell dead.

In a matter of seconds, silence fell on us once again.

I held up my hand, signaling for the others to wait while I went to check things out. With the barrel of my gun aimed straight ahead, I continued to the foyer where Jenna had met with Delgado.

There were four guards sprawled out on the floor, and they were so out of it they were practically drooling. I shot one in the head, and then the next and the next. It felt like I was giving them the easy way out, but I didn't want to take a chance on them waking up.

Once I was certain they'd all been dealt with, I called out to the others, "We're clear!"

When I spotted Jenna, I rushed over to make sure that she was okay. She was out, just like the others, but she was okay. Prez and the others had started to file into the room. Ghost came over, and with concern in his eyes, he asked, "She okay?"

"Yeah, she will be." I stood as I ordered, "Get Delgado to the clubhouse and take him to one of my rooms."

"You got it, brother."

I didn't want to leave Jenna. But I'd made a promise and Jenna would expect me to keep it. Besides, I knew they would keep an eye on her, so I started up the staircase leading to Delgado's office.

I had no idea what I would find when I reached the top.

I prayed that Luna was okay, and for Delgado's sake, I hoped he hadn't hurt her. But I wouldn't know for certain until I laid eyes on her. With a deep breath, I pushed open the door, and a wave of relief washed over me when I spotted Luna balled up on the sofa. She was sleeping soundly and looked to be okay.

My chest swelled with emotion as I lifted her into my arms and held her close. I gave her a kiss on the top of her head, and her little eyes fluttered open. With a tiny gasp, she muttered, "Hey."

"Hey, kiddo." I gave her a quick once over as I asked, "You okay?"

She nodded, then whispered, "I want Momma."

"I know you do. She's here, and I'm gonna take you to her, but I need you to do something for me."

I sat her down on Delgado's desk just long enough to take off my cut. I'd all but forgotten about being shot until Luna muttered, "You got another booboo."

"Shit." I glanced down at my bloodstained shirt, and I could see through the tear that it was just a bad graze. "I'm okay. Just need a Band-Aid."

"You said shit."

"It's been a day, kid. You're just gonna have to give me that one." She nodded, then listened as I said, "I'm gonna take you to your mother. You gotta keep your head down and your eyes closed until I tell you it's okay. Do you think you could do that for me?"

She nodded, and as soon as I lifted her back in my arms, she closed her eyes and nestled her head between my shoulder and jaw. Damn. The kid was killing me. I held her close against my chest, covered her with my cut, and started my descent back down the stairs. I was about halfway down when I spotted Skid in the center of the foyer with Jenna cradled in his arms.

Even though he was my kid and I knew he'd never step against me, I saw red. The second he saw that I wasn't pleased, he shook his head and said, "Don't look at me like that. I know she's your girl. I'm just trying to help."

I didn't respond.

I just continued down the steps and right out the front door. With Skid following close behind, I took Luna out to the SUV and got her settled in the back with her mother. There were still things that needed to be done, so I turned to Skid and ordered, "Stay with them. It shouldn't be long."

Without waiting for a response, I went back to check on Prez and the others. They were all making their way out front, preparing to leave. "How do you wanna handle the cleanup?"

"I called in Cletus."

Cletus was ex-military, and while he spent most of his day working as a school janitor, he had a real talent for making problems go away. I had no doubt that he would take care of Delgado's men. He would either make them disappear or ensure that no one would ever suspect that we had anything to do with their murder.

"So, we're good?"

"For the moment. Now, let's get your girls home and call it a day."

"Now, that's a plan I can get behind."

With that, we loaded up and headed back to the clubhouse. As we pulled in, I looked over to Jenna and Luna, and it hit me. I thought I was helping Jenna when I let her and Luna come stay with me, but it was the other way around. They were the ones who'd helped me. They'd brought me back to reality and showed me what it was like to have it all.

Now that I had it, there was no way in hell I was ever letting it go.

Jenna

I had Luna back. She was lying right here in the bed next to me, and I owed it all to Lawson and his brothers. They brought her back to me, and I felt like my world was finally back on its axis. It would've never happened without Lawson.

There was no doubt that I'd fallen for him. I'd fallen hard and fast. I didn't know what was going to come of us. I wanted to believe we had something special and would make it to the end.

But there was a piece of me that wondered if he was just another lesson that life had to teach me and that I wouldn't get to keep him. I didn't doubt that we had something good—something special. I knew that we did, but I wasn't the kind of girl who got something special.

I'd already lost so much. It was what I knew. It was

what I'd become accustomed to. But I loved Lawson. I really, really loved him.

And for my sake and for Luna's, I was going to hold on to the hope that we could make a life together because I couldn't imagine making it through the day without him.

I slipped my arm around Luna and pulled her close. It wasn't long before she started squirming. "Momma, you're squishing me."

"Sorry, honey. I just can't seem to help myself." I'd already checked her over. There wasn't a scratch on her, and she assured me that the mean man hadn't touched her. While it could've been much worse, I knew the experience would leave its mark, and I wanted to do everything in my power to make sure that it was a small one. "How are you feeling?"

"I'm okay."

"Are you sure? Are you hungry? Do you wanna go get a snack?"

"I'm not hungry." She sat up and asked, "When are we going home?"

"Soon." I thought it was sweet that she thought of Lawson's place as home. It was the first one she'd really had. "We just have to give Lawson some time to take care of a few things."

"What's he doing?"

Before I could answer, there was a tap on the door. I'd hoped it was Lawson, but I opened it to find Skid standing there with a tray full of coffee and snacks. "I thought you girls might want a bite to eat."

"Skid!" Luna gasped.

"Hey there, kiddo." He walked over and placed the tray on the desk. "How you doing?"

"Momma keeps asking me that."

"She's just worried." He knelt down in front of her and smiled. "That's what moms do."

She nodded, then turned her focus over to the tray of food. Once she saw the animal crackers, her eyes lit up. She quickly grabbed them and handed them to me, waiting patiently as I opened them for her. "You want to play your game on my phone?"

She nodded excitedly.

I pulled it out of my purse and offered it to her. With her crackers in hand, she crawled back up on the bed and started playing. Knowing she wasn't paying us any mind, I turned to Skid and asked, "Where's Lawson?"

"He's taking care of a few things."

"I feel like I haven't really seen him. I was out of it when he brought us here."

"Yeah, you were, but don't worry. You'll be seeing him soon enough." He leaned against the desk and smiled. "So, you two are a thing, huh?"

"I'm not the one to ask about that."

"I don't know. I think you are."

"Well, if I have a say in it, and I'm not all that sure I

do, I'd say yeah." I gave him a shrug. "There's definitely something there."

"Oh, there's no doubt about that. I've never seen him like this before."

"Like what?"

"I don't know. It's hard to explain. It's like he's finally alive. You know... Not just going through the motions but actually living. I started noticing the change in him right around the time you moved in, but I didn't actually piece it together until the night he showed up at the bar."

"Yeah, that was a telling night." I sat down on the edge of the bed. "I still don't understand one thing."

"Oh, and what's that?"

"Why didn't you tell me that you were his son? He told me about the thing with the club and you not wanting there to be any influence there, but I had no part in that. You could've at least mentioned it."

"You're right. I should have, and I have no idea why I didn't. I guess I was just hoping that things would go another way. But don't get me wrong, I'm glad they went the way they did."

"Thanks, Skid."

"It's the truth. I may not always show it, but I love my ol' man. He's gotten us both through some tough times."

"He said the same about you."

"He's not one for showing emotion."

"I've noticed." I giggled. "But when he does..."

"Yeah, it's something."

"So, what happens now?"

"There are some loose strings still needing to be tied up, but I figure he will be back soon."

"And what about Delgado?"

"You know I can't say much, but I don't think you'll have to worry about him anymore."

"Thank goodness for that."

"So, you're doing okay?"

"Yeah, I'm good."

"You sure?" he pushed. "I know last night had to be rough."

"Yeah, that's putting it lightly." I glanced over at Luna as I whispered, "I was so scared. I'd tried so hard, but the fear of messing things up had me wondering if either of us was going to make it out of there. One wrong move..."

One tear rolled into the next, and before I realized it, I was full-on crying—something I'd tried desperately not to do, especially in front of Luna. Trying his best to console me, Skid placed his hand on my arm and said, "You did good, Jen. You did real good."

Hearing him say that only made me cry more. I was becoming a blubbering mess when the door opened, and Lawson stepped in. "What the hell is this?"

I didn't answer. I simply stepped over to him and wrapped my arms around his waist, hugging him. I held him close, letting the warmth of his touch calm me, and when my tears began to subside, I kept holding on.

I just didn't want to let go. After several moments, he placed his mouth next to my ear and whispered, "I've got ya, baby. I'm not letting go."

"I'm sorry. I don't know what got into me."

"No need to apologize." He gave me a light squeeze. "You good?"

"Better now." I looked up at him with a smile. "Are you done doing whatever you had to do?"

"No, but I'm in dire need of some shut-eye. You ready to head home?"

"Absolutely."

"I'm ready, too," Luna announced as she stood and jumped into Lawson's arms. He winced for a slight moment, which was surprising, but I let the thought go when she asked, "Can Skid come, too?"

"Awe, that's sweet, Lune Bug, but I..."

"Yeah," Lawson interrupted. "Skid can come, too."

"Don't we need to clean up a bit before we go?"

"Nah, one of the girls will get it."

Lawson was still carrying Luna when he reached down and took my hand. With Skid following behind, we headed outside to his truck. When he opened the back door, I was surprised to find that Luna's car seat was secured inside. It had been in my car the day before, which led me to ask, "What about my car?"

"We'll take care of it." When I hesitated, he added, "I'll have one of the guys bring it over later."

I nodded and then waited as he put Luna in her car seat. Once she was buckled in, he and I got inside, and with Skid following on his bike, we headed over to his place. When we pulled up, there were several unfamiliar vehicles parked along the curb. Lawson didn't seem bothered by the fact, so I didn't mention anything.

Once we were parked, I got out and grabbed Luna, and we all started up the front steps. That's when I noticed that there were boxes lined up in the garage. I turned to Lawson and asked, "What's all this?"

"Just had some stuff boxed up. Probably send to Goodwill or something."

He didn't have to tell me. I knew what was inside them. It was all the stuff I'd unboxed months ago that should've never been unboxed. We continued up the steps, and when Lawson opened the door, I was surprised to hear laughter and talking drifting down from the hallway. I immediately turned to Lawson and asked, "What's going on?"

"I don't know. Why don't you and Luna go check it out?"

I could tell by his expression that he was up to something, so I gave him a look. "What's happening?"

"Go see for yourself."

With a mixture of curiosity and trepidation, I started down the hallway, and as I entered the room Luna and I shared, I was hit with the surprise of my life. Star and several of the girls were busy working on Luna's room, and they'd turned it into a wonderland. The room was full color, every corner adorned in shades of pink and purple, and a mountain of stuffed animals piled on a new princess bed.

It was amazing, but it was the sight of Star and the other girls being so excited that brought tears to my eyes. When Star spotted us, she threw up her arms and shouted, "Surprise!"

"Oh, my goodness!"

"Do you like it?"

"Are you kidding? It's amazing." I lowered Luna to the floor as I told her, "It looks like you have a new room."

"This is mine?"

"Yeah, kiddo," Lawson answered. "It's all yours."

With that, Luna darted inside the room, and she was practically beaming as she checked out all her new toys. The girls were so sweet and showed her all her new things. They opened the closet, showing her all the new clothes inside—clothes I could've never afforded on my own. It brought tears to my eyes. "She's never had a room of her own before."

"Well, she does now."

"It's just..." I wiped the tears from my cheeks as I said, "I can't believe you did this."

"I wanted her to have a place of her own. I want you both to have it."

"Don't you just love it?" Star asked as she and Nikki rushed over. "I think the stuffed rabbits are just the cutest!"

"Yeah, it's amazing."

I was at a loss for words. Lawson had already done so much for us. He'd not only brought us into his home and kept us off the streets, but he got me a job and helped me find my pride again. He saved my daughter from a monster and gave her the most beautiful room I'd ever seen.

It was all too much.

I was struggling to contain my emotions.

I was overflowing with love and appreciation when Luna rushed over to Lawson and wrapped her arms around his legs, hugging him as she shouted, "Thank you!"

"You're welcome, kiddo."

"Damn." Skid stepped up beside us. "You went all out."

"Yeah, well, they couldn't just keep sharing that old room if they're gonna be living here for the long haul."

"Whoa. *Long haul?*" I turned to Lawson with a gasp. "You're asking us to live with you for real? Like a permanent thing?"

"I wasn't exactly asking." He cocked his brow. "I was more telling."

"Oh, is that right?"

"Yeah, that's right." He slipped his arms around my waist. "You got a problem with that?"

"Nope. No problem at all."

I slipped my arms around his neck and eased up on my tiptoes as I pressed my lips to his. His arms tightened around my waist, quickly pulling me closer as he took over the kiss. There was no denying it. I was in love with him, and with each moment I'd spent with him, I'd found myself loving him even more. People would probably think I was crazy for falling for a man like Lawson, especially when I had a young daughter.

But she was one of the many reasons why I loved him the way I did.

He put everything at stake to save her.

I may never know why he'd chosen to do the things he'd done, but the fact remained that he *knew*. He knew that lives were at stake—Luna's, mine, his brothers', and his own, but that didn't stop him. He did what it took to get her back.

And the truth be known, his life would always be filled with danger, and I would have to learn to accept that. I would have to learn to live with the worry. It was worth it to have him in our lives. I eased back from our embrace just long enough to whisper, "I love you."

He stared at me for a moment, and emotion filled his eyes as my words started to sink in. I could see the wheels turning in his head, but I had no idea what he was thinking. I started thinking I shouldn't have said it, that maybe it was too soon, so I started babbling, "I know it's a lot, and it's okay if you don't feel the same. I just..."

"I love you, too, Jenna." He motioned his head towards Luna. "I love you both."

"And you're sure about all this? The moving into together? The having a kid around? It's a lot."

"I wouldn't have done this if I wasn't."

It was fast, probably too fast, but everything I wanted was in that room, and there was no way I was giving up a chance to keep it. This was one dream I was going to let myself have, and no one was going to take it from me.

No one.

Grim

❧

"I can't believe you didn't tell me."

"I don't know what to tell ya. It just slipped my mind."

"How does getting shot just slip your mind?"

"We had other stuff going on."

"I don't care what's going on. You tell me when you get shot." Jenna's face twisted into a worried frown as she checked my wound and said, "You need stitches."

"I'm fine," I assured her.

"You're not fine. Doc needs to look at it and..."

"You're looking at it. Don't need Doc."

I dropped my towel to the floor and reached for my sweats. Jenna's face flushed red with desire as she watched me slowly pull them over my hips. Damn. I loved the way she looked at my body like she'd never be able to get enough of me.

I stared at her standing there in my t-shirt, looking

sexy as fuck, and it was all I could do to keep myself from taking her right there in the bathroom. Sensing my thoughts, Jenna took a step back and said, "*I cannot believe you!*"

"What?"

"You know what!"

"Come on now." I gave her a playful smirk. "You tell me you love me, and I don't get to do anything about it?"

"You've been shot!"

"*It's just a graze.*"

"That came from a bullet!"

"I'm fine. Now, come here."

"*Lawson.*"

"*Jenna,*" I said firmly as I leaned against the dresser. My lips immediately curled into a smile when she did as I requested and stepped closer, settling between my legs. She placed the palms of her hands on my chest, looking up at me with anticipation. I lowered my mouth to hers, kissing her with a promise of what was to come.

The beat of her heart next to mine calmed me, refueled me, and that's when I knew. She wasn't my first, but she would be my *last*. I pulled back, and she gave me a puzzled look until I stated, "You said I love you."

"Yeah?"

"You said it in front of everyone."

"My timing wasn't exactly the best."

"Your timing was perfect. I just didn't get a chance

to make it official and let you know that I'm claiming you."

"Claiming me?" Her brows furrowed. "As your ol' lady?"

"To start." I pulled her closer as I added, "But I want it all. I want my ring on your finger and you with my last name."

"Seriously?"

"Without question."

"I like the sound of that," she answered before pressing her lips to mine. With just a simple touch, the kiss became heated, full of need and want. I couldn't get enough of her. I reached for the hem of her t-shirt but quickly stopped when there was a knock on the door.

"Momma?" Luna cried.

Jenna eased back from our embrace as she answered, "Just a minute!"

She waited for me to put on a clean shirt, then opened the door and smiled at Luna. "Good morning, sweetheart."

"I'm hungry."

"Oh, okay. I'll see what's in the fridge." Jenna took Luna's hand and started out of the room. "I'll be back."

While I hated that we were interrupted, I figured it was for the best. I had been putting something off, and it was time to deal with it. So, I walked over to the dresser and grabbed some clean clothes. I'd told Jenna that I was fine and that my wound wasn't a big deal, and it wasn't. I'd had far worse, but it was starting to tighten up on me and made it a little difficult to get on my shirt.

But I managed.

I also managed to get on my jeans and was about to put on my boots when Jenna came waltzing back in. I could hear the disappointment in her voice as she asked, "What are you doing?"

"Gotta run to the clubhouse for a bit."

"But I was going to fix dinner tonight. Will you be gone all day?"

"Go ahead." I slipped on my boot as I told her, "It shouldn't take me long."

"Okay, but you have to promise to call if you're gonna be late."

"Not a problem."

"And go by and see Blade while you're there," she ordered. "I want him to check that wound."

"Sure thing, boss." I stood and walked over to her. After a quick kiss, I told her, "I'll be back when I can."

"Be careful."

"Always."

On my way out, I spotted Luna in her room. She was sitting on her bed, eating a pack of animal crackers, and she looked perfectly content as she talked with one of her stuffed rabbits. It did my soul good to see her so happy. It made it hard to walk out of the house and head out to my bike.

But I had loose ends to tie up, and it was time to tie the knot.

I got on my Harley, and a weird sensation washed over me as I backed out of the drive. At first, I didn't know what the feeling was, and then, it hit me. I didn't want to leave them—either of them. Goddamn it. I needed to get my fucking balls in check.

Thankfully, I would be doing that sooner than later.

When I got to the clubhouse, I swung by Blade's room and let him patch me up, then went directly down to Prez's office. I knocked, then stuck my head inside and was pleased to see that he was sitting at his desk. "Hey, brother. I wasn't expecting you back so soon."

"Figured I would pay Delgado a visit but wanted to check in with you first."

"About?"

"Shep mentioned that there's a strong possibility that Delgado is Tyrone's supplier. I wanted to make sure we have a plan B in place before I took him out."

"Yeah, I talked to Gus a couple of hours ago. He said he can hook us up with some pretty good shit. He seems to think it's the best he's ever had."

"No shit? Is this the stuff coming out of Nashville?"

"Yeah, it's Ruthless Sinners. They're growing it themselves, and apparently, it's the real deal. He said we could make a pretty penny with it."

"Sounds good."

"Yeah, I thought so, too. We're gonna head over to Memphis tomorrow morning so he can give us all the ins and outs."

"Mind if I tag along?"

"Wouldn't go without ya."

"Good deal. I'll be ready." I started for the door as I told him, "You might wanna grab your headphones for a bit."

"Thanks for the heads up."

I left Prez's office and made a beeline for the holding room where they'd taken Delgado. He'd been there for more than twenty-four hours, and even though it hadn't been all that long, he wasn't looking that great. He wasn't smelling all that great either.

We'd given him a little water here and there, but other than that, he'd been left to his own devices and that hadn't fared well with him, especially since he had his hands bound behind his back and his feet chained to the chair.

Dude was stuck sitting in his excrement, and that had to suck.

But it was nothing compared to what he had come coming.

He started with the theatrics the second he spotted me coming towards him. "If you know what's good for you, you'll let me go."

"Um-hmm. Not gonna happen."

"You don't know who you're dealing with."

"But I do." I stepped in front of him and fought the urge to plow my fist in his face. "I know exactly who you are. You've made quite a name for yourself."

"I've lived with the belief that a man without enemies is no man at all."

"Well, from the looks of it, that's not going so well for you."

"My people will come for me."

"Your people are dead."

"So, what is this?" He glared at me with a snarl. "You gonna torture me? Try to get information out of me?"

"That's not what this is about. I already know everything I need to know."

His face grew red with rage as he roared, "Then, what the fuck do you want?"

"You should've never touched her."

"Oh, this is about the girl," he scoffed. "I didn't do anything you or your crew wouldn't do."

"We don't fuck with women or kids."

"Well, you're missing out. There's a lot of money there."

"There are a lot of things in this life that are more important than money."

"Ha!" he chuckled. "Like what?"

"My integrity." I walked over and grabbed the bottle of lighter fluid. "But you wouldn't know anything about that."

"What are you going to do with that?"

"There's an old adage that says, 'Build a man a fire, and he's warm for a day'." I started dousing him with lighter fluid. "Set him on fire, and he's warm for the rest of his life."

"Oh, fuck." His eyes widened with horror. "You

don't have to do this. I've got money. I'll pay you whatever you want."

"It's always money with you." I shook my head and opened the box of matches. "Let's see how far that money will get you in hell."

I struck the match, then tossed it at him.

Within seconds, he was engulfed in flames and screaming for mercy. I had none to give, so I opened the door and walked out, leaving him there to burn. I walked out feeling no remorse. The man was evil, through and through, and the world was a better place without him.

I could still hear his screams as I made my way out to my bike. I sent Seven a text, letting him know that Delgado had been dealt with and told him to have a couple of prospects deal with the mess. Once he'd confirmed, I put on my helmet, turned the key and started the engine, revving it a few times to drown out the ruckus. I was pretty spun up, so I decided to take the long way home, hoping it would give me some time to unwind.

And it did.

By the time I made it back to the house, I was ready to get inside and put my cares away for the day. When I walked in, Jenna was standing at the stove. She was wearing this white, sleeveless nightgown that had a sweet and innocent look about it, but I didn't get sweet and innocent thoughts when I saw her in it.

Just the opposite.

I never expected to like having a woman in my kitchen, making a mess while she cooked dinner, and treating my house like a home.

But I did.

I liked it more than I ever thought I could. She had me wanting things I'd never imagined I'd ever want or need. She had me wanting a future, a future with her and Luna.

Unaware of the thoughts racing through my mind, she asked, "Did you see Blade?"

"Yep." I lifted my shirt, revealing my fresh bandage. "I'm all fixed up."

"Good."

I walked over and slipped my arms around her, pulling her closer. She watched me with those beautiful dark eyes as I dropped my mouth to hers.

The kiss quickly became heated, and a slight whimper escaped her lips when I stepped forward, pressing her back against the refrigerator. Her arms wound around my neck, and just as we were about to lose ourselves in the moment, the oven timer went off.

"Damn."

She quickly pulled away from me and rushed over to the stove. A wonderful aroma filled the air when she opened the oven door, making my mouth water. I stepped over to get a better look as I asked, "What'd ya fix?"

"Poppyseed chicken and mashed potatoes and some rolls and some brownies for dessert."

"Damn, woman. You went all out."

"Just a little thank you for everything."

"You gotta stop with all that. I didn't do anything I didn't want to do."

"Okay, then... It's a welcome home dinner."

"I like the sound of that."

I gave her a kiss on the temple before helping her get everything to the table. We called Luna in, and together, we ate a hell of a meal. When we were done, Jenna gave Luna a bath and put her to bed. She wasn't used to having her own room, much less sleeping alone. I figured it would take her some time to adjust, so I went to the bedroom and took a quick shower.

I'd just gotten out and had thrown on some fresh boxers when Jenna came tiptoeing into the bedroom with a big smile on her face. "She's out like a light."

"That was fast."

"I know!" She stepped over to me and placed her hand carefully on my fresh bandage. "I know your club means a lot to you, but I'm going to need you

not to get shot again. Okay?"

"I'll do my best."

"Does it hurt?" she asked with concern.

"I'm fine, babe." I looked down at her nightgown as I ordered, "Now, lose the PJs, so I can show you just how fine I am."

A wicked smile crossed her face as she slipped the nightgown over her head and tossed it across the room. I dropped my boxers, then reached down and lifted her into my arms. Her legs instinctively wrapped around my waist as I carried her to the bed.

As soon as I lowered her down onto the mattress, she slipped off her lace panties, and my cock began to throb as I reached over and grabbed a condom from my bedside table. My eyes were locked on hers as I rolled it on, then settled between her legs.

I hovered there for a moment, gazing down at Jenna in all her splendor, and it amazed me that she had no idea just how incredible she really was. I lowered my mouth to her shoulder, let my tongue trail along the delicate line between her neck and ear lobe, then whispered, "You ready for me?"

She nodded, then spread her thighs and wrapped her legs around my waist, pulling me close and grinding her hips against mine. I pulled back and raked the head of my throbbing cock against her. I wasn't gentle about it. I let her know my intentions, and she didn't give me a moment's hesitation.

She simply pressed her lips to mine in a possessive, demanding kiss as she used her legs to pull me forward. I felt her tremble beneath me as I slid every inch of my throbbing cock deep inside her, then slowly withdrew. A slight hiss slipped through her teeth as I drove into her again and again—each time a bit faster and more unforgiving.

My girl was insatiable.

She took everything I had to give and wanted more.

And I did my damnedest to give it to her.

Her heels dug into my back as she repeated my name over and over again. As much as I loved having her that way, I wanted more. I placed my hands on her hips as I slowly pulled out. I flipped her over, pulling her ass up high, so I could take her from behind.

I reached for her hair, fisting it in my hand as I gave it a gentle tug. Then I thrust forward, driving inside her once again. Unable to control myself, I slowly drew back and slammed into her again, fucking her hard and deep. A carnal moan vibrated through her as she started to rock back, meeting my every thrust. I slid my hand from her hip down between her legs, and feverish cries echoed through the room as I began teasing her clit.

Within seconds, I could feel her muscles start contracting all around me as she pleaded, "Don't stop."

She panted wildly, moaning and desperately gripping the sheets as I drove deeper. I felt her body tremble around me, urging me on as I thrust inside her, over and over. Seconds later, she submitted to her release and clamped down around me.

All too soon, I felt my own release building as the muscles in my abdomen and legs grew taut. Unable to stop and savor the moment, I continued to drive into her, and the sound of my body pounding against hers pushed me over the edge. I gave her hair another tug as I held her ass tight to me and came deep inside her.

After several moments, I finally caught my breath and lowered myself down onto the bed next to her. I tossed the condom in the trash beside the bed, then turned to her and teased, "How was that for wounded?"

"That was pretty damn good." She gave me a playful smirk. "My man doesn't disappoint."

"Say it again."

Confused, she paused for a moment, then smiled and repeated, "My man."

"Yeah, I like the sound of that."

She nestled close to me, and I found myself wondering if it was possible for a man like me to have it all. I didn't deserve it, not after the life I'd lived, but having her there next to me, it certainly felt close.

I might not deserve it, but I damn well was going to hold on to it.

Jenna
THREE MONTHS LATER

Spring had officially sprung. The daffodils were blooming, along with every flowered tree in a hundred-mile radius, and the grass had gone from a tired brown to a lively green. It was my favorite time of year, which was why I'd decided to take Luna outside and work on the flower beds—or lack thereof. Lawson had a beautiful home with all the basic necessities, but it lacked the flare of a woman's touch.

He gave me the okay to do whatever I wanted to liven things up, and I'd taken full advantage. It had taken some time. I'd added a picture here and there and changed out a blanket or two. And it had made a subtle but real difference in the place. I thought a few flowers outside might help perk things up, so Luna and I grabbed a few from the local nursery and set out to plant them next to the front steps.

As expected, it didn't take long for Luna to grow

tired of planting, and she moved to the front porch and started playing with her dolls. She played a few minutes before asking, "When can we go inside?"

"It's a pretty day. Let's just try to enjoy it, okay?"

"Okay." Her eyes drifted over to the flowers I'd just planted. "They look nice, Momma."

"Thank you, punkin. Hopefully, Lawson will think so, too."

I went back to my planting, and just as I was finishing up, I heard the familiar rumble of Lawson's motorcycle coming down the street. I quickly gathered all the empty pots and bags and tossed them in the garbage, then swept away the loose dirt. I wanted him to get a good look at everything, so I stepped on the front porch and waited with Luna as he pulled into the driveway.

Once he'd parked, he removed his helmet and said, "Wow. You two have been busy."

"What do you think?"

"It looks great." He got off and started over to us. "You did good."

"It's not too girly?"

"It's flowers, babe."

"You know what I mean." I motioned my hand over to the little white blooms. "I tried to do simple."

"And it worked. It looks really good." He smiled, then leaned down and gave me a quick kiss. "We've got a party at the club this weekend."

"Oh? Any particular reason?"

"Yeah, you could say that." He smiled but didn't actually tell me what the reason was. "It's been a long few weeks. The guys need to blow off some steam. I do, too."

He was right. There had been a lot going on, especially at the club. I didn't know what they were dealing with, but Lawson had been on one run after the next. He'd been to Memphis countless times, and then, it was on to Nashville. It wasn't a terribly long drive, but it had taken its toll. It was understandable that they'd want to cut loose for a bit.

"Okay, I'll call Stacie and see if she can watch Luna."

"About that..."

"What's wrong?"

"I went by Rosie's and saw Jud." He came over and kissed me. "Stacie was there too, so I invited them to come by."

"To the party?"

"Yeah, I thought they might enjoy it."

"And what'd they say?"

"They were all for it."

"Really?" While we were a few weeks late, we'd made it to the zoo with her and even went to the movies a couple of times. She seemed to really enjoy getting out, but I didn't get the feeling that she was ready for a party—especially one at the clubhouse. "Are you sure Stacie's ready for that?"

"No, but it might be good for her."

"Yeah, as long as Duggar and Goose behave themselves."

They were known for using their boyish charms to pick up the ladies, so I wasn't surprised when Lawson replied, "Can't promise anything there."

"I was afraid you were going to say that." I giggled, and then reality hit. "So, what are we going to do about Luna?"

"I was thinking we could ask Star or Nikki to come by."

Both Star and Nikki loved Luna. They couldn't help but dote on her, and they were great ladies with good heads on their shoulders. I trusted them both to take care of her, so I told him, "Yeah, that would be great. If one of them can do it."

"I'll give them a call and see if they can work it into their schedule."

"That'd be great."

Three days later, I was on the back of Lawson's bike, and we were headed to the clubhouse. I felt a little guilty about leaving Luna behind, but she was with Nikki, and Luna couldn't have been happier about spending the night with her. I'd been to the clubhouse several times over the past few months and I'd gotten to know most of the guys, but I was still a little anxious. I'd never actually been to a club party and didn't know what to expect.

My heart was racing as we pulled up through the gate. Just as I expected, the place was packed. There were cars and bikes parked everywhere, but Lawson managed to find us a spot in the back. We both got off his bike, and when Lawson got over to me, he smiled and asked, "You ready?"

"As ready as I'm gonna be."

"Hey." He took my hand in his. "Don't be nervous. You girls are gonna have a great time."

"I'll feel better after I have a drink."

"Then, let's go grab you one."

I was excited.

It had been a few weeks since Lawson and I had been out, and I was looking forward to having a good time with him. The bonfire was casting a glow over the grounds, making it easier to see as we got closer to the group. Everyone was talking and drinking, and it was clear by all the laughter that they were having a great time. Ghost yelled out to Lawson and motioned us over to the fire where he was standing with Memphis and Preacher.

I was relieved to see so many familiar faces as we walked over to him. They each greeted us with nods and friendly banter, making me feel instantly at ease. Lawson grabbed us both a beer from the cooler and offered it to me. I'd just taken my first sip when Ghost leaned over and whispered something in his ear. Lawson nodded, then turned to me and said, "We gotta head inside for a bit."

"Why? Is something going on?"

"Yeah, you could say that."

He gave me a wink, then took my hand and together we followed the others inside. I hung back while Lawson and the others gathered around Preacher and Skid. Preacher was talking to Skid, but I couldn't make out what he was saying. I had no idea what was going on, but I could tell from Lawson's expression that something big was about to happen.

Preacher grabbed a box from the counter and offered it to Skid as he told him, "Welcome to the brotherhood."

Skid hugged him, then reached into the box and pulled out a leather jacket with Satan's Fury MC Little Rock embroidered on the back. I wanted to congratulate him, so I walked over and stood next to Lawson. Skid was beaming with pride as he slipped on his new cut. Emotion filled his eyes as he ran his fingers across the embroidery.

Lawson's voice was strained as he told him, "Looks good on ya."

"I can't believe it." Skid was all smiles as he said, "I really did it."

"Never doubted you for a second." Lawson gave him a big hug and a pat on the shoulder. "You did good, son. You did real good."

"Thanks, Dad."

I don't know who looked more excited- father or son. Not that it mattered. It was a special moment that was made even more special because they were able to share it with each other. They talked for a few minutes, and then Lawson went over and grabbed a couple of cold beers from the cooler and headed back over to me. As he offered me one, I told him, "I didn't know Skid was patching in tonight."

"It was supposed to be a surprise."

"Well, I think it was great. He seemed really happy."

"He deserved it. He worked hard and it paid off."

Once he finished talking to one of the other brothers, I stepped over and gave him a quick hug as I said, "Congratulations."

"Thanks, Jen. Appreciate it."

I'd just released him from my hug when Lawson leaned over to me and said, "Jud and Stacie are here."

"Really?" A strange look marked Skid's face as he turned and started searching for them. "I didn't know they were coming."

As soon as he spotted them, Skid left us and went over to greet them. He spoke to Jud for a moment, then turned his attention to Stacie. It was obvious by the way he was talking to her that he was interested in her, and I couldn't blame him.

She looked stunning in her short skirt and black cowboy boots. Her sweater was slightly fitted and showed off all of her curves, but not overly so. She had her hair down, and it was curled loose around her shoulders. It was clear she'd taken a good bit of time and care to get ready for the party, and it had paid off.

She'd drawn the attention of one of the nicest guys around. I could see her blushing from across the room, so I told Lawson, "I'm gonna go over and say hey."

"Go ahead. I'll catch you in a bit."

"Grab a beer for Stacie. Looks like she's gonna need it."

"Sure thing."

I walked over, and Stacie's face lit up when she saw me. "Hey! You're here!"

"I wouldn't miss it." I reached over and hugged her. "Grim told me you guys might stop by. I'm really glad you decided to come."

"I don't think we'll stay long."

"That's okay. We'll make the best of it while you're here." I motioned to the back. "Why don't we go find a table?"

"That would be great."

We wedged our way through the crowd, and by the time we got to a table, Lawson had made his way over with the beers. We sat down, and it wasn't long before Memphis and Ghost came over and sat down with us. Stacie leaned in close as she whispered, "I never knew bikers were so hot."

"Yeah, they're not so bad."

"No, not bad at all."

Stacie drank her beer and then another. She wasn't much of a drinker, so it was no surprise that it only took the two to give her a buzz. She was all smiles as she looked over to Memphis and asked, "I hope you don't mind, but I gotta ask... How'd you get a nickname like

Memphis? Is there a hidden meaning behind it, or did you like Elvis or something?"

"Nah, it ain't got nothing to do with Elvis." Memphis had a Jax Teller look about him with his shaggy blond hair and baby blues, and he had a similar gruff attitude. "It's where I was conceived."

"Seriously?"

"Yeah, the guys have a sick sense of humor."

"I don't know. I kind of get it." Stacie glanced to her left. "But I'm not so sure about Ghost. Does he see dead people or something?"

"No, he just has a way of sneaking up on ya, and it'll scare the hell out of ya when he does."

"OH." She took another drink. "I certainly hope he doesn't ever try sneaking up on me, or we'll both get a scare."

The guys chuckled, even Ghost, and that tickled Stacie.

I was glad she was having a good time. I was, too. It was nice getting to know the guys a little better. It was also nice seeing Lawson in his element. He seemed truly at home with his brothers, and it meant a great deal that he was sharing that with me.

Stacie had just finished off her beer and was about to ask for another when Duggar started walking over. She immediately leaned over to me and whispered, "Who's that?"

"That's Duggar. He's one of the club's prospects."

"What's a prospect?"

"It's someone who's working to be a brother but isn't one yet."

"Oh."

She appeared a bit skeptical as he approached and offered her a drink. "I thought you might like a cold one."

"Thanks." She took it from his hand and smiled. "I appreciate it."

"You interested in a dance or a game of pool?"

"Oh, I don't know." She glanced over at me, then right back to him. "It's really nice of you to offer, but I think I'm going to pass."

"Okay. Suit yourself." He raised his bottle and smiled. "You ladies have a nice night."

I wasn't surprised that she'd turned it down. She'd had her eye on Skid the entire night, and he had been eyeing her, too. I had a feeling there was something going on there, but it was clear that neither of them was going to do anything about it. So, I left it alone and hoped they would figure it out on their own.

After another hour or so, the party started to fizzle out. Most of the guys had already left, and it was quiet, with a low rumble of a song playing on the jukebox. Lawson stood by the doorway, looking sexy as hell as he waited for me to make my way over to him. Even from across the room, I could see that lustful spark in his eyes, making me want him even more. There was no better feeling than seeing that look and knowing it was just for me.

I walked over to him and smiled, "Hey there. How's my man making it tonight?"

"Better now." He slipped his arm around my waist. "You ready?"

"Absolutely."

"You gonna be able to ride back, or should we take the truck?"

"I can ride," I assured him. "I only had a few."

He nodded, then took my hand and led me out to his bike. When we got home, Nikki and Luna were sound asleep on the sofa. Lawson walked over and carefully lifted Luna into his arms, then carried her to her bedroom. I saw no point in waking Nikki, so I covered her with a blanket and left her there to sleep.

When I got to our bedroom, Lawson was there waiting for me, and he'd already taken off his shirt. And oh, man. He was looking mighty fine. I could've just eaten him up right then and there. He must've noticed me admiring him because his lips curled into a smirk. "You like what you see?"

"Oh, yeah. My man is looking good tonight."

"You think so?"

"I know so."

The sound of his zipper sliding down sent a jolt of excitement through me. This man had me imagining all sorts of things—very naughty, wicked things. Unable to hide the thoughts that were going through my head, a devious smile crept across my face. I walked over to him and slowly dropped to my knees, reaching out for the waistband of his jeans.

His eyes widened when I started to inch his jeans down his hips.

A torturous groan vibrated through his chest when I took him in my hand and began to stroke up and down his hard, rigid shaft. His fingers clamped around the edge of the dresser, and his eyes shut when I brushed my tongue across the head of his dick.

"Fuck," he mumbled as I took him deep in my mouth. I continued to stroke him slowly, with my fingers wound tightly around his cock, feeling him throb against my tongue. His fingers tangled in my hair as his hips thrust forward, guiding me to take him deeper.

I loved seeing how his body responded to my touch. It gave me such a sense of power. The thought of making this man lose control with just my mouth exhilarated me, fueled my desire, and made me want him even more. With just the twist of my hand, a guttural moan echoed through the room, and a pained expression crossed his face.

I could feel him pulsing beneath my fingertips. He was getting close, really close, and I was shocked when I was suddenly yanked up from the floor and carried over to the bed. He dropped me, with my back lying flat against the mattress.

He didn't say a word.

He didn't have to. I knew what he wanted.

He lowered his hands to the waistband of my jeans and unfastened the button before slowly lowering them down my legs. I could tell by the hungry look in his eyes that he was in the mood for taking, and I was good with that. He could take whatever he needed, and more, and that's exactly what he did. He took into the wee hours of the morning, and by the time he was done, I was weak-kneed and fully sated.

I was also absolutely, positively, madly in love.

And I was happy.

Truly happy.

My man does not disappoint.

Epilogue

Grim
Christmas- One Year Later

I could feel them watching me.

I knew they were worried about me.

They had every right to be. Hell, it was Christmas. I should've been home in Little Rock, spending the day with my brothers. Instead, I was in Washington, sitting in the back corner of the Fury clubhouse, and I was downing one drink after the next. I was trying to make myself forget. I wasn't being all that successful.

It had been a year.

Maybe it was the holidays or just the fact that it was the anniversary of his death, but I couldn't get Beckett out of my head. The memories were weighing on me and being around Preacher and Memphis only made it worse. I couldn't imagine how they were doing with it. I had no doubt it was rough spending their first Christmas without him, and that only made me feel worse. I'd gone to Washington in hopes of escaping it all.

I figured the Washington boys would understand.

They knew there was nothing worse than the sting of losing someone you cared about. That shit comes with a sting you won't forget. We all had blood on our hands and had to live with the guilt of that, but this was different for me.

My guilt ran deeper. It ate at me like rust on a nail. Hell, even after all this time, I was still trying to make peace with what happened. I couldn't get over the fact that I'd failed. I'd failed my club and my president.

But most of all, I'd failed myself.

I could spend the entire day drinking, but I would never forget that.

It haunted me, and it always would.

I was about to grab another beer from the cooler when I spotted Jenna and Luna walking towards me. The second Luna saw a clear path, she darted towards me and lunged into my lap. She slipped her arms around my neck as she announced, "Momma said it's time to go."

"She did, did she?"

"Um-hmm." Luna nodded. "She said we need to go get on the plane."

"We got a little time before we do that."

"Actually..." Jenna held out her watch so I could see. "We should leave in about fifteen if we wanna make our flight back home."

"I don't see why we gotta rush."

"You promised Luna that we would be home for Christmas." She cocked her brow. "Question is, are you going to keep that promise?"

I looked at Luna, and when I saw the hopeful look in her eyes, I smiled and said, "A promise made is a promise kept. I just need to go pack up my things."

"It's already done and in the car."

"Oh, you weren't messing around."

"I'm just ready to get home."

"Okay. Just give me a minute to tell the guys I'm leaving."

"We'll wait for you in the car."

Luna got up and went over to Jenna, and together, they started making their way through the crowd. Several people stopped them and said their farewells, but eventually, they made their escape. Once they were gone, I collected my empty bottles and tossed them in the trash. I made my way over to Maverick and said, "I appreciate the hospitality, but we're gonna head out."

"You get your head right?"

"I'm gettin' there."

"These things take time." Maverick extended his hand and shook mine as he told me, "You guys are welcome here any time."

"I appreciate that, brother. You're a good man. Keep things hunkered down around here, and I'll see ya when I see ya."

"Look forward to it."

I left Maverick and made my way over to Rooster and Torch. I took a moment to thank them and tell them goodbye, and then I was out. I got in the passenger side, and I didn't say a word as Jenna started the engine and drove us out the gate. I don't know how long we'd been riding when she stated, "You know I'm here for you. For anything."

"I know."

"I hope so, 'cause I really am." She reached over and placed her hand on my thigh. "I know you have to deal with your anger and your pain in your own way and in your own time, but babe... if Beckett cared about you half as much as I think he did, he wouldn't want this for you. Deep down, you know that."

"You're right."

"I know I am." She gave me one of her smiles. "You're a good man with a big heart, and I love you more than you'll ever know."

"Love you, too, babe."

It took about an hour for us to get to Seattle, and once we did, it was a rush to get to the right gate. We returned the rental, then rushed to check in. A few minutes later, we were on the plane and on our way back home. We were about an hour out when Jenna pulled out a little box and said, "I have a little surprise gift for you."

"I thought we were opening our gifts when we got back."

"We are." She shrugged. "I was just a little excited about this one."

"So, you want me to open it now?"

"Well, yeah, but if you don't want to..."

She started to put it away, but I quickly grabbed it from her hand. "No, I want to."

"Okay, but I want you to know that this wasn't planned."

"What?"

"It wasn't planned, and I just don't know how you're gonna feel about it."

"I'm not following."

"Just open it."

I didn't have a good feeling as I pulled the paper back and removed the top of the box. As soon as I saw the blue and white testing strip, I knew she was pregnant. I put the top back on and leaned back in my seat. "How did this happen?"

It was a dick question. I knew how it happened, but we'd talked about it. She knew my worries about the age difference, so my reaction shouldn't have come as a complete surprise. "Well, I was sick last month. I guess the antibiotics made my birth control less effective or something."

When I didn't respond, she let out an exasperated breath. "I knew you wouldn't be thrilled with the idea, but I hoped you would be at least a little happy about it."

"Ten years ago, I would've been good with it. Hell, I would have been more than good with it. But you gotta know I'm too old for a baby."

"You're not too old," Luna interjected. "You're just right."

"You think so?"

"Um-hmm." She nodded with a smile. "You play Barbies good, and you let me paint your fingernails."

"Kid, that's between you and me."

"I know." She smiled. "But I really want a baby sister."

"Is that right?"

"Yeah, and I want her to have your hair and Momma's eyes. And I want her to be nice like me. And you can fix the other room for her and make it pretty like mine. And I can share my toys with her."

"You've really thought this out."

The kid never failed to amaze me. She made the impossible possible, and I could not only picture bringing a new baby into our lives but found myself happy about the idea. My DNA or not, Luna felt as much mine as any kid could be, and if she thought I'd be a good dad to this kid, then who was I to tell her any different?

And hell, maybe she was right.

Thatch had turned out alright, and Luna was holding her own.

Maybe, just maybe, I could do this father thing one more time.

I turned my attention back to Jenna, and I wasn't surprised to find her looking out the window with a blank expression on her face. If I didn't know better, I'd say she was thinking of all the different ways she could kill me in my sleep. I wouldn't exactly blame her. I'd been an ass, so I leaned over to her and whispered, "I'm sorry. I'm not very good with surprises."

"It's okay."

"No, it's not. None of this has been okay." I reached over and took her hand in mine. "Can we start this over?"

"I don't really think that's possible."

"Sure it is." I took the box in my hand and slowly opened it. I reached in and took out the test, then looked at her with a smile. "You're gonna have my baby?"

"Yeah, in about eight months."

"Holy shit." I looked back at the test. "I can't believe it. We're gonna have a kid."

"I know it's a lot, but..."

"It's gonna be good. We're gonna bring another one of you into this world."

"It could be another you."

"Lord, let's hope not." I leaned over and kissed her. "Boy or girl, I don't care. I just have one request."

"Okay, what's that?"

"If it's a boy, we name him Lenard."

"Lenard?" She gasped, then started giggling. "I'm not naming our baby Lenard."

I gave her a wink. "There's that smile I've been looking for."

"You're a mess."

"It comes with age." I leaned back and sighed. "Damn. I gotta start working out. It's hard enough to keep up with you."

"Yeah, but you love me."

"More than I ever thought possible."

This woman had taken a bad day and turned it completely around. She'd done the same thing with my life. She'd made it worth living, and I would spend the rest of my life thanking her for it.

The End

More from the Little Rock Chapter coming soon!
Excerpt from Rooster following Acknowledgments.

Acknowledgments

I am blessed to have so many wonderful people who are willing to give their time and effort to making my books the best they can be. Without them, I wouldn't be able to breathe life into my characters and share their stories with you. To the people I've listed below and so many others, I want to say thank you for taking this journey with me. Your support means the world to me, and I truly mean it when I say I appreciate everything you do. I love you all!

PA: Natalie Weston (And dearest friend)
Editing/Proofing: Marie Peyton
Promoting: Amy Jones, Veronica Ines Garcia,
BETAS/Early Readers: Tawyna Rae and Amanda Quiles- you two are the best!
L. Wilder's Read and Review Team: Thank you for reading early and reviewing. You are amazing!
Street Team: All the wonderful members of Wilder's Women (You rock!)
Best Friend and biggest supporter: My mother (Love you to the moon and back.)

EXCERPT FROM ROOSTER: SATAN'S FURY SG

Prologue

"I don't do this."

"Yeah, okay."

"No, I'm serious." She motioned her hand between our hips. "I don't do this. I'm a mom. I've got kids. Two of them."

"You saying you don't wanna do this?"

"No, no. I'm not saying that." She raked her teeth over her bottom lip. "I just wanted you to know that I don't do this sort of thing."

The movie theater bathroom was a new one for me, too, but I didn't see any need in telling her that. Besides, she was already feeling a bit leery, and the last thing I wanted to do was scare her off, especially when her hot little body was pressed against mine, and I had a raging hard-on. I gave her one of my most charming smiles and said, "Baby, I don't care if you do or don't. It's not like we're courtin' here. We're just *fuu...*"

"Yeah, yeah. I got it."

The crease in her brow faded, and I knew I had her when a smile swept across her face. She nodded, and that was that. I lowered my mouth to hers once again, drawing her closer as I kissed her with everything I had.

She didn't resist. Instead, she wound her arms around my neck and kissed me back. Need surged throughout me like a fucking wildfire as she eased her hips forward and started grinding against me. It was all I could do to keep from taking her right there in the hallway.

I was on the brink of losing control when she placed her hand on my chest and pulled away from me yet again. "I'm not a bad person for this, right? I mean, people do this kind of thing all the time, don't they?"

"Yeah, I guess, but that doesn't mean you gotta do it."

"I know, but I deserve this. I always take care of everybody else. This time, I'm going to treat myself." Her eyes skirted over me. "Instead of some chocolate, I'm having the hot guy I met at the movies."

"Ah, you think I'm hot?"

"Oh yeah." A wicked smile swept across her face. "You're way hot."

"Right back at ya, babe."

I pulled her closer and pressed my mouth to hers. This kiss was different. This kiss wasn't laced with doubt or any resistance at all. Instead, it was smoking hot and filled with a hunger that matched my own. Her body melted into me as her tongue brushed against mine, and then it was over. I'd taken all I could take.

I dropped my hands to her waist and started to unbuckle her jeans. "You sure you're good with this?"

"Oh, yeah. I'm definitely good."

The tip of her tongue slowly dragged across her bottom lip as she kicked off her boots, then lowered her jeans and panties to the floor. She stood there staring at me with a wanton look in her eyes as I grabbed a condom from my wallet before lowering my jeans and boxers.

From the moment we'd first kissed, she'd had me all tangled up. My cock pulsated against my fingers while I slipped on a condom. I gave it a hard squeeze, trying to relieve some of the throbbing pressure, but it did little to help. I needed her, and I needed her now.

Unable to resist a moment longer, I reached for her, pulling her close. Anticipation flashed through her eyes as my hands dropped to her hips and lifted her up, pressing her back against the wall. She bit her lip and wrapped her legs around me, making my cock grow even harder. My need for her was palpable, burning deep inside my gut.

Fuck.

I didn't know what it was about this woman, but she had me spiraling out of control. With one hard thrust, I buried myself deep inside her. A rush of air hissed through her teeth as I withdrew and drove into her again and again. With her arms wound tightly around my neck, I growled into her shoulder and started thrusting harder and deeper, building up to a relentless pace.

I'd been with many women in my time, but never had a woman made me feel so on edge. Needing more, I turned around and carried her over to the sink counter. Her legs widened, giving me better access as I lowered her onto the edge of the cold porcelain. She immediately leaned back and propped her hands on the sink's ledge.

I lowered my mouth to her neck, kissing her like a hungry animal as I drove deeper, harder. Her head reared back with a sated groan. That was it. That was exactly what I wanted to fucking hear. Her nails dug into my lower back as her hips rocked against mine, meeting my every thrust with more intensity. I could feel the pressure building, forcing a growl from my chest.

"Fuck," I groaned as she tightened around me. She panted wildly, and her thighs clamped down around my hips when I tried to increase my pace. I knew she was close, unable to stop the inevitable torment of her building release. I lowered my hand between her thighs, raking my thumb across her clit, and that was all it took. The muscles in her body grew taut as her orgasm took hold. I continued to drive into her; the sounds of my body pounding against hers echoed throughout the room until I finally came inside her. With a ragged breath, I panted, "Wow."

"Yeah, that was pretty freaking incredible." She gave me a warm smile as she glanced down at her boots. "Even better than I thought it would be."

"You doubted me?"

"No, it was me that I doubted."

"Got no reason to doubt yourself, babe." I slowly withdrew, then quickly tossed the condom in the trash. "You're amazing."

As I was pulling up my boxer briefs and jeans, she hopped down from the countertop and started to get dressed. "Tell my ex that."

And just like that, there was a shift in her mood. I couldn't stand the thought of her thinking she was anything but incredible, so I told her, "Your ex is a fucking idiot."

"Oh, yeah? What makes you say that?"

"He'd have to be to let you go."

Her smile returned as she said, "Thanks, you didn't have to say that."

"Just tellin' it like it is." I stepped over to her and placed the tips of my fingers on her chin, forcing her to look up at me. "Why don't you give me your number so I can remind you whenever you forget?"

"I would, but I don't think it's a good idea." She stood up and fastened the last button of her jeans. "I've only been divorced a few months."

"Okay, then give me your phone."

"Hmm?"

"Your phone." To my surprise, she grabbed her

phone from her purse and handed it to me. I put my name and number in her contacts as I told her, "My name's Ronin. If you change your mind or need something, just give me a call."

"Okay, thanks." She dropped her phone back in her purse, then eased up on her tiptoes and gave me a quick kiss on the cheek. "Thanks for this. I really enjoyed it."

"Yeah, me too."

She studied me for a moment, and just as I thought she was going to say something, she turned and walked out the door. I wanted to believe that I hadn't seen the last of the beautiful brunette, but with the way my luck had been lately, I wasn't so sure. Regardless, she'd given me a night I wouldn't soon forget, and I could only hope I'd done the same for her.

Rooster

"It's gotta be a password, right?"

"Yeah, but to what? We checked the house and his office. There was nothing there." Bones sounded frustrated as he added, "And I already have access to his laptop, emails, and bank accounts. What else could there be?"

"I don't know, but there's gotta be something. Otherwise, he wouldn't have kept repeating that Sawyer 247 bullshit."

"Could it be one of his kids or grandkids?"

"Nope," Bones answered. "Already checked."

"What about an employee? Or some woman he screwed around with?"

"Maybe."

I'd been listening to my brothers go back and forth for over an hour, and I couldn't help but notice how much had changed over the past couple of months. I'd patched in more than ten years ago, and back then, Cotton sat at the front of the table with Guardrail and Stitch at his side. They were a force to be reckoned with.

Now, Maverick sat in Cotton's place, and Savage and Wrath were his right-hand men. They were just as fierce and determined, but unlike their older, wiser, more mellow predecessors, Savage and Wrath were still young and quick-tempered. Most of the young ones were. I fell somewhere in between and considered myself to be a decent mix of the two.

Except when I was hungry or hung over.

And today, I just happened to be both, and I was teetering on the edge when Smokey asked, "When were we supposed to deliver the next load, or is that still on?"

"Next week, but we got no idea about the who or the where," Prez answered. "We'll figure it out, but you know Bruton. He only told us what he felt like we needed to know."

"Yeah, he was a real gem about that."

"Maybe there was a reason for that. For all we know, we're worrying over nothing," Clutch suggested. "It's not like his death wasn't plastered all over the fucking news. Surely whoever he was working with saw it."

He was right.

Everyone was talking about it.

I couldn't really blame them. It wasn't every day that a councilman died in our small town, much less one who was gunned down in broad daylight. Add in the fact that

EXCERPT FROM ROOSTER: SATAN'S FURY SG

he was shot over an accident due to a traffic light he'd petitioned for, and you had a real story on your hands.

But it's only half the story.

None of them knew he was a notorious arms dealer who worked with some of the most dangerous men in the world. I wasn't sold on going into business with Bruton in the first place. We didn't know much about the guy—just that he'd gone to an extreme to get us all on board, and since then, he'd been a blessing and a curse. He'd really come through for us when we had an issue with the Demarco brothers, only to turn around and buy us trouble with the Stingers.

He had us do a drop in their territory, and they weren't happy about it. Even tried to get a hold of Savage's ol' lady and their kid, but yet again, Bruton swooped in and took care of it. That's when I learned just how cold and heartless our new partner could be—which made it all that much harder to believe that he was shot by an everyday citizen over a fucking traffic light.

I didn't give a fuck how the guy died.

He was gone, and all he'd left us with was some dying last words that made no sense to any of us—which led me to say, "But there's no way to be sure that they saw it or if they even cared. They could still be expecting the shipment, and when they don't get it, they're gonna come looking for it."

"Rooster is right," Prez agreed. "We got no idea what they're expecting or what Bruton told 'em."

"So, we just wait here like a bunch of sittin' ducks and see if they come lookin' for their shit?"

"We've still got some time before the delivery is due." Prez turned to Bones as he said, "We need to work fast and find out everything we need to know about Bruton and his business dealings. Even if that means going through every fucking email and receipt that has ever passed his hands."

"I'm on it," Bones assured him.

Big was quick to add, "And I'll be there to help any way I can."

"Appreciate that, brother."

"I'll be there, too." Torch shrugged. "I don't know what I'll do, but I'll help if I can."

Prez nodded, then stood as he told us, "None of us are happy about the way things have played out with Bruton, but these are the cards we've been dealt, and we've gotta act accordingly. Be careful out there and don't take any unnecessary chances."

Without saying anything more, he slammed the gavel on the table and dismissed church. The brothers quickly started to disperse, and those who could stick around began filing into the bar. I followed Savage and Smokey up to the front counter, and we all sat down next to Cotton. We hadn't even opened our beer when Cotton turned to Savage and asked, "How's Londyn doing with the big move?"

"Good." He popped the cap as he continued, "She

EXCERPT FROM ROOSTER: SATAN'S FURY SG

finally got Dalton's room the way she wants it and has moved to organizing the bathroom."

"Which means she's moving out most of your stuff," Cotton chuckled.

"Oh, yeah. My stuff has come and gone." Savage shook his head. "Never seen so many different kinds of shampoo and lotions. Won't be long and I'll be swimming in the stuff."

"It's the same way with your mother... I have my drawer, and she has the rest."

"I need to claim a drawer."

"*If it's not already gone.*" Cotton smiled as he asked, "What about Dalton? How's he doing?"

"He's adjusting."

"You don't sound so sure."

"Cause I'm not." Savage shook his head and shrugged. "I was kind of hoping we could just step right into all this family shit, and that would be that. But there's a lot to it, and I have no fucking clue what I'm doing."

"I'm sure you're doing better than you think."

"I don't know." Savage turned to his father. "The other night I was just minding my own business, watching TV, and he crawled in my lap. I felt like my chest was gonna explode. Hell, it damn near brought tears to my eyes. What the hell is that?"

"That's being a father," Cotton answered. "And I got news for ya. That feeling never goes away."

"I don't know if I can take it."

"You can, and you will."

"I'm gonna try." A proud smile crossed his face as he said, "Dalton's an amazing kid. Hell, I'd claim him even if he wasn't mine."

"He really is something." Cotton cocked his brow. "So, when are your mom and I gonna get to spend some more time with him?"

"Whenever is good with me." Savage took a pull from his beer. "Let me check with Londyn, and if all is well, he can hang with you guys this weekend. Then, he won't be underfoot while we're putting together his swing set."

"A swing set?" I groaned. "That's great. Our VP's getting all domesticated and shit."

"Says the man who's yet to find an ol' lady. You know, you could use some domestication yourself." He gave me a playful nudge. "An ol' lady might do you some good. She could settle your ass down."

"Never gonna happen, brother." I was tempted to tell him about the gorgeous brunette I'd met at the movies a few months back, but it didn't feel right. So, I ran my hand over my beard. "I'm a beast that can't be tamed."

"Yeah, keep telling yourself that. One day, the right girl will come along..."

"I wouldn't hold my breath." I wasn't in the mood to discuss my love life, so I turned to Smokey and asked, "How are things going out at the orchard?"

And just like that, the conversation turned to MJ

and all they had going on at the farm. From the sounds of it, my brother had his hands full, but that was nothing new. He and MJ were always busy doing something, but we were all busy. Each of us had our own lives outside of the club, and I'll admit, some were more hectic than others. And from the sounds of it, things were pretty hectic over at the orchard.

Hoping to lift his mood, I leaned over to him and smiled, "Do you know the difference between an apple and an orphan?"

Smokey gave me a look, then shook his head and sighed. "Nope. Can't say that I do."

"An apple gets picked."

It took a second for my answer to sink in, but when it did, it got the reaction I expected. "You're going to hell. You know that, right?"

"What?" I asked innocently. "You didn't like my joke? I've got more. What do you get when you cross a dick with a potato?"

Again, Smokey shook his head.

I chuckled as I answered, "A dictator."

There was a low rumble of laughter which quickly faded when Torch appeared in the doorway and said, "I think they found something."

No one responded.

We simply stood and followed Torch down the hall to Bone's computer room. When we walked in, Big was at the back table sifting through a stack of files while Bones sat at his laptop spouting off dates. It was always impressive to see them work, especially together. From the beginning, Big had an uncanny gift for finding information no one else could find and doing things no one else could do. Bones was just like him, but he had a focus like none other. And when he set his mind to something, he didn't stop until he got it done.

I stood there in the doorway listening as Bones called out another date. "April 1st, 1998... 87256038."

"Yep. Got it."

"Got what?" Savage asked as he stepped over to Big and glanced over his shoulder. Big lifted one of the pages and said, "Deposits from one of Bruton's offshore accounts. They go out every month. Sometimes more than once, but always to a Sawyer Grant, account number 87256038. Been making deposits since '98."

"Oh, yeah?" Savage studied the receipt for a moment. "Wait... '98? Isn't that when Bruton started teaching at the high school?"

"I don't know, but it wouldn't be hard to find out."

"Something to keep in mind." Savage continued to study the receipt as he asked, "Got any idea who this Sawyer guy is?"

"No, but we're working on it."

I felt like we were finally getting somewhere when Clutch stepped into the room and said, "We've got company."

"What?" Savage sounded annoyed as he asked, "Who the fuck is it?"

"We got somebody at the gate." Clutch cocked his

brow as he looked over to me and said, "He asked to speak with whoever's in charge."

"And?"

"And we were about to turn him away until he mentioned he had ties to Bruton."

"Damn. He's six feet under and still bringing the surprises."

"That he is." Clutch started for the door as he said, "Prez is waiting for you in the bar."

Savage gave him a nod, then started out of the room. He hadn't gotten far when I started after him and said, "Hold on. I'm coming with."

When we walked into the bar, Wrath was standing next to Prez, and they were both glaring at the back door. You could literally feel the tension radiating off them as they waited for our guest to make his way inside. We stepped up beside them, and the silence was deafening as the heavy double door swung open.

Seconds later, a man dressed in a jet-black business suit stepped inside. His dark, piercing eyes scanned the room, and he exuded an aura of menace and authority as he took in every detail of the room. A subtle twitch of his jaw represented a warning that he wasn't a man to be trifled with.

With every step, his polished leather shoes echoed through the bar, intensifying the tension in the room as he started towards us. His back was straight, his chin was out, and his expression was blank. He wasn't the least bit shaken that he'd just entered the Satan's Fury clubhouse and was about to face its president, but I couldn't say the same for me.

Just being around this dude had me rattled.

Fuck.

This dude was no joke.

He walked straight up to Prez and asked, "You the one in charge?"

"Who the fuck's asking?"

"I go by many names, but you boys can call me Maltese."

"Why don't you tell us why you're here, Maltese?"

"I simply need to deliver a message." His face remained void of expression as he said, "My boss is a very busy man, and he is expecting his goods to be delivered as scheduled."

"What makes you think we know anything about your boss or his fucking goods?"

"Let's not play games. We are well aware of your ties with Bruton and that you have been making his deliveries. I'm just here to let you know that it's in your best interest, *and ours*, that you fulfill your commitments."

"And how are we supposed to do that without Bruton?"

"Oh, come now." A sly smile crossed his face. "You fellas have made quite a name for yourselves, and you don't do that without crossing a line or two."

"We'll take care of it."

"That's what I wanted to hear." His eyes skirted over

to me and Clutch, then back to Prez. "I won't waste any more of your time. You boys have a good night."

Before any of us had a chance for a rebuttal, he turned and walked out of the room. Savage was still glaring at the door as he growled, "Well, fuck."

"Yeah. My thoughts exactly."

"How many more of these assholes are gonna show up at our door?"

"One is more than enough." Prez turned to Savage as he said, "We need to figure out this Sawyer situation, and we need to figure it out now."

Maggie

"I don't want to go."

"I know, but you have to."

"But why?"

"Because he's your father, and *it's his weekend*."

"Well, that's stupid," Nathan huffed. "I don't even see why we gotta go. He's never even there. He's either hunting or playing golf or off on some work thing, and we're stuck with his stupid girlfriend."

"Fiancé."

"*Whatever*." He rolled his eyes. "She sucks... She smells funny and can't even make a peanut butter and jelly sandwich right."

"What?"

"She just slaps everything on there. Doesn't even cut it in half or take off the crust. It's gross, and so is she." Nathan sat down at the kitchen table and poured himself a bowl of cereal as he continued, "I don't want to be there with her, and neither does Sam."

I understood his frustration. In fact, I felt the same, but there wasn't much I could do about it. It was Chad's weekend, and, like it or not, they had to go. It didn't make it any less frustrating. He rarely spent time with the kids when we were together, but during the divorce, he did his best to portray 'father of the year' and pleaded for every other weekend and various holidays and summer break.

I wanted the kids to have a relationship with their father, so I agreed. At the time, I had no way of knowing that he would pawn them off on Crissy—his personal secretary and new girlfriend. It infuriated me, but there was little I could do. The courts had granted him every other weekend, and I had no choice but to comply.

I wished I had some great words of wisdom for my precious son, but there were none to give. "I'm sorry, honey, but there's not much I can do about that."

"I wish he'd get hit by a bus."

"Nathan," I fussed. "Don't say things like that."

"Well, I do." He gave me a disgruntled shrug. "He's the worst."

"Maybe so, but he loves you and wants to spend some time with you." I feigned a smile as I suggested, "Maybe you could get him to take you shopping, and you could look for a new pair of jeans to replace the ones with the ripped pocket."

"Maybe."

"And you've been saying you needed a pair of new boots. Your sister could use a new pair, too."

"New pair of what?" Samantha asked as she strolled into the kitchen.

"Boots and any other clothes you might need. I was thinking your dad could take you to do some shopping." I'd already spent a small fortune on their back-to-school clothes. It was only fair for Chad to pitch in with their fall clothes, so I told her, "You really need a jacket and maybe a couple of new hoodies, too."

"I don't like shopping with Dad," Samantha whined. "He's always fussin' about how much stuff costs."

Printed in Great Britain
by Amazon